DOOMSDAY: Anarchy

The Doomsday Series

Book Three

by

Bobby Akart

Other Works by Amazon Top 50 Author, Bobby Akart

The Doomsday Series

Apocalypse
Haven
Anarchy
Minutemen
Civil War

The Yellowstone Series

Hellfire
Inferno
Fallout
Survival

The Lone Star Series

Axis of Evil
Beyond Borders
Lines in the Sand
Texas Strong
Fifth Column
Suicide Six

The Pandemic Series

Beginnings
The Innocents
Level 6
Quietus

The Blackout Series

36 Hours

Zero Hour

Turning Point

Shiloh Ranch

Hornet's Nest

Devil's Homecoming

The Boston Brahmin Series

The Loyal Nine

Cyber Attack

Martial Law

False Flag

The Mechanics

Choose Freedom

Patriot's Farewell

Seeds of Liberty (Companion Guide)

The Prepping for Tomorrow Series

Cyber Warfare

EMP: Electromagnetic Pulse

Economic Collapse

DEDICATIONS

For many years, I have lived by the following premise:

Because you never know when the day before
is the day before, prepare for tomorrow.

My friends, I study and write about the threats we face, not only to both entertain and inform you, but because I am constantly learning how to prepare for the benefit of my family as well. There is nothing more important on this planet than my darling wife, Dani, and our two girls, Bullie and Boom. One day, doomsday will come, and I'll be damned if I'm gonna let it stand in the way of our life together.

The Doomsday series is dedicated to the love and support of my family. I will always protect you from anything that threatens us.

ACKNOWLEDGEMENTS

Writing a book that is both informative and entertaining requires a tremendous team effort. Writing is the easy part. For their efforts in making the Doomsday series a reality, I would like to thank Hristo Argirov Kovatliev for his incredible cover art, Pauline Nolet for her editorial prowess, Stef Mcdaid for making this manuscript decipherable in so many formats, Chris Abernathy for his memorable performance in narrating this novel, and the Team—Denise, Joe, Jim, and Shirley—whose advice, friendship and attention to detail is priceless.

In addition, my loyal readers who interact with me on social media know that Dani and I have been fans of the television reality show *Big Brother* since it began broadcasting on CBS in the summer of 2000. The program was one of the greatest social experiments ever imagined. Each season, more than a dozen contestants compete for a half-million-dollar cash prize.

During the months-long airing of the program, the houseguests are isolated from the outside world, but we, the viewers, get to watch their every move via more than a hundred cameras and microphones. The opportunity to study how people interact under these unusual stressful circumstances has allowed me to create diverse and interesting characters for you, dear readers.

Over the years, we've been fortunate to meet several of the past *Big Brother* contestants, and this year, for the second time (the first being our friend Judd Daugherty, who was a doctor in the Boston Brahmin series), I've actually written four of them into the characters through the use of their first name and unique character attributes.

During the airing of season twenty during the summer of 2018, early on in the show, an alliance formed between a group of six who controlled the game from start to finish. You can imagine the high fives Dani and I exchanged when they named their alliance *Level 6*, the title of book three in my Pandemic series released in the summer of 2017.

To season twenty winner, Kaycee Clark; our favorite *showmance* of all time, Angela Rummans and Tyler Crispen; and to one of the funniest, most real people I've ever seen on television, "JC" Mounduix—thank you for inspiring the Rankin family in the Doomsday series!

Thank you all!
Choose Freedom and Godspeed, Patriots!

ABOUT THE AUTHOR

Bobby Akart

Author Bobby Akart has been ranked by Amazon as #55 in its Top 100 list of most popular, bestselling authors. He has achieved #1 bestselling Horror Author, #2 bestselling Science Fiction Author, #3 bestselling Religion & Spirituality Author, #5 bestselling Action & Adventure Author, and #7 bestselling Historical Author.

He has written over twenty international bestsellers, in nearly fifty fiction and nonfiction genres, including the chart-busting Yellowstone series, the reader-favorite Lone Star series, the critically acclaimed Boston Brahmin series, the bestselling Blackout series, the frighteningly realistic Pandemic series, his highly cited nonfiction Prepping for Tomorrow series, and his latest project—the Doomsday series, seen by many as the horrifying future of our nation if we can't find a way to come together.

His novel *Yellowstone: Fallout* reached #50 on the Amazon bestsellers list and earned him two Kindle All-Star awards for most pages read in a month and most pages read as an author. The Yellowstone series vaulted him to the #1 best selling horror author on Amazon, and the #2 best selling science fiction author.

Bobby has provided his readers a diverse range of topics that are both informative and entertaining. His attention to detail and impeccable research have allowed him to capture the imaginations of his readers through his fictional works and bring them valuable knowledge through his nonfiction books.

SIGN UP for Bobby Akart's mailing list to receive special offers, bonus content, and you'll be the first to receive news about new releases in the Doomsday series.

VISIT Amazon.com/BobbyAkart, a dedicated feature page created by Amazon for his work, to view more information on his thriller fiction novels and post-apocalyptic book series, as well as his nonfiction Prepping for Tomorrow series. Visit Bobby Akart's website for informative blog entries on preparedness, writing, and a behind-the-scenes look into his novels.

BobbyAkart.com

Author's Introduction to the Doomsday Series

November 8, 2018

Are we on the brink of destroying ourselves?

Some argue that our nation is deeply divided, with each side condemning the other as the enemy of America. By way of example, one can point to the events leading up to the Civil War in the latter part of the 1850s, right up until the first cannon fire rained upon Fort Sumter in Charleston, South Carolina. It's happened before, and it could happen again.

The war of words has intensified over the last several decades, and now deranged people on the fringe of society have taken matters into their own hands. Ranging from pipe-bomb packages mailed to political leaders and supporters, to a gunman shooting congressmen at a softball practice, words are being replaced with deadly, violent acts.

To be sure, we've experienced violence and intense social strife in this country as a result of political differences. The Civil War was one example. The assassination of Martin Luther King Jr., followed by the raging street battles over civil rights and the Vietnam War, is another.

This moment in America's history feels worse because we are growing much more divisive. Our shared values are being forgotten, and a breakdown is occurring between us and our government, and between us and the office of the presidency.

Our ability to find common ground is gradually disappearing. We shout at the television or quit watching altogether. Social media has become anything but *social.* We unfollow friends or write things in a post that we'd never dream of saying to someone's face.

Friends and family avoid one another at gatherings because they fear political discussions will result in an uncomfortable, even hostile exchange. Many in our nation no longer look at their fellow Americans as being from a different race or religion but, rather, as supporting one political party or another.

This is where America is today, and it is far different from the months leading up to the Civil War. Liberal historians label the conflict as a battle over slavery, while conservative historians tend to argue the issue was over states' rights. At the time, the only thing agreed upon was the field of battle—farms and open country from Pennsylvania to Georgia.

Today, there are many battlefronts. Media—news, entertainment, and social—is a major battlefield. The halls of Congress and within the inner workings of governments at all levels is another. Between everyday Americans—based upon class warfare, cultural distinctions, and race-religion-gender—highlighting our differences pervades every aspect of our lives.

Make no mistake, on both sides of the political spectrum, a new generation of leaders has emerged who've made fueling our divisions their political modus operandi. I remember the bipartisan efforts of Ronald Reagan and Tip O'Neill in the eighties. Also, Bill Clinton and Newt Gingrich in the mid-nineties. The turn of the century hasn't provided us the types of bipartisan working relationships that those leaders of the recent past have generated.

So, here we are at each other's throats. What stops the political rancor and division? The answer to this question results in even more partisan arguments and finger-pointing.

Which leads me to the purpose of the Doomsday series. The term *doomsday* evokes images of the end of times, the day the world ends, or a time when something terrible or dangerous will happen. Sounds dramatic, but everything is relative.

I've repeated this often, and I will again for those who haven't heard it.

All empires collapse eventually. Their reign ends when they are either defeated by a larger and more powerful enemy, or when their financing runs out. America will be no exception.

Now, couple this theory with the words often attributed to President Abraham Lincoln in an 1838 speech interpreted as follows:

America will never be destroyed from the outside. If we falter and lose our freedoms, it will be because we destroyed ourselves.

The Doomsday series depicts an America hell-bent upon destroying itself. It is a dystopian look at what will happen if we don't find a way to deescalate the attacks upon one another. Both sides will shoulder the blame for what will happen when the war of words becomes increasingly more violent to the point where one side brings out the *big guns.*

That's when an ideological battle will result in the bloodshed of innocent Americans caught in the crossfire. Truly, for the future of our nation, doomsday would be upon us.

Thank you for reading with an open mind and not through the lens of political glasses. I hope we can come together for the sake of our families and our nation. God bless America.

Epigraph

In the beginning of a change, the patriot is a scarce man, and brave, and hated and scorned. When his cause succeeds, the timid join him, for then it costs nothing to be a patriot.

~ Mark Twain

*****

The following five attributes marked Rome at its end; first, a mounting love of show and luxury; second, a widening gap between the very rich and the very poor; third, an obsession with sex; fourth, freakishness in the arts, masquerading as originality and enthusiasms pretending to be creativity; and fifth, an increased desire to live off the state.

~ Edward Gibbon (1737–1794)
in his *Decline and Fall of the Roman Empire*

*****

Those who cannot remember the past are condemned to repeat it.

~ George Santayana, philosopher and novelist

*****

The real rulers, you'll never see.

~ Anonymous

*****

Previously in the Doomsday Series

Dramatis Personae

PRIMARY CHARACTERS

George Trowbridge — A wealthy, powerful Washington insider. Lives on his estate in East Haven, Connecticut. Yale graduate. Suffers from kidney failure. Father of Meredith Cortland.

The Sheltons — Tom is retired from the United States Navy and is a former commander at Joint Base Charleston. Married to his wife of forty years, Donna. They have two daughters. Tommie, single, is with Naval Intelligence and stationed on a spy ship in the Persian Gulf. Their oldest daughter, Willa, is married with two young children. The family lives north of Las Vegas. Willa is a captain at Creech Air Force Base, where she serves as a drone pilot. Tom and Donna reside in downtown Charleston.

The Rankin Family — Formerly of Hilton Head, South Carolina, now residing in Richmond, Virginia. Dr. Angela Rankin is a critical care physician at Virginia Commonwealth Medical Center in Richmond. Her husband, Tyler, is a firefighter and a trained emergency medical technician. He was formerly a lifeguard. They have two children. Their daughter, Kaycee, age eleven, nearly died in a helicopter crash as a child. Their youngest child, J.C., age eight, loves history and is a devoted student of America's founding.

The Cortland Family — Michael *Cort* Cortland is chief of staff to a prominent United States Senator from Alabama. His wife, Meredith, is a teacher and the daughter of George Trowbridge. The couple met while they attended Yale University. They have one child, twelve-year-old daughter Hannah. They live in Cort's hometown of Mobile, Alabama. They have an English bulldog named after Yale's mascot, Handsome Dan.

The Hightower Family — Will Hightower is retired from the Philadelphia Police Department and in his mid-forties. After he left Philly SWAT, he got divorced from his wife, Karen. He moved to Atlanta to work for Mercedes-Benz security, only seeing his children—Ethan, age fifteen, and daughter Skylar, age eleven—periodically. Will also has a second job as *Delta*.

Hayden Blount — Born in North Carolina, but now resides in the Washington, DC, area. She is an attorney with a powerful law firm that represents the president in front of the Supreme Court. She formerly clerked for Justice Samuel Alito, a Yale graduate. Single, she lives alone with her Maine coon cat, Prowler.

Ryan and Blair Smart, Chubby and the Roo — Former residents of Florida, and now founders of the Haven, a prepper community built on the former location of the Hunger Games movie set in Henry River Mill Village, North Carolina, just west of Charlotte. The Smarts, together with their two English Bulldog sisters, Chubby and the Roo, now reside at Haven House within the community and have surrounded them with like minded thinkers as they prepare for the coming collapse.

Alpha, Bravo, Charlie — The Haven needed a security team, but these individuals needed to have other skills that contributed to the daily operations and development of the community. The Smart's first hire was Alpha. Ex-military with an expertise in building primitive, log structures, he was a perfect fit and became the head of the security detail which included recruits Bravo and Charlie. Will

Hightower, who was referred to as Delta at the Haven, was also a member of the team.

Echo — given name, Justin Echols, and his wife, Charlotte, were the oldest members of the Haven until the Sheltons arrived. Although not a member of the security team, Echo was part of the Haven's hierarchy. He and Charlotte were former farmers who had an expertise in sustainable living and caring for livestock. Their role as providers to the Haven community was invaluable.

X-Ray — real name, Eugene O'Reilly, was the newest member of the Haven community, having arrived on the afternoon of New Year's Eve. Bearing the same name as the famous character on the *M*A*S*H* television show, his grandfather provided him the nickname X-Ray, and it fit his perfectly. A science nerd growing up, X-Ray was especially adept at all things electronic or associated with the internet. His elaborate Faraday Cages and computer setups seemed to be a perfect fit for the Haven.

Book One: *Doomsday: Apocalypse*

It was the beginning of great internal strife, neighbor versus neighbor, warrior versus warrior. The fuse was lit with a simple message, understood by a select few, but impacting the lives of all Americans. It read:

On the day of the feast of Saint Sylvester,
Tear down locked,
Green light burning.
Love, MM

And so it begins…

In *Doomsday: Apocalypse*, all events occur on New Year's Eve

New York City

It was New Year's Eve, and New York City was the center of the annual celebration's universe. Over a million people had crowded into Times Square to bid a collective farewell to the old year and to express hope and joy for the year ahead.

There were some, however, who had other plans for the night's festivities. A clandestine meeting atop the newly constructed One World Trade Center, ground zero for the most heinous terrorist attack on the United States in history, revealed that another attack was afoot. One that sprang from a meeting in a remote farmhouse in Maryland and was perpetrated by a shadowy group.

In New York, Tom and Donna Shelton, retirees from Charleston, South Carolina, belatedly celebrated their fortieth anniversary atop the Hyatt Centric Hotel overlooking Times Square. Caught up in the moment, they made the fateful decision to join the revelers on the streets for a once-in-a-lifetime opportunity to be part of the famous ball drop and countdown to New Year's.

However, terror reared its ugly head as a squadron of quadcopter drones descended upon Midtown Manhattan, detonating bombs over Times Square and other major landmarks in the city. Chaos ensued and the Sheltons found themselves fighting for their lives.

After an injury to Donna, the couple made their way back to their hotel room, where they thought they were safe. However, Tom received a mysterious text, one that he was afraid to reveal to his wife. It came from a sender whom he considered a part of his distant past. It was an ominous warning that weighed heavily on his mind.

The text message read:

The real danger on the ocean, as well as the land, is people.
Fare thee well and Godspeed, Patriot!
MM

Six Flags Great Adventure, New Jersey

Dr. Angela Rankin and her husband, Tyler, were in the second leg of their educational vacation with their two children, Kaycee and J.C., although the New Year's Eve portion of the trip was supposed to be the fun part. They had arrived at Six Flags Great Adventure, the self-proclaimed scariest theme park on the planet.

Following a trip to Boston to visit historic sites related to our nation's founding, they were headed home to Richmond, Virginia, with planned stops in Philadelphia and Washington to see more landmarks. The planned stop at Six Flags was to be a highlight of the trip for the kids.

The night was full of thrills and chills as they rode one roller coaster after another. Young J.C., their son, wanted to save the *wildest, gut-wrenchingest* roller coaster for last—Kingda Ka. The tallest roller coaster in America, Kingda Ka, in just a matter of seconds, shot its coaster up a four-hundred-fifty-six-foot track until the riders reached the top, where they were suspended for a moment, only to be sent down the other side. Except on New Year's Eve, some of them never made it down, on the coaster, that is.

When the Rankin family hit the top of the Kingda Ka ride, an electromagnetic pulse attack struck the area around Philadelphia, which included a part of the Mid-Atlantic states stretching from Wilmington, Delaware, into northern New Jersey. The devastating EMP destroyed electronics, power grids, and the computers used to operate modern vehicles.

It also brought Kingda Ka to a standstill with the Rankins and others suspended facedown at the apex of the ride. At first, the riders avoided panicking. To be sure, they were all frightened, but they felt safe thanks to Tyler's reassurances, and they waited to be rescued.

However, one man became impatient and felt sure he and his wife could make their way to safety. On his four-seat coaster car, with the assistance of a college-age man, they broke loose the safety bar in order to crawl out of the coaster. This turned out to be a bad idea.

The young man immediately flew head over heels, four hundred feet to his death.

The man who came up with the self-rescue plan and his wife attempted to shimmy down a support post to a safety platform within Kingda Ka but lost their grip. Both of them plunged to their deaths.

Safety personnel finally arrived on the scene, and they began the arduous task of rescuing the remaining passengers, leaving the Rankins for last since they were at the front of the string of coaster cars. Unfortunately, as the safety bar was lifted, J.C. fell out of the car, only to be retrained by a safety harness that had been affixed to his body.

Despite the fact that he was suspended twenty feet below the coaster, held by only a rope, the family worked together to hoist him to safety and an eventual rescue. But their night was not done.

The Rankins made their way to the parking lot, where their 1974 Bronco awaited them. Tyler pulled Angela aside, retrieved his handgun that was hidden under the chassis of the truck, and explained. The EMP had disabled almost all of the vehicles around them. Thousands of people were milling about. Most likely, they had the only operating vehicle for miles. And the moment they started it, everyone would either want a ride or would want to take their truck. When they decided to leave, it would be mayhem. So they waited for the most opportune time—daylight.

Mobile, Alabama

Michael Cortland split his time between his home in Mobile—with wife, Meredith, and daughter, Hannah—and Washington, DC, where he served as the chief of staff to powerful United States Senator Hugh McNeil. Congress had remained in session during what would ordinarily be the Christmas recess due to the political wranglings concerning the President of the United States and attempts to have him removed from office. But that was not the reason Cort, as he was called by his friends and family, was taking the late evening flight home.

He had been summoned by his father-in-law, George Trowbridge, to his East Haven, Connecticut, estate. Trowbridge was considered one of the most powerful people in Washington despite the fact he'd never held public office. Cort was the son Trowbridge never had, and as a result, he had been taken under the patriarch's wing and groomed for great things.

The conversation was a difficult one, as the old man was bedridden and permanently connected to dialysis. However, as they conversed, Cort was left with these ominous words:

Either you control destiny, or destiny controls you.

Cort was consumed by what his father-in-law meant as he waited for a connecting flight from Atlanta, Georgia, to Mobile, Alabama. The flight that should have been routine was anything but. On final approach to Mobile, the plane suffered a total blackout of power. Nothing worked on board the aircraft, including battery backups, warning lights, or communications.

The pilots made every effort to ditch the plane in the Gulf of Mexico, but the impact on the water caused the fuselage to break in two before it sank towards the sandy bottom of the gulf.

Cort leapt into action to help save his surrounding passengers, including an important Alabama congressman from the other side of the aisle. His Good Samaritan efforts almost killed him. He almost drowned on that evening and was fortunate to be rescued and delivered to the emergency room in Mobile.

After a visit from Meredith and Hannah, Cort began to assess the devastating events around the country and then hearkened back to the words of his father-in-law regarding destiny. Deep down, he knew there was a connection.

Atlanta, Georgia

On the surface, Will Hightower appeared to be a man down on his luck although some might argue that he'd made his own bed, now he had to sleep in it, as the saying goes.

Will's life had changed dramatically in the course of two years since a single inartful use of words during a stressful situation caused his family's world to come crashing down. He had been a respected member of Philly SWAT, one of the most renowned special weapons and tactics teams in the nation. Until one night he lost that respect.

During the investigation and media firestorm, his ex-wife, Karen, turned to the arms of another man, one of his partners. His son, Ethan, and daughter, Skylar, were berated in school and alienated from him by their mother. And Will made the decision to leave Philadelphia to provide his family a respite from the continuous attacks from the media and groups who demanded Will be removed from the police force.

With a new start in Atlanta as part of the security team at Mercedes-Benz Stadium, Will looked forward to a new life in a new city, where his children could visit far away from his past. Ethan and Skylar arrived in Atlanta for a long New Year's weekend that was to begin with a concert, featuring Beyoncé and Jay-Z, at the stadium.

A poor choice by his son landed the kids on the field level of the concert in front of the stage, and then the lights went out. Saboteurs had infiltrated the stadium and caused all power to be disconnected. The thousands of concertgoers panicked, and the kids were in peril.

Will was able to find an injured Ethan and frightened Skylar. He whisked them away to the safety of his home; however, their evening was not over. Will was able to pick up on the tragic events occurring around the country. The collapse he'd feared was on the brink of occurring manifested itself.

Then he received a text. Four simple words that meant so much to his future and the safety of his children. It read:

Time to come home. H.

He'd been asked to come home. But not in the sense most would think. His home was not back in Philadelphia with an ex-wife who'd made his life miserable. It was in another place that he'd become a part of since he left the City of Brotherly Love.

It was time for him to go to the Haven, where he was simply known as Delta.

Washington, DC

Hayden Blount was young, attractive, and a brilliant attorney. She also represented the President of the United States as he fought to protect his presidency. After winning reelection, the president came under attack again, but this time, it was from his own side of the aisle.

Making history, his vice president and members of his cabinet invoked a little-known clause of the Twenty-Fifth Amendment to the Constitution to remove him from office because they deemed him unfit for the job.

Using Hayden's law firm to represent him, the president counterpunched by firing all of the signers of the letter and installing a new cabinet. This created chaos within Washington, and many considered the machinations to have created a constitutional crisis.

The matter was now before the Supreme Court, where Hayden once clerked, and she was putting the final touches on a brief that had to be filed before midnight on New Year's Eve. After a conversation with the senior partner who spearheaded the president's representation, and a brief appearance at the firm's year-end soiree, Hayden left for home.

Trouble seemed to be on the horizon for the young woman when she got stuck on the building's elevator for a brief time. After enduring two drunken carousers, the elevator was fixed, and she happily headed for the subway trains, which carried people around metropolitan Washington, DC.

She was headed south of the city toward Congress Heights when suddenly, just as the train was at its lowest point in a tunnel under the Anacostia River, the lights went out, and so did all power to the train.

A carefully orchestrated cyber attack had been used to shut down all transportation in Washington, DC, including the trains, public buses, and the airports. The city was brought to a standstill, and Hayden was stuck in the subway, in the dark, with a predator stalking her.

She got away from the man who would do her harm, using her survival skills and Krav Maga training. Then she helped some women and children to safety by climbing up a ladder and through a ventilation duct.

Once at home with her beloved Maine coon cat, Prowler, Hayden began to learn of the attacks around the country. She was shocked to learn the Washington transportation outage wasn't the lead story. It was far from it.

Monocacy Farm, South of Frederick, Maryland

The story ended as it began. The people who had initiated these attacks came together for a toast at the Civil War–era farmhouse overlooking the river. They weren't politicians or elected officials. They were spooks, spies, and soldiers. Government officials and bureaucrats—accountable to no one but themselves.

They shared a glass of champagne and cheered on their successes of the evening, hurtful as they were to their fellow Americans. They acknowledged their task had just begun. Standing before them, the host of the gathering closed the meeting with the following words:

"One man's luck is often generated by another man's misfortunes. I, for one, believe that we can make our own luck. It will be necessary to achieve our goals as laid out in our carefully crafted plans.

"With this New Year's toast, I urge all of you to trust the plan. Know that a storm is coming. It will be a storm upon which the blood of patriots and tyrants will spill."

He raised his champagne glass into the air, and everyone in the room followed suit.

"Godspeed, Patriots!"

And so it began…

Book Two: *Doomsday: Haven*

The story continues with the introduction of Ryan and Blair Smart, and their four-legged kids, Chubby and The Roo.

My mother taught me a German proverb that goes like this — *Wer im Spiel Pech hat, hat Glück in der Liebe.* Or something like that (My German is a little rusty). This translates to mean *he who is unlucky in game or gambling, is lucky at love.*

Well, Ryan and Blair Smart were lucky in both. The married couple from Florida spent each day of their lives together and loved every minute of it. They were not gamblers, but on one fateful night before Halloween, they decided to take a stab at winning the largest Megaball lottery in history.

They won. Now, they faced the daunting task of what to do with their money.

The Smarts were genuinely concerned about the direction their country was taking and vowed to never let outside influences disrupt their happiness. They wanted to find peace and serenity in their daily lives while preparing for the eventual collapse of American society.

Over the next two years, their lottery winnings were transformed into the Haven, a community developed on the site of the Hunger Games movie set located at Henry River Mill Village in North Carolina, an hour or so west of Charlotte.

The community was designed to use the existing structures on the land, plus modern ones specifically purposed for creating a preparedness community. The Smarts set about to assemble a team, all of whom had an important skill to contribute to the Haven. Through direct contact and the recruitment of like-minded thinkers they met on social media, the Haven became a reality.

And it was just in time. In the midst of a quiet New Year's Eve celebration, the proverbial crap hit the fan.

OUR OTHER CHARACTERS

As a new day dawned on a new year, our characters found themselves in various states of disarray. As the reader found out in book two, they all had a common goal—get to the Haven. The journey was not easy for any of them.

HAYDEN BLOUNT was in a state of limbo. She was scheduled to appear before the United States Supreme Court on behalf of the President as he fought the 25th Amendment action taken against him. She was self-reliant and confident in her capabilities, but by the same token, she wasn't going to risk her life unnecessarily by staying in the metropolitan Washington, DC area as society collapsed around her.

Hayden prepares for either eventuality and travels to a nearby Walmart to purchase additional ammunition and supplies. After stopping by the gun range to retrieve her firearms, she sees a group of people spray-painting graffiti on a bridge support. The drawing of a fist raising a black rose high into the air was unknown to her, but left an indelible mark, nonetheless.

TOM and DONNA SHELTON had survived the chaos of New Year's Eve with the only injury coming to Donna's ankle. As they rested in their hotel room, they were startled by a loud knocking at their door. The police were evacuating the area around Time Square due to a dirty bomb scare.

With the assistance of a wheelchair, Tom and Donna made their way through Midtown Manhattan to a staging area where buses were provided for refugees to flee the city. One of the destinations to choose from was East Haven, Connecticut, a place that Tom knew well.

While Donna slept by his side, Tom decided to call upon a resident of East Haven whom he'd met in the past — George Trowbridge. During this meeting in which Tom asked for assistance to get closer to home, it was revealed that the two men had been connected for many years.

Trowbridge was rich and powerful, and he'd purchased the loyalty of Tom Shelton with a handsome stipend in exchange for seemingly mundane tasks related to his command at Joint Base Charleston. The relationship had been hidden from Donna, but she accepted her husband's explanation as their benefactor assisted them to Norfolk.

During the meeting at the Trowbridge residence, the sickly man provided Tom a letter to deliver to Meredith Cortland. Tom did not know anything about her, but Trowbridge assured him that their paths might cross.

MICHAEL "CORT" CORTLAND, wife MEREDITH, and daughter, HANNAH

The Cortland family had to make a decision. Cort had recovered and was released to go home. After seeing the news reports and speaking with his boss, a powerful Washington Senator, Cort knew that he had to take his family to the Haven.

There was just one problem. They knew nothing about it. Following an emotional scene in which Cort revealed some, but not all, of what he knew about the state of affairs and his reason for becoming involved in the Haven to begin with, Meredith acquiesced to leaving Mobile.

Her bigger concern was now for her husband who wanted to fly. Gasoline shortages had struck the nation and societal unrest was rampant on the first day following the terrorist attacks. She as convinced that Cort was suffering from PTSD, but he insisted, and the family made the arrangements.

DR. ANGELA RANKIN, TYLER RANKIN, and their children, KAYCEE and J.C.

The Rankins were caught in the midst of a region decimated by an EMP attack. Electronics were destroyed, the rural parts of New Jersey where they were located had no power. But the Rankins were fortunate that Tyler had an old Ford Bronco that was not susceptible to the electromagnetic pulse.

This would become both a blessing and a curse for the family. Having the only operating vehicle for miles, they immediately became a target of their desperate fellow man. Their first challenge was to get away from the Six Flags parking lot that was packed with dazed and confused New Year's revelers.

Then, they had to traverse the back roads through New Jersey toward their home in Richmond, Virginia. Except for a few skirmishes along the way, the family was almost safely in Virginia when they came upon the Chesapeake Bay Bridge-Tunnel. They entered the dark tunnel not realizing that trouble lay ahead.

Tyler gets ambushed by thugs who were robbing travelers in the darkness of the tunnel, but Angela came to the rescue. The family persevered and eventually made it home to Richmond where they came to the realization that they needed to wind up their affairs and head for the Haven.

THE HAVEN

We were introduced to Ryan and Blair Smart and got a sense for what brought them to North Carolina, and why. They applied their organizational skills, their preparedness mindset, and their newly found wealth to create a community that could not only protect themselves from the inevitable collapse of society, but others as well.

Their team consisted of like-minded thinkers with valuable skills the Haven needed. After the events of New Year's Eve, they set their security plans into motion and waited for other residents to arrive. The first to arrive was WILL HIGHTOWER, a/k/a DELTA, and his kids, ETHAN and SKYLAR.

Delta blended in with the team and he tried to reassure his kids that they would be safe. Skylar took to the community immediately, but Ethan had his doubts. He was more focused on reaching out to his mother and possibly bringing her to the Haven than assimilating with the other residents.

Around the Haven, preparations were being made. Security was established, duties were assigned, and the Smarts tried to implement the detailed plans they'd created over the prior two years. They hoped for the best but prepared for the worst.

THE HEAVY HITTERS

It turns out, as the conspiracy surrounding George Trowbridge, his associates and the Schwartz family deepened. He assisted the Sheltons to travel quickly toward the Haven, providing Tom a letter to give to Meredith Trowbridge Cortland.

He had a pulse on a lot of things, although his own pulse was weakening due to a debilitating disease. Trowbridge began to have his doubts about what happened to Cort on the ill-fated Delta 322 flight. He suspected that his associates were going off the reservation, so to speak.

Meanwhile, György Schwartz and his son, Jonathan, plotted the further demise of the United States by inserting themselves into the chaos. Jonathan was the henchman of the family while his father played global financier.

One of the Schwartz family's favorite tool to manipulate financial markets was to fabricate societal unrest. To further their goals of collapsing the U.S. dollar, and destabilize American society, Jonathan calls upon the anarchist group known as the Black Rose, or Rosa Negra.

Well-financed by the Schwartz family organizations, the grassroots movement around the country was known for wreaking havoc on cities during political events. Now, they'd be called upon to take the fight to Main Street USA, America's heartland, where we all live in our neighborhoods, with two-car garages, and parks for our children to play in.

None of the following is supposed to happen around us. No sirree. Only in the big cities, or places like Portland, Seattle, Chicago, and DC, right?

Doomsday: Anarchy begins now…

January 2, The Dawn of a New Day

CHAPTER 1

American Airlines Flight 5463
Pensacola to Charlotte

Humans were not meant to be airborne. Michael Cortland repeated this to himself throughout the ninety-minute flight from Pensacola to Charlotte on that New Year's night. It had only been fifteen hours since he'd been plucked out of the Gulf of Mexico following the ill-fated Delta flight on New Year's Eve. Somewhere during the ordeal, he'd sworn off flying forever, he was sure of it.

Yet, there he was, buckled into a Canadair RJ-700, a sixty-eight-seat regional jet manufactured by Bombardier. Cort knew all of these details because during the preflight checks, he'd read the safety instructions backwards and forwards and insisted that Meredith and Hannah do the same.

His anxiety was so bad that he admonished a passenger seated in front of him to pay attention as the flight attendants went through their safety briefing. The two exchanged words before Meredith was able to calm Cort down. She'd pulled a bottle of water out of her carry-on and insisted he take two of her Zoloft tablets, a medication prescribed to her for premenstrual dysphoric disorder. PMDD was similar to PMS, except more serious.

Before they left the house, Meredith had researched whether Zoloft would help Cort with the aftereffects of the plane crash and the post-traumatic stress he would most likely encounter. Her online research, and a quick conversation with Cort's attending physician at the hospital, confirmed the medication would help.

The doctor made it abundantly clear that he did not approve of Cort's flying so soon, especially the same evening following the crash.

Meredith didn't approve either, but Cort was very convincing. He was genuinely concerned for the safety of his family.

The Mobile airport was still closed due to the investigation, so they made the one-hour drive into Florida to catch a flight from Pensacola to Charlotte. They'd purchased their tickets online but still had to go through the check-in process because Cort was traveling with weapons and Handsome Dan.

Interestingly, his ability to bring guns on board the aircraft was easier than convincing the American Airlines personnel that their seventy-pound English bulldog was an *emotional support animal* under the FAA guidelines.

Cort was unaware of any limits placed on the number of weapons that could be checked aboard an aircraft, but he assumed the handgun and two rifles he brought would not be a problem. Still, procedures would need to be followed. Cort lived in a time in which pocket knives, snow globes, and gel inserts for your shoes couldn't be brought through a TSA checkpoint.

His weapons were stored in sturdy, hard plastic cases that contained fitted foam made for each gun. His ammunition, because it was less than .75 caliber, could be stored in the same cases, and Cort ensured the magazines were empty.

The ticket agent studied Handsome Dan throughout the check-in process, even going so far as to call in two different supervisors to assess the situation. Meredith had obtained by fax an ESA letter from Cort's attending physician, the second reason for her phone call.

In recent years, the major airlines had tightened the leash on comfort animals as passengers began to abuse the privilege. Everything from squirrels to miniature ponies had emerged as candidates to help fearful passengers get from one destination to another. Passengers had become lax in their restraints of the animals as they were allowed to wander the cabin midflight, at times misbehaving, biting other passengers, or defecating at will.

It became incumbent upon the ticket agents to determine if the passenger had the proper paperwork, which included the ESA letter—a signed letter from a veterinarian stating the animal was trained to behave without a kennel—and a health vaccination record from the vet.

Meredith had the ESA letter and Handsome's vaccination history, but not the training letter. After explaining to the American Airlines agent the circumstances behind Cort's crash, the three personnel made a judgment call and allowed Handsome on board. To his credit, the stout pup sat quietly as he passed inspection, despite the fact that a yappy poodle disrupted the entire terminal.

The process helped distract Cort from the task at hand. It wasn't until the family was buckled in and the pilot had pushed the aircraft away from the gate that reality set in for Cort. His palms became moist and then sweat began to pour down his forehead. After his stomach rolled over the first time, he looked around to see how many rows he'd have to race down to reach the lavatory. This thought process reminded him of swimming through the Delta aircraft in search of Congressman Johnson Pratt, a noble gesture that almost got him killed.

Cort had applied some logic when he booked the flight. He wanted to sit with Handsome next to him, but Hannah and Meredith nearby. He pulled up the seating chart and found an entire row open. He purchased all six seats. Meredith and Hannah sat across the aisle, and he strapped Handsome in the middle seat next to him. Cort felt most comfortable in the aisle and immediately pulled down the window shade after they boarded. He had no intention of looking outside.

Several times throughout the flight, he second-guessed his decision to leave so abruptly and, especially, the choice of transportation. The news reports coming in from around the country indicated gas shortages had swept the nation as panicked Americans topped off their tanks and fuel trucks stopped running altogether due to the attacks.

Then there was the matter of the electronic failure of the Delta flight. Cort wasn't all that familiar with the operation of commercial jets, but he did understand the effect an electromagnetic pulse could have on one. He'd been part of many Pentagon briefings with his boss, Senator Hugh McNeil, in which the use of EMPs in warfare were discussed.

The development of directed-energy weapons capable of disabling electronics on a specific target was a high priority for the Department of Defense, as well as other military powerhouses around the world. The downing of Delta 322 had all the earmarks of a pulsed energy attack.

Now Cort needed to know why. *Was it purely coincidental?* Sure, Congressman Pratt, the man who would lead the impeachment charge against the president, might be a target of political opponents. But was murdering everyone on an airplane to get to one man necessary?

Or was there more than one target?

Cort's mind raced to many different scenarios and plausible explanations. The Zoloft managed to keep him in his seat and not throwing up in the lavatory, but it did little to calm his anxiety.

He kept a constant watch on the Flight Tracker display on the small monitor embedded in the back of the seat in front of him. They were making their final approach into Charlotte, and a sense of relief began to wash over him. Then he recalled he had been less than a mile from home when Delta 322 hit the water, and a wave of anxiety hit him again.

To reassure himself, he elected to open the window shade. He stretched to reach over their passed-out, snoring bulldog. "Some comfort you are," Cort whispered to his *bestest pal* with a grin. With a slight grunt to overcome the pain in his midsection, Cort reached the shade and forced it upward.

He closed his eyes and shook his head before opening them again to confirm they hadn't betrayed him. Fires roared out of control throughout the Charlotte cityscape.

CHAPTER 2

Schwartz Estate
Katonah, New York

György Schwartz knew that it didn't matter whether he was right or wrong. What mattered was how much money he'd made when he was right, and how much he lost when he was wrong. He was a rich man financially because he survived by recognizing his mistakes and admitting when he was wrong. He was rich spiritually because he'd had a profound impact on the geopolitical affairs of the world for decades.

When pressed on the issue of his political influence during an interview with the BBC, he dryly quipped, *I cannot and do not look at the social consequences of what I do.* Nobody believed that statement, least of all Schwartz, yet it was delivered with conviction and sincerity.

In the United States during this time, almost everyone had an agenda. News networks were identified by whether they leaned left or right on the political spectrum. Television networks were known to cater to certain demographic groups. Print media attracted journalists who were like-minded thinkers.

Even authors of fiction, those who conjure up characters and scenarios to provide entertainment for their readers, couldn't help but allow their personal beliefs to slip through in their writing. *We're all humans, after all.*

Schwartz was different. He had wealth, and with his vast riches, he was able to exert a tremendous amount of influence over political candidates at all levels of governments, in any country. Money runs campaigns, and Schwartz was generous with his contributions, provided the candidates fulfilled a commitment to advance his agenda.

There was, however, one matter that he had not yet addressed. Something that would either bankrupt him or make him the richest man on the planet. Today, he would complete his quest to collapse the U.S. economy and cause the collapse of the dollar.

"Good morning, Jonathan," he said in a cheerful voice as his son arrived in the estate's magnificently appointed conference room. Television monitors were installed and framed as if they were works of art. To break up the walls, exquisite paintings adorned the walls, and sconce lighting allowed an eerie glow to cast shadows on the ceiling.

"Did you sleep well?" his son responded, imperceptibly nodding to the butler, who poured his morning tea. Father and son were accustomed to making small talk while the staff served their breakfast. Most mornings, the two men met in the dining room, but today, one that would not be forgotten by financiers around the world, required them to have access to all the electronic tools necessary to effectuate their plan and monitor the results.

"*Tre bone, konsiderante*," Schwartz replied, relaying the fact he slept well under the circumstances. Schwartz chose to speak in Esperanto, an unusual, secretive language he'd learned from his father, a speaker and writer who'd traveled Europe following his release from a Siberian prison camp after World War One. Esperanto was designed to be an international language, loosely based upon Latin. "*Grava tago atendas.*"

An important day awaits. The words came out of his mouth with the singsong rhythm of an Italian cardinal speaking to one of his aides, or of Michael Corleone in *The Godfather III*.

"Shall I make the calls?" asked Jonathan, curtly dismissing the staff and directing them to close the doors as they departed. He'd been up for hours as the European markets opened. Before he went to bed, he'd alerted the family's business associates in Asia to be prepared for a busy day.

Schwartz wandered around the conference room, pausing to

survey the inhospitable winter landscape outside. The snow had fallen throughout the night, obliterating the line between the lawn and a small lake located behind the stately home. Schwartz chuckled to himself. Nature's stormy wrath had a similar effect on the world as his life's work—blurred lines and eliminated boundaries.

To a stranger, Schwartz might have appeared disinterested in making conversation with his son. As he focused on the white splendor that engulfed his home, one might mistake his faraway thoughts as unfocused, perhaps hearkening back to his native Hungary. But his mind was singularly focused on the task at hand.

When he began to speak, his son took meticulous notes. The Schwartz financial empire was comprised of many multinational corporations and organizations, utilizing a complex network of brokerage accounts enabling him to effectuate secretive transactions.

Schwartz continued to give his son direction, using his brilliant mind to announce his plan. A financial attack he'd plotted and dreamt about for many years.

"Dominica, St. Kitts, Providenciales, Cook Islands, Nevis, Panama." His voice was grave as he listed the most used tax havens in the world, where offshore accounts and shell companies were the norm.

The intricacy of the trades was remarkable. The sums of money, *billions*, were astounding. Jonathan typed furiously on his iPad, his longish fingernails tapping the glass screen as he recorded his father's directives.

"Father, this will take days," Jonathan lamented when Schwartz stopped to gather his thoughts.

"No, it will not!" he shot back, taking his son's demeanor as insolence. "We must complete these transactions before the opening of the Asian markets."

"That's in five hours." Jonathan was wounded by his father's rebuke. He shook it off, taking into account the magnitude of the moment. He added, "The Australian markets open an hour sooner."

"Understood, son. Currency trades of this magnitude will have repercussions throughout the global financial system. They will draw attention, and rightfully so. That's by design. I want them to notice. I want them to know their currency is under attack. Frightened animals act irrationally. We'll be prepared for the next step when they do."

Jonathan nodded and sipped his tea. He relaxed as his father's tone changed. "These will be scrutinized by the CFTC. Taking a one-point-three billion short position in the euro, coupled with a corresponding long position in the dollar, will not go unnoticed."

The CFTC, the United States Commodity Futures Trading Commission, had been established during Schwartz's early days as a hedge fund trader to regulate options and futures markets. He'd been navigating through their regulations for decades, which was ironic because his trading activities were responsible for quite a few of them.

"I'm aware, but Washington is in chaos. The president is hiding. With the help of your friends, the regulatory apparatus will be focused on things other than their jobs."

Jonathan continued to study the currency transactions. The size of these trades would rival those that triggered the Asian financial crisis in 1997 and the collapse of the British pound sterling in 1992. The process of short-selling and long-selling had been used by traders for decades to manipulate markets in their favor.

"There is more, son," Schwarz continued. "The U.S. markets will be closed indefinitely, but their equities will be sold internationally, nonetheless. I want to put pressure on corporate America to force Washington to intervene abroad. I want you to systematically dump our positions in American equities too."

"Father, we stand to lose a considerable amount of earned profits gained."

Schwartz sighed and managed a sigh. He pulled his maroon-colored silk housecoat closed and stuck his hands in his pockets. Looking at the winter wonderland outside, the thought of his goals being realized warmed his heart.

"It's all for the greater good, son."

CHAPTER 3

Haven House
The Haven

Ryan Smart sat in a comfortable, rolled-arm chair in the corner of their master bedroom, sipping his morning drink concoction, a fifty-fifty blend of Couple's Coffee and Fairlife two percent chocolate milk. His daily routine, when he didn't have to hit the ground running, began with perusing the day's news headlines on his iPad and waiting for his lovely wife to wake up. Blair started to stir on her own, and Ryan paused to admire her beauty.

"I'm so lucky to wake up next to someone so beautiful every day," he said in a soft tone as she sat upright in bed. His compliment was corny, yet sincere. He loved her more than life.

Blair's long blond hair covered half her face, and the half that was visible revealed an eye that was barely open. She slowly shook her head from side to side in disagreement.

"You can save that one for the Thanksgiving prayer, buddy." Blair immediately fell backwards onto her pillow and pulled the covers over her head. Then she added, her voice muffled by the covers, "It's too early. Go away."

Ryan laughed and took another sip of his coffee drink. He considered teasing Blair and even ripping all the covers off her to get her good and riled up, but he resisted his devious urges. They had a long day ahead, one of many to come, he presumed. He would need his wife and partner well rested.

"Can I talk to you?" he asked sheepishly.

Blair slowly removed the blankets covering her head. Her hair was now completely over her face, making her the perfect vision of

Cousin Itt from the classic *Addams Family* shows. "Go ahead. I may or may not be listening." She covered back up and got settled in to catch a few more winks.

Ryan ignored her efforts to hide. "Things are escalating. Overnight, riots broke out in cities across the country. I'm starting to see a pattern here. The locations aren't the usual high-profile targets to garner media attention. Instead I'm seeing places like Nashville, Phoenix, and Richmond. Even Charlotte."

Blair started to come to life, as Ryan knew she would. "What pattern?"

"In all the reports I could find, there's a noticeable effort to target the suburbs. Especially wealthy and middle-class neighborhoods. I've been looking at images of families driven out of their homes by fires. You know, mom, dad, and two small children holding nothing but their freakin' teddy bears."

Blair sat up and propped herself against several pillows. She reached for her bkr water bottle. The iconic glass-and-silicone bottle was a constant companion to Blair, as she'd vowed to stay hydrated. "We've talked about these rabble-rousers before. They always seek media attention. What's the point in going into the burbs?"

"I don't know, but it can't be coincidental. The national media hasn't mentioned it, really. They've shifted their focus back to what the president is going to do, and how all of this relates to the Supreme Court."

"Have they identified any specific groups who are behind the riots?" asked Blair, now fully awake and reaching for her own iPad.

"No, but there are some images that have emerged on Twitter. You know, thugs dressed in head-to-toe black outfits. Leather boots, faces covered in black bandanas and topped off with a black hat or mask. It's all intended to intimidate anyone who dares to stand in their way."

"They have their uniforms and we have ours—camo."

Ryan chuckled. "Just like the blues and the grays of the Civil War. Every army has their own colors."

"Well, there's also this," added Blair as she held up her iPad. She routinely checked news from Florida. She pointed to an image from the front page of the *Gainesville Sun* newspaper's website. It depicted a group of armed men patrolling the streets of an affluent neighborhood. All were carrying AR-15s and dressed in camouflage clothing.

"Exactly," said Ryan. "That's what I'm talking about. Newton's laws of quantum physics."

"Huh?" Blair wasn't *that* awake yet.

"You know, for every action, there is an equal and opposite reaction," Ryan explained. "On New Year's Eve, somebody, and I have no idea who, fired the first shots."

"Big ones," interjected Blair.

"Oh yeah. But now the ground war has begun. It's almost like a civil war between left and right. The Antifa bunch do what they do best—create a lawless environment. You know, anarchy. The guys on the opposite end of the spectrum bow up and show they're tough by walking down the street carrying their guns. In the past, everyone mouthed off at each other and then went home. Not now."

Blair continued to read through the article from Gainesville. "The good old boys from Ocala who came to join their friends in Gainesville shot and killed three UF students who were part of the Antifa protestors."

"Were they protesting or setting fires like in these other cities?" asked Ryan.

Blair scrolled further down the article. "Apparently, the students, dressed in black like the others, were carrying lit torches toward a gated community near Gainesville Country Club. Fires had already been set around town. Before they could scale the gates, the good old boys opened fire. Three were killed, and half a dozen were wounded."

"How would the guys from Ocala even know to be there?" asked Ryan.

Blair shrugged. "Beats me."

The two continued reading their respective news articles before Ryan went to the kitchen and prepared Blair's coffee. When he returned, he got down to business before he left for the morning briefing at the Haven Barn.

"I had a text from Alpha. We've had a few new arrivals, and I suspect more will be coming throughout the day. I wanna get jobs assigned to everyone so we can be ready for anything that comes our way."

Blair sipped her coffee. "Sounds good. I'll check the roster and try to make a few more calls, but, Ryan, I can't chase these people down. Either they're gonna take advantage of what we have here, or they're not."

"I totally agree. Do you need me to assign anyone to you? You know, admin, security, anything?"

"Nope," she replied with confidence. "Today, I'll do an orientation for some of the new peeps. My focus is going to be on establishing routines and a sense of normalcy. Idle time creates idle minds, and idle minds concoct drama that we don't need. This is not a time for sitting around commiserating or hand-wringing."

Ryan laughed at the tough nature of his wife. She was sweet and adorable on the exterior, but on the inside, she had a resolve that nobody should underestimate. He approached Blair and gave her a kiss, something he'd never failed to do in all of their years together.

"We know what to expect," he began. "Now we need to make sure everyone is on the same page. I love you."

They kissed again and the two embarked on the second day of the apocalypse, fully expecting more surprises to be thrown their way.

CHAPTER 4

CNN Center
Atlanta, Georgia

At This Hour host, Kate Bolduan, sat upright in her chair and addressed the camera. "As we continue to keep our viewers abreast of the situation with foreign exchange markets via the chyron on the screen, I'd like to move to another topic that has been heavily on the minds of legal analysts. I'm referring to the president's use of executive orders following a contentious election."

CNN had maintained its regular programming lineup as it continuously broadcast scenes from areas around the country that were directly impacted by the attacks of New Year's Eve. Bolduan was joined on the news set by two attorneys.

One was Jeannie Ray, a former attorney for the Clinton Foundation and a member of the now disbanded special prosecutor's team headed by Robert Mueller. The other, a longtime Washington insider, Rachel Black, had been the United States associate attorney general but was best known for her legal representation of President George W. Bush during the 2000 presidential election recount in Florida.

Bolduan began the conversation with a pointed question directed at Rachel Black. "Rachel, you've been down this road before, in a way. You have a contested election, the electorate is angry at the result, and political animus rules the day. What advice do you give the president?"

"Kate, today is a deeply divided time. There is an anger out there, a rage, that isn't healthy. In the lead-up to this election, the acrimony that we were seeing, um, we also saw in the 2016 election, and we saw it again this year. It is a bitterness, to the point of being apoplectic, that is tearing us apart. In my opinion, it's corroding the very fabric of our democracy."

Bolduan pressed further. "Rachel, isn't the president partly to blame for this hostility? I mean, take his use of executive orders and the recent firing of his cabinet. Why wouldn't that justify the anger and rage you referenced?"

"First of all, Kate, as I argued in 2000, just because one side doesn't like the results doesn't mean you can overturn the outcome afterwards. Bush versus Gore was the first attempt I've seen to delegitimize an election, and it happened again in 2004, 2016, and now in 2020. It's sour grapes from a bunch of sore losers, in my opinion."

Bolduan held up her hand and tried to tone her guest down, but before she could speak, Jeannie Ray, the other panelist, fired back, "I think Rachel is missing the point here. Or avoiding it, whichever. The matter before the Supreme Court has nothing to do with the allegations of election fraud and ballot manipulation. We're talking about the president's own cabinet speaking out to protect the nation from someone who is clearly mentally unstable. The Twenty-Fifth Amendment was put in place for a reason, and we were seeing it properly implemented until the *bloodletting*."

Black chuckled and shook her head condescendingly. "The *bloodletting*, a term coined by this network, is a farce. The cabinet serves at the pleasure of the president. He can fire any of them, or all of them, as he deems fit. Just because it doesn't suit your political agenda doesn't make it illegal."

"Politics has nothing to do with this," Ray shot back. "We're talking about a mentally unstable president who needs to be removed from office. The people who know him best—his cabinet, his co-workers, if you will—agreed. The law was followed, and he should've stepped aside in the best interests of the country."

"That's a load of crap, and you know it," countered Black. "The president has undergone more scrutiny from the media than any in history. He has submitted himself to frequent physicals and mental-acuity tests since the issue regarding his mental competence was raised on day one of his presidency. Besides, where was the vice president and the cabinet before the election? Hmm? They rode his coattails back into office, and lo and behold, the traitors to the nation tried to remove him in order to take over."

"*Traitors* is a pretty strong word, don't you think?" Bolduan interjected a question in an effort to take back control of the interview.

The two female panelists were having none of it. This was their stage now.

Ray ignored her question and was now glaring at Black. "Traitor? The vice president is a good man, widely respected on both sides of the aisle."

Black laughed at the statement. "Yeah, sure, when he's a convenient stooge for the left. Do I need to remind you of the names he's been called? The accusations made about his religious beliefs? The way he's been treated—"

"He is just one of the cabinet members. Look at all of the others, Rachel. Besides, none of that is relevant. The Twenty-Fifth Amendment was designed to create a process, and your president decided to shun the Constitution, a document that he tries to wrap himself in most times, or at least when it suits him. He fired his detractors, all good people, in order to save his presidency."

"That's his prerogative." Black shouted her response. "I'm sorry that the political lynching didn't work out for you."

"What? Lynching?" Ray was incredulous. "How dare you hearken back to the dark times in this nation when race relations were at their worst. That's a word that should never be used in the public discourse."

"Good grief! It's just a word. Would you rather me call it mob justice? Vigilantism?"

Bolduan interrupted. "Rachel, two members of the president's cabinet are African-American. One might construe your use of the–"

"Well, well, nice of you to notice, Kate," snarled Black. "How many times has this network referred to the president as being racist?

Yet he has diversity in cabinet. I stand by my statement."

Ray had a stack of notes in front of her on the table. She picked them up and slammed them on the desk in front of her. An awkward silence ensued until Bolduan touched her hand to her earpiece.

"It's time for a hard commercial break, but when we return, we'll look at the president's options in times like these, including the use of martial law."

Into her open microphone, Ray mumbled, "Every tyrant's favorite weapon."

Black and Ray were glaring at each other when one of the CNN producers, speaking into Bolduan's earpiece, instructed her to step away from the host's chair. She quietly excused herself although the two women seated across from her hardly noticed her departure.

She walked around the back of the rolling cameras and the bright lights that illuminated the set. She accepted a glass of water and a touch-up of her makeup as two of the show's producers approached her.

Bolduan spoke first. "These two don't like one another very much."

"Ray is seething. Look at her," said one of the producers, who nodded in the direction of the two panelists. The two women were not speaking, but their body language spoke volumes.

"Well, Black instigated the whole thing with her attitude," the other producer chimed in. "I thought Jeannie held her tongue pretty well."

Bolduan shook her head and laughed. "I thought they were going to come to blows."

"Good, let 'em," said the first producer. "It'll be ratings gold."

The group observed the two women, who sat with their arms folded in front of them, staring in different directions. Bolduan asked, "Did you guys catch what Ray said after I signed off? Did that come through the mic?"

"Oh yeah," said the second producer, "and guess what? It hit the airwaves too."

"You guys didn't cut it? You had seven seconds."

The first producer pointed her thumb over her shoulder. The big guys made a snap decision and said to run with it. The press will talk about it for a day or two."

"Publicity," muttered Bolduan.

"Name of the game, Kate," said the second producer. "You need to get back in the chair. This segment should be fun."

CHAPTER 5

Congress Heights
Washington, DC

Hayden Blount's mind was focused on the uncertainty of the upcoming Supreme Court hearing when she awoke that morning. As a single woman, her life didn't involve a partner or getting kids ready for their day. Her career was everything and garnered a hundred percent of her attention. From her early days as a clerk for Justice Samuel Alito until the present, a junior partner with the prestigious firm of Stein Mitchell, her employer was provided a dedicated lawyer who spent every waking hour thinking about the cases she was assigned.

Today was no different. To be sure, most people would be consumed by the signs of collapse occurring around them. The power grid had failed in large parts of New Jersey, Eastern Pennsylvania, and Northern Maryland. Curfews had been established from Baltimore to Trenton, but that didn't stop people from taking to the streets. Looting was rampant, and law enforcement was overwhelmed.

Similar unrest was being experienced closer to home as Washington, DC, was still attempting to restart its public transportation system in the aftermath of the cyber attacks. The mayor had commissioned an emergency advisory council that worked in conjunction with the Department of Homeland Security to conduct a cyber forensic investigation to determine the cause and the culprit.

However, the task of fixing the problem was almost

insurmountable. The malware inserted into the systems couldn't be easily removed, and therefore the computers themselves had to be replaced and the new ones programmed. The internet technology specialists were estimating this to take weeks, not days.

Hayden, however, was not consumed by the drama associated with the New Year's Eve attacks. Nor was she overly concerned about the status of Friday's hearing by the justices on the fate of the president's objection to the Twenty-Fifth Amendment removal from office. She was confident in her brief and the legal position she argued. Whether the hearing occurred on Friday would be determined in short order by the president's potential use of his martial law powers.

No, Hayden was singularly focused on two things. One was the series of text messages she'd received before she'd hustled off to Walmart. Ominous in their tone, it prompted her to go on a shopping spree for ammunition and supplies.

As she entered the kitchen to make coffee and feed Prowler, she picked up the television remote to turn on the news. Then she grabbed her phone and read the messages aloud.

"Luck can come from a tragic sequence of fortuitous events. For one, everything in life is luck. Godspeed, Patriot."

She fixed her coffee and glanced at the TV screen. The volume was muted, but the antics were unmistakable—two partisan contributors were going at it. She recognized Rachel Black immediately. Black was an icon for conservative, female attorneys, as she was somewhat of a glass-ceiling breaker in Washington.

Hayden looked at the phone a second time as she took her first sip of coffee.

Trust the plan.
MM

She'd tossed and turned all night replaying the words in her head. She searched the far recesses of her memory in an attempt to remember who talked like that. The term *patriot* was used often by those on the right who felt it was their duty to protect the Constitution.

In legal circles, conservatives often argued that the Constitution was under attack by activist judges who considered the Constitution to be a worn-out, out-of-date document that needed to be brought into the twenty-first century.

Whoever sent this anonymous message clearly considered her to fall within their definition of being a patriot. Hayden couldn't dispute that, although she always tried to see legal issues from both sides of an argument. That was her job, and failing to do so usually ended in disastrous results for a client.

But the second message still puzzled her. *Trust the plan.* She had no idea who the mysterious *MM* was who sent the message, nor did she have a clue as to what their *plan* was. The night before, she'd fallen asleep with Prowler curled up on her lap and her iPad resting on his side as she searched the internet for people whose initials were *MM*.

The results were as varied as the theories Hayden had generated about the events of New Year's Eve. Matthew McConaughey came to her mind first, naturally. She was single and generally uninterested in dating, but she wasn't oblivious to the man's sex appeal.

The next person who came to mind was Marilyn Monroe, but she was dead. Another Marilyn, Marilyn Manson was next, but, um, no, it wasn't her, or him, or whichever. Hayden wasn't sure on that point.

Marshall Mathers, also known as Eminem, was an option, but not likely. She ultimately found a website called *People By Initials*. The site listed hundreds of people with the initials MM, including the celebrities who came to mind. She researched them all, and none of them had government or political connections. Eventually she drifted off to sleep.

After feeding Prowler, she made her way into the living room with her coffee and a Yoplait blueberry yogurt. The commercial break ended, and the CNN discussion continued. Curious as to why Black and her fellow guest were so animated before the commercial, Hayden turned up the volume to listen in.

"And we're back with our panelists, fellow attorneys Rachel Black and Jeannie Ray," began Kate Bolduan. Hayden had met Bolduan at a dinner party in New York years ago. Bolduan had been pregnant with their daughter and had been accompanied by her husband, Michael David Gershenson, who'd just been named managing director of a major real estate client of Hayden's firm. Bolduan was a genuinely nice person and a respected journalist. Hayden's interest piqued as the discussion continued.

Bolduan took a deep breath and addressed her guests. "I'd like to get your take on the issue of martial law. We are in the throes of a crisis in this country following the attacks of New Year's Eve. Six major U.S. cities were brought to a standstill by various tools of terrorism. Local law enforcement is ill-equipped to handle the unrest, and some authorities are clamoring for the president to act. What should the president do? Rachel Black, you first."

Black sat a little taller in her chair and leaned onto the desk to look Bolduan in the eye. Her response was curt. "Whatever is within his legal authority."

Bolduan, caught off guard by the sudden change in Black's demeanor, pressed for more. "That's just a few words from an eloquent attorney. Would you care to expand on what those options might be?"

"Obviously, the elephant in the room that everyone wants to address is martial law," began Black in response. "So let's do it. The concept of martial law is not expressly mentioned in the Constitution, but the activation in time of rebellion or invasion is addressed in Article One, Section Eight. Also, the suspension of habeas corpus, which prevents someone to be held by the government without due process, is available under Article One, Section Nine."

Hayden knew all of this, and the arguments had been made many times. Several times in the history of the country, martial law had been declared to varying degrees. The most obvious and often-cited example was when President Abraham Lincoln declared martial law during the Civil War. Hayden's mind wandered as she equated the hostilities associated with the Civil War to today's sociopolitical climate. The similarities were remarkable.

"He needs to ask the Congress to make the declaration!"

The sudden outburst by Jeannie Ray brought Hayden back to the present.

Ray, red-faced from the previous exchange, continued. "Lincoln had the authorization of the Congress. This president, despite what he might think of himself, is not a dictator. If it's for the good of the country, the Congress will agree. In just a few days, the new Congress will convene, and he can get their answer. Not before then."

Black couldn't mask her distaste for Ray and her position. Looking at Bolduan, she said, "Kate, I'm pretty sure if the election had gone differently, Jeannie would take a counter position. The law is clear. Supreme Court precedent in the case of *Ex Parte Milligan* laid the groundwork. The president can declare martial law when circumstances warrant it. Look around you. These monitors of your live news feeds depict an America collapsing from these attacks."

Bolduan began to speak when Black cut her off and continued. She turned to Ray and said, "Come on, Jeannie. You spoke earlier of doing what's best for the country. Are you arguing against the president because you want America to descend into the abyss?"

Ray slammed her fist on the table in response. "No, I'm trying to argue against a tyrant of a president using this opportunity to avoid getting kicked out of office. I resent you saying otherwise."

The two women began shouting at one another, prompting Hayden to stand and approach the television monitor for a closer look.

"Prowler, get over here," she shouted to her Maine coon cat. His instincts were to fight and he'd enjoy a good *human catfight*. "I think they're gonna come to—"

Before Hayden could finish her sentence, it happened. Ray stood and shoved Black until her chair spun around on its swivel base. Black had barely caught her balance to avoid falling to the floor when Ray gave her another push. This time Black couldn't avoid the sudden plunge downward.

"I can't believe this!" shouted Hayden at the screen as Prowler hopped on the coffee table to get eye level to the action. The two of them had ringside seats to the scrap.

Black leapt to her feet and lunged at Ray headfirst, thrusting the crown of her skull into Ray's midsection, knocking her backwards. Ray, in an attempt to avoid falling, grabbed Black's hair with both hands, causing her adversary to scream in pain.

The two rolled over and over across the studio floor until they crashed into the supports of the news feed monitors Black had referred to earlier. After several blows were exchanged, members of the production team moved in to break it up.

Hayden watched with her mouth agape, more astonished that the CNN cameras continued to roll than she was at the fight itself. Only the ringing of her phone could drag her away from the spectacle befitting a Jerry Springer episode.

CHAPTER 6

Congress Heights
Washington, DC

Hayden had barely pressed the accept button on her iPhone when she heard Pat Cipollone's voice. "Blount! Are you watching CNN?"

"Um, yes."

"My money's on Rachel. She's a real fighter. I've squared off in court against her in the past. She's a take-no-prisoners type of litigator."

Hayden laughed and decided to play along, enjoying the playful banter with her boss. "It seemed to me she was blindsided by Jeannie Ray. She should've never let her guard down like that."

"Maybe, but how could she expect Ray to start throwing punches?" countered Cipollone.

"Because, sir, you should always expect the other side to fight dirty. We're at war." Hayden used the phrase facetiously, but deep down, she felt that one was coming.

"Interesting choice of words, Blount," said Cipollone. "My guess is the president agrees with you."

"Have you heard something?"

Cipollone chuckled and replied, "You know, unofficially, off the record. The usual malarkey."

"And?"

Cipollone hesitated, and Hayden turned her attention back to the television momentarily as CNN broke away from its coverage of the catfight to update a report from Richmond. There, news crews showed buildings on fire near the Virginia State Capitol building, the location of the capitol of the Confederacy during the Civil War.

"Richmond?" muttered Cipollone into the phone. "This is spreading like the plague."

"No doubt," responded Hayden, who brought the conversation back to what her boss had called about. "Sir, have you heard something from the president?"

Cipollone returned to the conversation. "His chief of staff, actually. Without saying so officially, he told me that, with ninety percent certainty, the matter before the Supreme Court will be postponed indefinitely."

"Wow, the president is going to declare martial law."

"It appears so. But, interestingly, he may not specifically suspend habeas corpus. A decision hasn't been made yet."

"But, sir, they go hand in hand. I don't know how—"

Cipollone cut her off. "It's political brinkmanship, Blount. You're right, naturally. By exercising his executive privileges under Article One, Section Eight, all governmental functions will come to a standstill while the military gets things under control. I'd be shocked if that process took less than a month."

"Just in time to get inaugurated and to regain the public trust."

"Exactly," said Cipollone. "Listen, his chief of staff is very politically astute. He single-handedly turned this presidency around. On the political battlefield, he was more of a general than the general who occupied his position before him."

"What does that mean for the case, and us?"

"The hearing will be postponed indefinitely," replied Cipollone. "The president, his new cabinet, and the justices will be taken into the government's labyrinth of protective bunker complexes around the country for safekeeping."

"Continuity of government," added Hayden.

"Yes, and frankly, at least in my lifetime, I can't think of a more appropriate time to do so. 9/11 was the closest thing to a war on our soil, and the use of the airplanes pointed directly to a specific group of terrorists. This is different. The weaponry and planning were far more sophisticated. The targets were diverse, yet they weren't."

"Sir, what do you mean by that?" asked Hayden.

Cipollone hesitated. "Um, never mind that. It's rambling speculation from someone who hasn't taken a shower to fully wake up yet. Blount, are you comfortable remaining in Congress Heights? That part of the District has the potential to get ugly."

Hayden had the sense he was giving her a nudge to move to safer surroundings. "I have a place to go, sir, thank you. Might I ask you about something else, off topic?"

"Sure."

"Have you ever run across a political movement symbolized by a black rose? Yesterday, I saw a group of people dressed in black with face masks to obscure their identities. They were spray-painting a fist holding a black rose on a bridge abutment near my condo."

Cipollone gave his opinion. "A black rose, something that doesn't exist naturally, usually symbolizes death or something coming to an end. You know, like a relationship breaking up. I'm unaware of any relationship to political movements, if that's what you're driving at. Do you think it's connected to these attacks?"

"I don't know," replied Hayden. "I just found it unusual that in the midst of all of this, graffiti artists would be taking to the streets unless they had a specific purpose or agenda in mind."

"Well, if you think it's related, call our contacts at the FBI. Let them sort it out."

"Okay, it's probably nothing. Thank you for calling me, sir. Is there anything else?"

"No, Blount, that's it. Keep safe and we'll stay in touch by phone. If something changes, I'll let you know, but watch for the president's declaration today. I suspect they're working on the verbiage now."

The two said their goodbyes and disconnected the call, neither aware that it would be many months before they spoke again.

CHAPTER 7

Rankin Residence
East Clay Street
Richmond, Virginia

It was almost midnight on New Year's Day when the Rankins pulled into the driveway of their 1920s Craftsman-style home in downtown Richmond. Angela was curled up in the front seat with her head leaning against the window, while the kids had crawled under their respective blankets in the back. Tyler had pulled into the short driveway and turned off the ignition, yet none of his family stirred. For a moment, he contemplated leaving them there because they were sleeping so soundly, but when he heard a group of teenagers yelling down the street, he thought better of it.

That night, the family had slept hard. Their ordeal since New Year's Eve was more than most could endure, yet they'd managed to get home safely. Angela was the first to rise, as was often the case. It wasn't unusual for her to be up as early as five thirty so she could go for a run. That morning, she allowed herself to sleep in. It was almost seven.

The house was quiet as she spun the cap off a Starbucks Cold Brew coffee drink. She wore Tyler's pink Hilton Head sweatshirt that she'd commandeered out of his closet when they first met and claimed as her own since. It had become a security blanket, a reminder of his love and ability to protect her, as she'd vowed to love and protect him forever.

Angela walked around their modest home, which had been renovated before they purchased it several years earlier. The home was their place of refuge. It was a place where the family gathered at the end of a long day and ate supper together when her schedule as an emergency room resident allowed. Oftentimes, the family played board games or spent time together in a local park.

The Rankins were a family, but moreover, they were close-knit friends and an *alliance*, of sorts. Kaycee and J.C. would much rather spend time with each other, or their parents, than with the other kids in school or the neighborhood. Angela credited that family closeness to helping them survive the harrowing experience aboard Kingda Ka and their ability to avoid being killed in the tunnel under the Chesapeake Bay.

As she strolled barefoot on the wood floor, admiring the ornate woodwork and the period pieces of furniture she'd purchased at yard sales, she began to question whether Richmond was a long-term home for them.

She liked the vibrant atmosphere that downtown Richmond offered. Their home was within walking distance to the convention center, the Richmond Coliseum, and the Downtown YMCA where they frequently worked out. Both she and Tyler could walk or jog to work if they wanted to. The kids' school was close, and overall, despite being in an inner-city neighborhood, they felt safe.

But her heart was still in the Carolinas. Richmond, and her position as an emergency room physician at the Virginia Commonwealth University Medical Center, was a means to an end. Her goal was to make it through her residency and immediately hope to land a job closer to Hilton Head.

She was staring aimlessly out the front windows when Tyler eased up behind her and wrapped his arms around her waist. He nuzzled against her neck and kissed her, a gesture she'd never tire of.

"Good morning, Dr. Rankin," he whispered in her ear as she turned to kiss him back.

"I guess so," she responded in a melancholy tone.

Tyler immediately noticed and pulled away so he could get a better look at her. A rare tear streamed out of her right eye.

He showed his concern but tried to lighten the mood at the same time. "Hey, hey, why the gloom and doom?"

Angela sniffled and wiped her cheeks with her sleeve. "More doom than gloom," she replied before pausing. "Um, well, maybe a little gloom."

Tyler took her by the hand and led her to the sofa, where they sat next to one another. Angela scooted up against the back and tucked her legs underneath her. He looked her in the eyes and said, "Talk to me."

"We both know what needs to be done," she began. She pointed her thumb over her shoulder towards the bedrooms. "We have two miracles asleep in there, and we've always vowed to do whatever it takes to protect them."

Tyler squeezed her hand and gave his wife a reassuring smile. Half-jokingly, he said, "We've done a great job, too. They're both still alive."

Angela laughed and playfully swatted at him. "Barely! But protecting them means more than keeping them alive, Dad. It means insulating them from the ugliness of the world, too."

Tyler sensed where she was going with the conversation. His words were simple, but emphatic. "We have to go."

She nodded and allowed another tear to escape. "We're so close, Tyler. Six more months at VCU and I could start looking for something closer to home. The kids are flexible and ready to go wherever we go. Now this crap has messed up the whole program."

"I thought about everything last night after you guys fell asleep in the truck. What if you asked for a leave of absence? You know, pause your residency program while we go to the Haven."

"I don't know. The whole thing is regimented. It definitely would take me off schedule for getting into a fellowship, not to mention the fact it will give my future employers a reason not to hire me."

"Okay," said Tyler as the realities began to set in.

"I'll probably have to drop out, but I think it's worth a try. It doesn't matter. What matters is taking care of our kids."

Tyler glanced past Angela and looked down the hallway. A sleepy-eyed J.C. had wandered out of his bedroom in his Feast Mode pajamas featuring a dog wearing a red-stocking cap and salivating over a line strung with fish, a turkey leg, and pumpkin pie. Tyler nodded to Angela to turn and look at their son.

"He's adorable," she said, her heart warmed by the sight of her sleepy man. "This is why we make sacrifices. For him and Kaycee."

Tyler nodded. "Agreed."

The family spent the next hour waking up and unpacking their things from the trip, and then they sat down to discuss their plans. Although Tyler and Angela had made up their minds, they wanted to include their kids in the conversation.

Their home was never run like a top-down dictatorship. Certainly, the kids had their moments when they were growing up. Both Tyler and Angela handled disciplinary duties equally. Usually, all it took was a disapproving look from their mother, and the kids would stop what they were doing immediately. Tyler was more of a softie and a little easier to be manipulated. To their credit, the kids never played their parents against each other. That wouldn't have ended well.

"Guys, here's the plan," began Tyler after they'd finished breakfast. "We're gonna run some errands today, and this afternoon, hopefully before dark sets in, we're gonna head down to the Carolinas to our place at the Haven. How does that sound?"

"Yeah! I love it there!" replied an exuberant J.C., who was always up for an adventure. Then he turned to his sister. "How about you, Peanut?"

"I can be ready in five minutes," added Kaycee. The events of the last two days had had a profound impact upon her. Perhaps, being older than J.C., she had a better appreciation of how much danger the family had been in. Her younger brother saw everything as an adventure that always worked out, just like on television.

"Well, that's good," said Angela, who noticed Kaycee's demeanor. "We do have some errands to take care of, and you two have important jobs to do while we're gone."

"What's that?" asked Kaycee.

"Well, for starters, can I trust you guys to do the laundry from our trip?"

"Piece of cake," replied J.C.

Tyler started laughing. "Let your sister run point on laundry duties, okay, buddy?"

"I got it, Dad," Kaycee replied. "What else?"

Angela scooted her chair up to the table. "We don't know how long we're gonna be gone, so I need you guys to pack both summer and winter clothes. We'll stuff jackets in the truck, so don't put them in your suitcases. If you have any special toys to bring, put them in our grocery tote bags."

"Roger that, Mom," said J.C., a lover of military action movies.

Tyler and Angela exchanged glances and shared an eye roll. The boy was gonna be a handful someday. He was a miniature version of the president, only without a Twitter account.

"Where are you guys going?" asked Kaycee.

"Well, I'm gonna head down to the hospital and talk to my administrator."

"Mom, do you have to quit your job?" asked Kaycee.

"I hope not, but—" began Angela before J.C. interrupted.

"Maybe you could take a *yatus*?"

Since J.C. was a toddler, he'd become enamored with the word *hiatus*, although he could never manage to pronounce it correctly. When he used it, it came out as *yah-toose*, not that it mattered. Everyone in the family knew what he meant.

"That's right, buddy. Mom is gonna see what they say."

"Your dad has errands to run as well, right?" Angela looked at Tyler to elaborate.

"I need to get replacements for our cell phones, for starters. Also, I need to replace the evidence taken by the police last night."

"The gun?" Angela mouthed the words.

Tyler nodded and continued. "We need some food and supplies for the cabin, and I think that I'm going to buy us another truck, something more reliable and a little faster." He mumbled his way through the last part of his answer.

J.C. became distraught. "But, Dad, what about the Bronco? You can't sell it!"

Angela reached over and touched Tyler's arm. "I kinda agree. That was your dad's truck. Besides, they'd never give you what it's worth, anyway."

"What if I keep the Bronco, buy a good used truck with a trailer, and use it to bring the Bronco with us?"

"Sounds like a plan," replied Kaycee. "We can bring more stuff that way."

Angela leaned back in her chair and laughed. "That's your daughter the prepper talking."

Tyler beamed. He'd taught his family well.

CHAPTER 8

**George Trowbridge's Residence
Near Pine Orchard, Connecticut**

George Trowbridge's trusted aide, Harris, led the lanky visitor up the wide marble stairwell of the expansive home overlooking the ocean. The snowstorm had moved out to sea, and the sun was shining brightly, reflecting off the white blanket that still covered the estate's grounds.

The visitor had been summoned overnight, and the inhospitable weather was not an excuse for nonattendance by the man who'd set the events of New Year's Eve into motion. Despite his failing health, Trowbridge was still very much in charge, but he was angry. Someone within his trusted circle had gone *off the reservation*, as they say, nearly resulting in the death of his son-in-law, Michael Cortland.

Nathaniel Hanson Briscoe, a descendent of John Hanson, the president of the First Continental Congress, was also the owner of Monocacy Farm, the location of the secretive meetings that launched the New Year's Eve attacks. Briscoe, who used his middle name when he introduced himself, was an aristocratic, cerebral ex-politician who'd made a name for himself in the defense industry.

Hanson Briscoe's contacts throughout the military-industrial complex needed high-level access to those in government who held the purse strings of the U.S. budget. Trowbridge was the gatekeeper who could make the introductions, in exchange for a quid pro quo, or two.

As is often the case in politics, one side to a backroom deal needed the other more than vice versa. Trowbridge always maintained the upper hand in a negotiation, and as a result, he was owed many favors from those he assisted. Of all those who owed George Trowbridge, Hanson Briscoe was at the top of the list.

Harris escorted Briscoe into Trowbridge's master suite, where the elderly man was receiving his morning medications and checkup. The two visitors stood casually as the medical team completed their work. Quietly and efficiently, they prepared Trowbridge for another day in which he operated from the confines of his bedroom. After they left, Harris nodded and slowly backed out of the room, leaving the two powerful men alone.

"George, you are looking well under the circumstances," began Briscoe as he slowly approached Trowbridge's bedside. Briscoe always dressed in his finest suit and an ankle-length herringbone overcoat in the winter. He held the coat over his arm, refusing to surrender it to the estate's staff when he entered the home.

Trowbridge sized up his business associate, noticing the jacket draped over his forearm. He surmised that Briscoe didn't plan on staying long, or expected he'd be dismissed in short order. Trowbridge had learned in his past dealings with Briscoe that the man had several hang-ups, the biggest of which was his continuous quest to gain recognition for the efforts of his ancestor John Hanson.

Briscoe argued, as many others in his family had before him, that John Hanson was in fact the first president of the United States, not George Washington. The Hanson family maintained for centuries that in November 1781, when John Hanson became the first President of Congress under the Articles of Confederation, that bestowed the honor of *first president* upon him. At the time, the U.S. Constitution had not been ratified, but the government was in place.

Be that as it may, history hadn't been kind to the Hanson family's efforts, and it continued to be a point of contention for Briscoe. He worked overtime to make a name for himself, working in the shadows and reminding anyone who'd listen that his lineage was every bit as important as the Founding Fathers'.

Trowbridge didn't care about such matters. He was interested in the present and what needed to be done to direct a nation into the future. A nation, in his opinion, that had lost its way. The events of

New Year's Eve, although orchestrated and planned in large part by Briscoe, would've never come to pass without Trowbridge's blessing.

All of the attacks that evening had been known to Trowbridge in advance, including the use of the directed-energy weapon on Delta Flight 322. During the planning phase, those operatives within his employ inside the government had been responsible for delivering travel plans and flight manifests to Briscoe.

It was Briscoe who'd made the final decision on whether to call off a particular operation or not. In fact, one of the planned attacks had included an intentionally failed attempt on the president's life. Trowbridge theorized that the president's most ardent supporters would rise up in arms at the botched assassination. When the logistics of the attempt didn't lend themselves to the desired result, Briscoe wisely called off the plan.

What Trowbridge needed to know was why the attack on Delta 322 wasn't called off considering his son-in-law was on board the flight. It was a question he needed to ask directly so he could study the body language of the man whom he trusted, but who also had motive to clear the playing field as Trowbridge neared the end of his life.

There would be a successor to the throne of power. Hanson Briscoe wanted to take the seat next. George Trowbridge had other plans.

CHAPTER 9

George Trowbridge's Residence
Near Pine Orchard, Connecticut

"Please, Hanson, pull up a chair," began Trowbridge as he pressed a button that maneuvered the back of his bed a little taller. He was now sitting upright and could see his guest's body completely. "I trust you had an uneventful flight."

Briscoe looked around warily before setting his jacket on a side chair underneath a nearby window. He settled into the leather chair adjacent to Trowbridge's bed. The man appeared nervous, a telling sign. It was also a mistake. Trowbridge immediately smelled blood and was more cautious with his words. If his suspicions were correct, then Briscoe was to be considered a dangerous threat to the Trowbridge dynasty and would have to be eliminated.

"Yes, George, it was uneventful, and the invitation was wholly unexpected. I appreciate the use of your helo."

"This weather is not conducive to traveling three hundred miles by car," Trowbridge added. He took a deep breath and began, choosing to make small talk, but establishing how their meeting would go. Trowbridge wanted Briscoe to do all the talking while he assessed the man's responses and demeanor. "How are you feeling about the first phase of the plan?"

"I thought it went very well," he began to reply with confidence. "As you know, we had to abandon the Mar-a-Lago operation, and we—"

Briscoe's cell phone began to chirp in his jacket pocket, immediately drawing a scowl from Trowbridge. When he met with someone, he expected their undivided attention. Briscoe gave his host an apologetic look before reaching into his pocket. He took a moment to study the display before shutting off the ring volume.

"George, it's the markets," he said as he shoved the phone into his pocket. "Schwartz is making his move."

Trowbridge nodded his head. "To be expected."

Briscoe continued. "I assume you've confirmed the appropriate course of action with the Treasury Secretary."

"I have, and with the fed chairman," replied Trowbridge. "Schwartz pulled these shenanigans once and caught everyone off guard. Kudos to him, as it made him a rich man. You can't fool this old fool twice. His efforts will backfire, and he won't realize the mistake he's made until it's too late."

"What about Interpol?"

"They've been alerted," replied Trowbridge. "International wiretaps and warrants have been issued for the offshore accounts that Jonathan Schwartz uses for these types of dealings. Our contacts in the FBI's financial crimes division are closely monitoring his U.S.-based activities. Justice will be meted out with lightning speed."

"The media?" asked Briscoe.

"Our friends at the *Financial Times* will break the story, and the Fox Business Network will make sure it is disseminated throughout the U.S. He'll be as toxic as a nuclear waste dump within days."

Briscoe smiled and rubbed his hands, lending the appearance of a miserly scrooge celebrating the bankruptcy of another. The man's body relaxed, and he slid down into the comfortable chair as if he were enjoying a casual chat with an old friend over cognac and cigars.

A wry smile came across Trowbridge's face as he saw the noticeable change in Briscoe's demeanor. Trowbridge often laughed at the so-called expert poker players who bragged about their ability to read their opponents. Those people had never played the kind of high-stakes card games that Trowbridge was accustomed to.

"I've received reports that unrest has spread across the country, especially in unexpected locales. May I assume these are organized efforts?"

"They are, George," Briscoe replied. "Our network has responded quickly and with equal violence."

"Any problems?"

Briscoe grimaced. "Only in Richmond, but we have teams descending upon the city this morning. The public will applaud our efforts."

Trowbridge appeared to be uninterested, casually refolding the end of the blanket that was tucked just below his shoulders to keep him warm. "What about the death toll from the Delta flight? How many?"

Briscoe's body stiffened in his chair. The question caught him off guard, as intended. "Um, one-oh-nine, passengers and crew. The target, um, Congressman Pratt was one of the dead."

"Survivors?" Trowbridge asked the questions that he already knew the answers to. He'd conducted his own, independent investigation of the downing of Delta Flight 322.

While it was true that Cort was a late addition to the flight, the manifest with his name on it had been filed with the FAA. For over an hour, Briscoe's team was, or should have been, aware of Cort's presence on that flight.

Trowbridge's investigation had revealed that the Frenchman, who had been one of their top operatives because of his development and knowledge of radio frequency weapons, a highly prized tool of terror, had been inadvertently killed as he slipped off the oil rig's elevated platform. The ex-military operators hired to protect the man had disappeared by prearrangement.

For Trowbridge, it was all too convenient. Briscoe had the answers and Trowbridge expected him to volunteer them. A lie of omission was just as big a lie as one of words. He was going to give Briscoe the opportunity to admit his operation almost killed Cort, whether by accident or design.

A few beads of sweat appeared on Briscoe's forehead. "They keep it warm in here for you, don't they?"

Trowbridge glared at his contemporary and nodded. He wasn't acknowledging the fact that the room was kept warm. He was relishing the fact that the room, and its suddenly hot feel, was closing in on Hanson Briscoe.

Trowbridge offered the younger man a glass of water and subtly changed the conversation to the next part of their intricate plan to push the nation to the edge of a second civil war. As the two discussed the arrangements, Trowbridge slid his hand under the blanket and pressed a buzzer, summoning Harris.

When his aide arrived, Trowbridge held his hand up, indicating that Briscoe should halt the conversation. Trowbridge waved his hand for Harris to approach, and then he pointed to his ear. Harris picked up on the cue and pretended to whisper in his boss's ear.

"Hanson, old friend, would you excuse us for just a moment?"

Briscoe nodded and left. Just as the door shut, Trowbridge mustered the strength to push himself up a little taller in the bed. Harris awaited his instructions.

"Not now. Not here. But soon. I want him gone. Without a trace."

"No message?" asked Harris.

"Oh, it will be loud and clear."

"Sir, I was unable to install the GPS tracking device in his jacket as you requested. Shall I send a team with—"

Trowbridge waggled his finger at his aide and pointed his thumb over his shoulder. "Quickly, so we don't raise suspicion."

Harris didn't hesitate, pulling the wafer-thin piece of electronic circuitry out of his pocket. He flicked open a spring-assisted knife and created a small incision where the outer pocket met the main body of the overcoat. Within seconds, the device was inserted, and Briscoe, who kept his jacket with him like a security blanket, could be found anywhere, anytime.

Trowbridge nodded his approval, and Harris exited the room, holding the door open for Briscoe—the dead man walking.

CHAPTER 10

Hilton Garden Inn, Airport
Charlotte, North Carolina

"Okay," began Cort cheerily as he returned to the hotel room, wiggling a key fob over his head. "How does a brand-new, barely broken-in Chevy Suburban sound to you guys?"

Handsome Dan was the most vocal in his response, immediately attempting to jump as high as his eight-inch legs could hoist his oversized girth of a waistline. The key fob was the target of his excitement, as the big boy couldn't care less about Suburbans.

"Too excited for words," said Hannah as she threw a pillow at her father. She enjoyed the slumber-party atmosphere of the night's stay in the hotel. She'd never slept on a pull-out sofa bed and enjoyed creating a wall of cushions and excess pillows to build a lean-to structure on top. She'd said it was her way of getting ready to sleep in the woods.

Meredith didn't respond, reacting instead by pointing toward the local news she was watching on the television. Cort slipped the fob in his pocket, much to the chagrin of Handsome, who immediately found his way to the tile-floored foyer to stay cool.

"Is this about the fire?" Cort said as he slid onto the edge of the bed next to his wife. She had the volume turned down with the closed-captioning scrolling across the bottom, Cort suspected it was because she didn't want their young daughter to hear all the gory details that the news media liked to relay.

"That's part of it," she replied with a sigh. "They have no idea what started the fires, and there was no discernible pattern to the targets. They were clearly arson, with the locations ranging from high-end homes to government buildings. The media is calling it the *Night of Rage*."

Cort took the remote from his wife and turned up the volume slightly. "Why?"

"Apparently, mobs were seen in the vicinity of all the fires before they were set. Last night, around ten o'clock, groups started congregating in different parts of the city. Cort, it wasn't just inner-city violence, either. I mean, the homes that were set on fire were big McMansions. Even their historic district was hit."

"The graphic reads coordinated."

"Right," added Meredith. "Their newly appointed fire chief said the fires were set in a way that prevented his department from responding to all of them. As he put it, he had to *play God with the Lord's water*."

"What did he do?" asked Cort.

Meredith grimaced as she replied, "He protected homes first and businesses only if he had the resources. Makes sense to me, but not to the business owners, many of whom were minorities, apparently. They're crying racism."

"That's the chief in the picture," said Cort, pointing to the split screen. "Um, he's black."

Meredith shrugged, and her eyebrows rose. "I guess that didn't matter."

The two watched the news a little longer until the coverage shifted to the mug shots of several white men whose faces were covered in tattoos. Cort shook his head in disbelief at the men's appearance and turned the volume up louder. The reporter explained.

"The Ghost Face Gangsters are a prison-based gang that has been operating in Georgia for twenty years until their recent expansion into other large Southern cities. In the last three weeks, several incidents have been attributed to suspected members of the gang, including a deadly jailbreak in nearby Gaston County that left two corrections officers dead.

"According to the Anti-Defamation League, they are one of dozens of white supremacist prison gangs operating in the greater

Mecklenburg County area. The three escaped men shown on the screen are on the lam and considered considerably dangerous."

The station's news host asked the reporter, "We've received reports that the Ghost Face Gangsters may have been involved in last night's Night of Rage, is that correct?"

The reporter nodded and his facial expression turned serious. "That's right. Police sources tell us there has been a turf war brewing between the Ghost Face gang and the Trinitarios, a New York-based gang composed primarily of Dominican Americans. Like the Ghost Face Gangsters, the Trinitarios members rose out of the penal system, this time in New York State. Their numbers have swelled over the past decade and so have their areas of influence. Their territory now includes Charlotte."

Cort turned off the television and tossed the remote over his shoulder, where it landed squarely on top of a pillow, emulating a trick basketball shot he'd perfected as a teen in which he'd shoot the ball blindly over his shoulder, finding the hoop every time.

"I have an idea," he said with a chuckle. "Why don't we load up and get the heck out of Charlotte?"

Meredith leaned over and hugged her husband while she gave him a long kiss on the cheek. "I really love you, Cort."

"That's a good thing, Mrs. Cortland. Our daughter, who's watching our every move, probably appreciates that."

"No, I mean it. The Haven, and your ability to overcome your fears to get us there, takes a tremendous amount of courage. I love you for that."

Cort genuinely blushed and smiled. "Aw, shucks, ma'am. 'Tweren't nothin'."

"Yes, Cort it was. I woke up several times last night as you fought through the nightmares. You were knocked out by the Zoloft, so you probably don't remember. There were several times that you began kicking and flailing about. The moans were what saddened me the most. It was heart-wrenching."

"Honey, I'm sorry. I had no—well, um, I don't remember the dreams from last night, but the night before. Those were awful."

She hugged him again and stood, using her arms to help Cort up. "We'll get through this together, as soon as we're safe at the Haven."

"Sounds good," said Cort as he reached into his coat pocket. He pulled out a small single-page map of the area surrounding the airport. "I picked this up at the front desk. If we head out this back way through Pinecrest, we can stop at Walmart and pick some things up for the cabin."

"Sounds good to me," said Meredith. "Once we get there, I'd like to stay put until all of this mess blows over."

The Cortlands quickly gathered their things, coaxed Handsome off the floor, and made their way to the rental car to start the final leg of their journey.

CHAPTER 11

Delta's Cabin
The Haven

Will Hightower was having difficulty transitioning to his role as Delta, one of the lead security personnel at the Haven. When he signed on with Ryan and Blair, he'd assumed he'd be flying solo. He was estranged from his ex-wife, who'd done little to rehabilitate his image as a father in the eyes of their kids. If anything, she'd torn him down further as it related to his fifteen-year-old son, Ethan.

Skylar, however, was a different matter. She had been somewhat shielded from the media circus inflicted upon the Hightower family two years prior, and for whatever reason, she hadn't succumbed to the onslaught of negativity directed at Will. She was still a daddy's girl and probably would remain so as long as Will didn't screw it up.

This was their second full day at the Haven, and routines were being established for the single dad. He awoke early to prepare breakfast for his kids. He dressed in his uniform that now consisted of a full military kit that held his sidearm, extra magazines for both the pistol and the AR-15 he carried, as well as a radio. He stopped once to check himself in the mirror before he gave final instructions to the kids. He looked more like Rambo than the former uniformed security guard for a stadium, his job of just three days ago.

"Okay, here's the plan for today," Delta began, trying to be upbeat. He sensed his kids were bored with this new arrangement, and he wasn't ready to explain to them how bad it really was beyond their secured perimeter, because he wasn't totally sure himself. This was one of the items on his agenda during today's morning briefing. "I've got my meeting and then I'll be making rounds. I plan on seeing you guys back here at noon for lunch. Cool?"

"That'll be cool, Daddy," replied Skylar enthusiastically. "I've got my paintings, and Miss Blair has commissioned some artwork."

"Whoa!" exclaimed Delta. He was impressed with his daughter's *big-girl speak*. "She commissioned some artwork? What are you supposed to do?"

Skylar proudly sat up in her chair as she finished off another scoop of oatmeal mixed with a cinnamon-sugar blend. "I'd asked her about things kids could do around here. Miss Blair said we were all living a simpler life now and that wasn't such a bad thing. She talked about the tire swing we have in front. That tire has been here since before the *Hunger Games* movie. She said she wouldn't be surprised if Katniss played on that swing."

Delta began laughing at the sincerity of Skylar's statements. He loved her innocence. Delta glanced over at Ethan, who continued to shovel oatmeal into his mouth in an effort to avoid interacting with the rest of the family.

"Sky, does she want a painting of the swing?" asked Delta.

"Yes. The cabin, too. She said this was one of her favorite spots when they bought the place. I promised her a beautiful painting for her wall."

"I'll bet you do a fantastic job." Delta leaned over and kissed his daughter on the forehead. He turned his attention to Ethan. "Son, you'll stay here with your sister, right?"

Ethan didn't look up from his bowl. He toyed with a clump of oatmeal and nodded his head. Will had hoped the change of scenery and a new adventure might bring Ethan around. He was beginning to wonder whether his son's attitude was normal for fifteen-year-old boys. He tried to remember what he was like at that age. Although he couldn't conjure up any specific memories, he certainly didn't remember being perpetually sullen and ill-tempered.

"Right, Ethan?" he reiterated his request.

"Sure, Dad, whatever. Are you gonna find me a charger for my phone today?"

"Top of my list, son." The lies continued. Delta walked over to

45

muss his son's hair, but Ethan just pulled away. The attempt to make some kind of contact with his son failed, again. "Okay, I love you guys. Be good, and I'll be back for lunch."

"Okay, Daddy. Love you!"

Ethan didn't reply. He stood and took his empty bowl into the kitchen without saying goodbye. Delta grabbed his gear and left, pulling the door tight behind him.

Skylar began to gather her sketching materials and headed toward the door.

Ethan interrupted her. "Where are you going?"

"Um, in the front yard to sketch the house and tire swing. I'll paint it inside because it's too cold out."

"Hang on." Ethan stopped her. He sat on the sofa and motioned for Skylar to join him. Although she was anxious to get started on her project, she reluctantly joined him.

"Okay," she said hesitantly as she set her materials down and plopped down on the slip-covered sofa.

Ethan began. "What do you think about Mom? I mean, do you think she's back from her cruise and home safe, or what?"

"I dunno. Daddy said he'd try to call her."

"Do you think he is?"

Skylar hesitated, indicating she wasn't so sure. "Um, I guess so. I mean, he said he would."

Ethan had a quick comeback. "He also said he would find me a charger for my cell phone, and he hasn't so far."

Skylar was growing uncomfortable with the conversation. She didn't like it when her mother criticized her dad, and she didn't like it when Ethan did either. She began to stand and leave when Ethan gently touched her arm and pulled her back down.

"Ethan, I don't know. What's the big deal. Mom's probably safe at home with Freddie, or they're still on the cruise ship. Either way, I'm happy here with Daddy."

Ethan rolled his eyes. "You mean you're not bored out of your mind?"

"We just got here," she replied. "I haven't had time to get bored yet. Besides, Miss Blair has given me a job, and Daddy said there would be other things for us to do."

"Like what?" asked Ethan.

"I don't know, but he'll tell us when it's time."

Ethan stood and walked around the room. "Well, I don't think he has any intention of talking to Mom. He sure isn't gonna go get her."

"Yes, he will," Skylar shot back.

"No, Sky, he won't. They hate each other, and Dad has everything he wants now. We're here with him, and Mom is out there somewhere, probably in trouble."

"You don't know that!" Skylar was becoming afraid for her mother now. "Besides, living with Dad isn't so bad. You'll see."

"Whatever," Ethan grumbled. He wasn't hearing what he wanted to from Skylar, so he rudely dismissed her. "Go on, do your painting or whatever. I'm gonna play with my new Nintendo until the batteries die. Then we'll see how long it takes Dad to get me more batteries."

Ethan angrily swiped the handheld Nintendo device off the coffee table and stormed off to their bedroom. Skylar sat on the sofa for a moment, staring at the fire through the small glass opening on the wood-burning stove.

She contemplated the fate of her mother and what her father's true intentions were. At eleven, she knew she had little, if any, control over what her parents decided. She was still of the opinion to go with the flow because they knew what was best for her.

There was one thing she vowed, however, as she considered the circumstances her family was in. She'd never grow up to be like her brother.

CHAPTER 12

West Clay Street
Richmond, Virginia

Joseph Jose Acuff was also known as *Chepe*, a Spanish name of endearment bestowed upon him as a boy because of his cherublike face. Chepe, however, was anything but a cherub. He had a master's in public administration from Cal-Berkley and was well respected as an advocate for reforming payday loan practices. He was widely recognized as he walked the halls of Congress, running in the same circles as congressional aides and those who had the ears of powerful politicians in DC.

Chepe led a second life, however, one that was unknown to the politicians whom he lobbied. He was a radical communist and Antifa leader who advocated the violent overthrow of the U.S. government. His platform on social media was one of the most widely followed by anarchists around the world.

As far as Chepe was concerned, nothing was off-limits. Regime change, murder of the rich and powerful, and harassment of public officials and media personalities were just some of the things on his bucket list. He was a student of Saul Alinsky's *Rules for Radicals*, a manifesto authored for communist activists on how to run a movement for change.

Encouraging charismatic leaders like Chepe, Alinsky provided simple guidance on how to organize low-income communities, the proverbial *have-nots*, into a powerful voice. Many grassroots political movements over the past fifty years could be attributed to the techniques suggested in *Rules for Radicals*.

Chepe was on Jonathan Schwartz's payroll. He'd been recruited while attending graduate school in Berkley after making headlines for leading protests against conservative commentators on the Cal-Berkley campus. Once on the radar of the FBI because of his ties to radical leftist organizations, Chepe was instructed to avoid the limelight and public displays of protest. He was turned into an insider, one who knew his way around Washington, while still being able to recruit operatives for Antifa.

Chepe excelled in his role and had become a rising star in the shadow organizations controlled by Schwartz. The events of New Year's Eve triggered the chaotic scenario he'd been waiting for. His dream was to take advantage of government dysfunction during which the rule of law could not be enforced.

He was a cerebral radical, oftentimes engaging in elaborate conversations with his contemporaries about the impact Saul Alinsky had on the American political landscape. His favorite of Alinsky's rules, rule number nine, posited *the threat is usually more terrifying than the thing itself.*

For decades, political change in America was effectuated by scaring people via the media until laws were passed to meet a certain ideological goal. Chepe's job was to create the news headlines at the most opportune moment to benefit his political allies in Washington. The opportunity to back up those threats with real violence was a dream that Chepe thought would never materialize, until now.

He'd been tasked with setting Richmond on fire, literally. His teams worked throughout Richmond to occupy first responders with widespread arson fires. While the fires raged, the members of his teams raged as well, smashing windows, destroying businesses, terrorizing and killing innocent homeowners while law enforcement officers chased ghosts.

He'd been so successful on the night of January first that his boss, under direct orders from Jonathan Schwartz, instructed Chepe to pick a handful of his top people and travel to Charlotte. Just as General William Tecumseh Sherman had carved a wide swath of death and destruction through the South in the final year of the Civil War, Chepe, one of Antifa's top field generals, would do the same.

From Richmond to Charlotte to Atlanta and beyond, he'd lead an army of have-nots on a fiery display of terror.

He was preparing to leave when a box truck arrived in front of the properties owned by the Schwartz foundation that acted as a rally point for the Richmond operation. Chepe wasn't expecting any type of delivery, especially since the normal signage or tee shirts weren't being used during the activities undertaken around Richmond. He stopped packing his duffle bags and peeked through the curtains of his upstairs apartment.

Two burly men dressed in black with gray beanie caps made their way to the front door. Most likely, based on Chepe's past dealings with his benefactors, the drivers were longshoremen from New Jersey. They nervously looked around before knocking.

Chepe bounded down the stairs to greet them. He opened the door. "Gentlemen."

The driver spoke up. "We have a delivery for Sabokitty."

Chepe smiled and took an envelope from the driver. He opened it and began reading the typewritten delivery notice. He glanced past the men toward the box truck. A vehicle trailer was attached to the truck's hitch with a small Nissan pickup in tow. He shook his head in disbelief.

"The pickup, too?"

"No, that's for our return trip. We're to leave all of this with you. It's my understanding you're heading to Charlotte today."

Chepe furrowed his brow, surprised that these men were aware of the plan. "Yeah."

The driver continued. "Take the truck. It has a crew cab capable of carrying you plus four more."

"Fuel? That's a real prob—"

"Both tanks are full," the driver responded abruptly. "If there's nothing else, we need to get back."

Chepe hesitated. "Um, I guess not." The men walked away, and he called after them, holding the delivery notice over his head. "Hey, do you need to teach me how to use this stuff?"

"The guys you'll meet up with will know."

For a moment, Chepe watched the men unhook their transportation. He read the list again, which included military-grade weapons such as shoulder-fired missiles, grenade launchers, automatic weapons, and the corresponding ammunition.

They had equipped him for a war.

CHAPTER 13

Congress Heights
Washington, DC

"Prowler, are you up for a road trip?" Hayden walked toward the ceiling-to-floor windows as her cat made figure eights through her legs, methodically moving between them and rubbing against her calves. Cats were not bred as a herding animal, like some dog breeds, but they'd acquired this behavior, known as *marking*, as a way to get attention or, at times, manipulate their owner into doing their bidding. Whether it be a good scruffing behind the ear or a bowl full of yummies, cats, like most dogs, learned to communicate to their human companions through a series of actions and reactions. Humans, for their part, enjoyed being manipulated by their furry friends.

"Okay, okay." Hayden relented to Prowler's persistent movements, mainly because the large cat threatened to trip her up by accident. She bent over and hoisted up the twenty-pounder and cradled him like a baby. Prowler nuzzled against her chest and purred his appreciation.

The Washington area had received a significant amount of snowfall overnight, but the skies showed signs of clearing. She looked across the Potomac River at the plumes of smoke rising from Arlington Ridge on the other side of Reagan Washington National Airport. The primary commercial airport servicing the DC-metro area and its twenty-three million passengers a year had sat dormant since the cyber attacks of two nights ago.

The lack of public transportation had caused commuters and travelers to take to their vehicles to get around the District, causing traffic jams and tempers to flare. Traffic on Interstate 295 between her building and the Potomac was slow but moving.

"I think we'll avoid the interstate, big boy," she said to an oblivious Prowler. "We'll head toward Joint Base Andrews and then pick up 301 toward Virginia. Whadya think?"

Prowler was asleep. He was a twenty-pound snuggle cat.

Hayden carried him to the sofa and gently laid him on a gray faux-fur blanket, Prowler's favorite, from Pottery Barn. CNN was now covering news from the London Stock Exchange about the impact the attacks on the U.S. were having on international markets. Hayden wasn't invested in the markets, opting instead to purchase physical silver and gold with her after-tax earnings. Both precious metals had skyrocketed in value as trading opened in foreign markets.

Before she began packing her Range Rover, she had to carefully consider what to bring. She had some things at her cabin already, namely food and clothing. Ryan had stored some of her weapons in the Haven's armory, and the ammunition she'd brought down on her previous trips had gone into storage as well.

She hadn't unloaded the truck from yesterday's shopping trip to Walmart, as everything was designed to be used for bugging out. As a result, her task was limited to stuffing a few duffle bags with additional clothing and personal toiletries. She retrieved her handguns out of a safe built into her closet and set them next to the door by the rifles retrieved from her gun-range locker.

If she got pulled over during the four-hundred-mile trip to Henry River Mill Village in North Carolina, it would take weeks to talk her way out of the legal trouble law enforcement would make for her. However, she expected the cops would be the least of her troubles.

She filled a large olive drab duffle bag with her weapons and readied them for transportation down the elevator to the secured parking garage. She made several trips down with her rucksacks and Prowler's gear first, surveying the garage and the building to determine if any looky-loos were present. Her building was remarkably devoid of activity, so on the fourth trip down, she carried the heavy bag of weapons.

Prowler, curious at the activity, conducted his potty business and was sitting patiently by the door when Hayden came up for him. Before she left, she looked around her loft, which she'd called home for years. It was her private space, decorated to reflect her taste, and perfectly suited the two of them.

In the moment, sadness came over her as she walked through one final time, as if she were checking a hotel room for a forgotten item. Prowler joined her side, periodically stopping to examine a piece of furniture or to swat at one of his many toys that were scattered about. It was their home, and he sensed they were leaving for a long time.

"We'll be back, buddy," said a melancholy Hayden. Her life revolved around the law and, most recently, defending the President of the United States. It was a dream job that surpassed her position as a clerk to Justice Alito on the Supreme Court.

Prowler responded with a meow, of sorts, using a deeper tone than he customarily used. *He's not so sure*, Hayden thought to herself.

Neither was she.

CHAPTER 14

DoubleTree Hotel
Norfolk, Virginia

Tom Shelton returned to their hotel room at the DoubleTree in Norfolk, frustrated and annoyed with the circumstances. He had been pleased to find the rental car counter open at the late hour the night before, but when the attendant revealed their GMC Yukon would be only half full of gas, Tom became agitated.

"But, sir, you only pay for the gas you use," explained the clueless young woman. She reminded him to return the vehicle with the same amount of gas as it had now. Tom didn't want to explain to the naïve woman that he expected gas shortages to become the norm after the attacks, and the gas-guzzling Yukon would consume half a tank in just a couple of hundred miles. They had nearly four hundred miles to travel to get to the Haven.

Donna Shelton greeted him as he entered the room, where she sat on the edge of the bed, watching the local news. "You were gone a long time."

"Yes, and unfortunately, I came back with less gas than when I started. As I suspected, the influx of travelers out of the northeast coupled with the attacks has stopped fuel trucks from running."

Donna stood and helped her husband remove his coat. She planted a kiss on his cheek and whispered reassuringly, "We'll be okay. Come sit down. There's more."

"Now what?" he asked, trying his best to shake off his fussy attitude.

"I'm surprised you didn't hear about this while you were out," she said, pointing at Norfolk's WAVY *News on Your Side* playing on the television. "A wildfire got out of control overnight. It's to the south of us, just beyond Chesapeake."

Tom read the news chyron. "The Great Dismal Swamp? Really? Dear, are you sure they're not referring to Washington?"

Donna gave him a playful slug and led him to the sofa to sit down. She had her iPad open to the Google Maps app. The Great Dismal Swamp extended from Southeastern Virginia into North Carolina. It was a vast area of forest combined with wetlands and tall grasses to create one of the most unique ecosystems along the Atlantic Seaboard. It was also no stranger to wildfires. A spark from a logging operation in the mid-1920s caused the Great Conflagration, which consumed nearly one hundred thousand acres. The fire raged for three years. More recently, in 2011, another fire caused by a lightning strike scorched six thousand acres and burned for weeks.

Donna was about to show Tom the road closures when he grabbed the remote and turned up the volume. The news crew on the scene was standing near a massive blaze that melted the light snow and the surrounding pine trees. The reporter explained what had happened.

"Here's how a peat fire occurs. Beneath the Great Dismal Swamp lies large areas of peat. You know, the partially decomposed organic matter resulting from fallen trees, leaves, and other plant material. Eventually, after a few million years or so, peat transforms into coal or oil. Even in its current state, it's highly flammable."

The news anchor interrupted the reporter with a question. "It's so damp out there. And we had a fresh snowfall. How does something like this begin to burn under those wet conditions?"

The reporter held his hand to his earpiece and turned as a sudden gust of wind blew dark smoke toward his position. "It does seem out of the ordinary, but here's how it works. Once the fire is ignited, and let me reiterate, we don't have an official cause as of yet although authorities have told me off the record that fireworks landing in the swamp is most likely the source of ignition."

"From New Year's Eve?" asked the news anchor.

"That's right. You see, it doesn't take much to ignite the peat.

Once the fire sets in, it sinks into the surface and spreads down to the peat layer, which can be as deep as fifteen feet below ground. That's why a peat fire is so difficult to extinguish. You have to saturate the swampland with more water. In 2011, folks around here were praying for a tropical storm to move through after the fire began. As you might recall, the rains never came."

The reporter's voice trailed off and Tom lowered the volume. He turned his attention to Donna, who was holding her iPad to show him the route options.

"All the major roads leading south of us are closed," she began. "Traffic is being diverted to our west."

"Richmond," interjected Tom. "I suppose we could make our way to I-95. It's a little out of the way to begin with, but then we should be able to make up time. Listen, it's only a six-hour drive from here under heavy traffic. If we get going, we can be there by dark."

"I'm almost packed and we've already checked out. All we have to do is load up."

Tom patted his wife on the knee and stood to gather their belongings. He went to the bathroom, and while he finished, Donna told him about her phone call with Blair Smart.

"How are they holdin' up?" asked Tom.

"They are incredibly prepared," Donna replied. "They have a plan and they've stuck to it."

Tom washed his hands and looked at the mirror. *There's that word again*—plan. *Everybody seems to have a plan.*

"Oh?" he said inquisitively.

"She's reached out to all of the property owners and heard back from most. Except for a few who intend to wait and see, as she put it, almost everyone who has a cabin is on their way. They only have limited space for property owners who haven't built yet, but some have campers or motor homes. Plus, they have some kind of dormitory set up too."

Tom emerged from the bathroom still drying his hands on a towel. He dropped it into a pile on the floor created by Donna to make housekeeping's job easier. He helped Donna pack the last of their things. As they made their way to the door, they both looked around the room one last time to confirm they hadn't forgotten anything.

Tom asked, "Do they have an opinion about all of this?"

The conversation continued as they walked alone down the hallway to the elevator.

"She said they've been too busy getting everything in order to give it an honest assessment," replied Donna. "And she reminded me that they felt your military experience would be useful in sorting through the hyperbole seen in the news media. Remember, neither Ryan nor Blair have a very high opinion of the media."

"I don't blame them," quipped Tom as the elevator made its way to the first floor. They stopped their conversation as they walked through the hotel lobby. Several groups of people were standing around, watching television monitors and talking on cell phones. Travelers and refugees alike were at a loss as to what they should do next.

The Yukon was parked near the front door and Tom quickly loaded the bags. Always the gentlemen, he helped his wife into the truck and walked around to the driver's side. Just as he opened the door, his cell phone rang. It was their daughter Tommie.

CHAPTER 15

Norfolk, Virginia

"Hey, Dad, can you talk?" His daughter's voice was hushed and sounded hurried. Tommie Shelton, their youngest daughter, was a Naval Intelligence officer stationed aboard the USNS *Invincible* in the Persian Gulf. Her full-time job was to lead a team that tracked terrorist activity emerging from Iran and Yemen. He hadn't heard from her since their conversation on New Year's Eve prior to the attacks.

Tom stopped short of entering the truck and replied, "Um, sure. Are you okay?"

"I'm fine, Dad. I'm worried about you two, but this is my first opportunity to get an outside, secure line."

"Honey, we're fine. We're in Norfolk, making our way to the safe place. You remember the Haven, right?"

"Good, Dad. I'm sorry, but I have to hurry. Is Mom within earshot of you?"

Tom noticed Donna was intently watching him. She motioned for him to get into the truck. He shook his head and raised his left hand with his index finger in the air, indicating she should wait just a moment. He quickly backed out of the truck and shut the door. As he spoke with Tommie, he wandered around the side of the truck, fully aware that Donna was following his every step.

"Not anymore," he replied. "What've you got?"

"Dad, I can't believe I'm about to say this. I mean…" Her voice trailed off, causing Tom to grow concerned.

"Spill it, Commander!" he ordered somewhat jokingly.

"Dad, this is being analyzed from a lot of different angles, do you understand?"

"Yes, but how do *you* see it?" he asked.

"It's not just us. It's several intelligence agencies." She paused and then continued. "Dad, it's not an external threat."

"A cell? They've been embedded within our borders for—"

"No, Dad." Tommie cut him off. "It's not a cell either. Internal."

Her words soaked into Tom.

Internal. Not from outside, but from within.

"Do you have any kind of confirmation of this?" he asked.

"It's fluid, but the process of elimination is leading several agencies to this conclusion," she replied. She paused again. "Dad, I can't say any more, and we're on strict time limits for our communiques. Tell Mom I love her. Bye."

Just like that, his daughter, the *terrorist catcher*, abruptly hung up. Tom stared at the icons on his phone's screen and then slowly shoved the device in his pocket. He thought back to the number of times he'd been called upon to perform some innocuous task on behalf of George Trowbridge. His mind wandered to the immense power that people like Trowbridge wielded, and then he considered the advanced weaponry available to Trowbridge's minions—just as he once was.

Tom slowly entered the truck and started the engine. He plugged Richmond into the navigation system in the Yukon and started them on their journey to the Haven. Donna sat in silence, clearly aggravated that Tom had found it necessary to exclude her from his side of the conversation. After several minutes, he tried to explain.

"Dear, that was Tommie," he began sheepishly. "She could only talk for a minute."

"A minute that obviously required you to exclude me."

Tom nervously gripped the steering wheel and chose his words carefully. "Tommie is very protective of you, and I have a tendency to overreact sometimes. We just didn't want to worry you."

Donna turned sideways in her seat and leaned against the passenger door. "Tom, no more secrets. You promised. I've barely gotten over your *special relationship* with that man Trowbridge, and now you find it necessary to talk to our daughter without me? I'm worried about her, too, you know. We could be at war and she's sitting on a boat at the devil's doorstep."

Tom felt terrible. He had assured her there would be no more secrets. He considered assuaging her concerns by telling her that Tommie was not at the *devil's doorstep*, as she put it. Most likely, the two of them were. Somehow, he wasn't sure that would provide her a sense of relief.

"She's fine and she wanted me to tell you that she loves you." Tom reached over the console to take his wife's hand in his. He felt bad and saw how hurt his wife was. He needed to stop coddling her, and now was as good a time as any. "Donna, you're right. I've hidden too many things from you for too long. We have a new lease on life, and after what you've been through, I doubt anything I tell you could be worse."

Donna bristled. "Exactly, Tom. Or is it *Commander*?"

Ouch.

Now he knew he had to come clean about everything, from the mysterious text message to Tommie's revelation.

"Let me go back to New Year's Eve first," he began. He took a deep breath and exhaled. "Donna, I love you, and I'm sorry."

"I love you, too. You have to believe in me, Tom. Please."

"Okay," he said with a smile. He reached into his pocket and retrieved his cell phone. With one eye on the road, he retrieved the deleted text message he'd received that night. He quickly logged into his iCloud account, found the deleted text message and restored it to his phone. As he went through the motions, he considered how the message had impacted him. It was signed in a way that reminded him of his past dealings with Trowbridge. "Here's a text I received after we'd fought our way back to the Hyatt."

Donna took the phone from Tom read the message.

The real danger on the ocean, as well as the land, is people.
Fare thee well and Godspeed, Patriot!
MM

"Who is MM?" asked Donna.

"Truthfully, I don't know for certain," he replied. "It could be the initials for one person, or it might have been sent by any of a number of people with access to my cell phone number."

"But it was meant for you, right?"

"I think so, and that's based upon the reference to the ocean and my career in the Navy. However, it's the sign-off that caught my attention."

"You mean Godspeed, Patriot?"

"Yes. When I was still commander at JB Charleston, after my agreement with Trowbridge, I'd receive instructions via text message. They weren't as cryptic as this, but they were signed with Godspeed, Patriot."

Donna read the message again and then gingerly returned the phone to Tom as if the device were some type of material evidence in a conspiracy. "What does it mean?"

"It was an expression of good wishes, or safe journey. The word *patriot* was always included because the people I worked for considered themselves patriots and defenders of more than the Constitution. They thought of themselves along the lines of caretakers of the American way of life."

"Do you mean like throwbacks to Revolutionary times?"

"Yes, I suppose. Back then, loyalists were those who opposed independence and wished to remain under British rule. Patriots were the continentals, the rebels, the revolutionaries who sought to break away. Over time, defenders of the Constitution, or, in many cases, the so-called American way of life, considered themselves to be patriots."

Donna thought for a moment. "I guess I'm a patriot, but then I'm old-fashioned. This is a topic we can debate for hours. Why did they send you this message?"

"I don't know. It didn't require me to do anything, so I didn't think it was important enough to trouble you with."

Donna pointed to the phone that sat in the cupholder of the console. "Is this why you chose to take the bus to New Haven?"

"That was coincidental," he quickly replied. "I considered it to be the least likely destination for people fleeing the city. It was while you were sleeping that my mind raced, considering the possible connection between Trowbridge and the text. Frankly, I thought the man owed me an audience considering the years of service I'd given him."

Donna relaxed and rubbed her husband's shoulder. Tom rolled his head on his neck again, welcoming his wife's touch.

"Well, I'm glad it worked out because he got us farther along than we could've done on our own. From what I saw on the news this morning while you were out, the highways from New York to Philadelphia to Washington are filled with violence and mayhem. Each day gets worse."

Tom slowed the truck as he approached Richmond. I-295 southbound was closed, and they were being routed north on the freeway.

"Now what?" said Tom out of frustration as he followed the string of cars onto the interstate that looped around Richmond. "At this rate, we'll be back in New York before we know it."

Donna used her iPhone to pull up the Apple app store. She searched for Richmond traffic and found the WTVR News 6 traffic app.

"Okay, this is not fire related. All it says on here is *disturbance*, whatever that means. Anyway, the good news is that you run directly into I-95, which takes us through the city."

Tom shook his head and moved along with the flow of the traffic. The Dismal Swamp fire had sent them sixty or seventy miles out of their way. It wasn't the time they'd lost that concerned him. It was the wasted gasoline. They couldn't make it all the way to the Haven, so a stop was necessary anyway.

"Well, imagine that," said Tom as they pulled onto I-95 southbound. A traffic jam."

Donna continued to study her phone. "There's nothing about it on the traffic app. I'm thinking this is just a temporary slowdown caused by refugees out of the northeast like us."

Tom stretched his arm to reach into the backseat of the rental to find his Navy cap. He'd worn the dark navy cap for years after he'd retired. He joked that it kept his head on straight.

They crept along the highway, making slow progress, when Donna interrupted the silence and pointed to their right. "Look at that, Tom."

Tom leaned forward in his seat to look past his wife at a spray-painting under the overpass. It was a black rose held high by a fist.

"I've seen that before somewhere. Um, maybe in Europe during the unrest."

"You mean in Paris?" asked Donna.

"Well, it started there before spreading to Belgium and the Netherlands. It was the beginning of that uprising a few years back."

They were both staring at the black rose, and Donna had raised her phone to take a picture when Tom suddenly slammed on the brakes, throwing her forward in her seat.

"Watch out!" he shouted as he quickly confirmed that the doors to the truck were locked.

CHAPTER 16

George Trowbridge's Residence
Near Pine Orchard, Connecticut

"Harris," Trowbridge began as he was handed reports on financial market trading to open the day, "bankers and executives in the high-tech industries have been preparing for the inevitable decline of the U.S. dollar for decades. From dinner parties in Silicon Valley to cocktail soirees on the Upper East Side, the rich not only expect the collapse of our currency, but they plan to profit from it. We are no different."

Harris handed his boss a Microsoft tablet. The screen was filled with a chart showing the U.S. Dollar Index. The index measured the value of the dollar relative to select international currencies including the euro, the Japanese yen, the pound sterling, the Canadian dollar, the Swiss franc and the Swedish krona.

The index was established in 1973 soon after the Bretton Woods agreement and the abandonment of the gold standard. The dollar has traded as high as 164.72 during the middle of the Reagan administration to a low in the early days of the real estate market collapse of 2008 at 70.70.

"Sixty-eight and falling," muttered Trowbridge as he handed the tablet back to his aide.

"Sir, is it time to step in?" asked Harris.

"No, let's give the feds time to raise the alarm, get their warrants from our judges, and move in."

"That could take days," added Harris, a former attorney.

"Ordinarily, but not today. The calls have already been placed."

"What about equity markets?" asked Harris.

"Under the circumstances, only the currency markets are impacted by Schwartz's moves. With stock markets closed indefinitely, the central banks will act to shore up asset prices. The nation will just have to endure until we can set up Schwartz to take the fall."

Harris nodded and stood quietly for a moment, and then he spoke his mind. "Sir, this is a re-creation of 1968, only the catalyst is more pronounced."

In 1968, America was teetering on the brink of societal collapse. The Vietnam War had polarized the nation. Two prominent leaders, Robert F. Kennedy Jr. and Martin Luther King Jr., had been assassinated. Political rancor had elevated to a fever pitch as the presidential election approached. Social tensions had boiled in a similar manner to current conditions.

"Harris, when society comes apart at the seams, the elite, the ones capable of controlling the masses, don't stand by to watch the carnage. They have contingency plans, just as we do. These circumstances are different."

"How so, sir?" asked Harris. "I mean, the results are similar, just more pronounced."

"Ah, there is a difference, as time will reveal. I like to call it *managed mayhem*. There will be a period where a purge occurs. My goal is to ensure that those who agree with my philosophies, and those of our Founders, prevail. Over the past two decades, the balance of power has tilted in favor of a European-socialist form of governance. I'm simply trying to tilt it back to its Constitution-based roots."

"Isn't this likely to be temporary?"

Trowbridge sighed. "Maybe, depending on how our nation's leaders respond. First, the cleansing must take place. And then a leader will step forward to bring America back to her former greatness."

Harris was about to speak when his cell phone rang. "My apologies, sir. I should take this."

He listened intently to the other end of the line. He nodded several times, occasionally mumbling a response.

"Thank you. I will let him know."

"What?" demanded Trowbridge.

"Two things, sir. First, your daughter and son-in-law have left their hotel and are en route to the Haven."

"How trustworthy is our surveillance team?"

"The best, sir, at your request. They will shadow them the entire trip, only intervening in the event the family is in grave danger."

"Good, I cannot risk pushing my daughter further away. If she senses I'm trying to meddle in their lives, even under these dire circumstances, I could lose her forever."

Trowbridge showed a rare sign of emotion. He'd become estranged from his daughter when she'd learned that her father had established a blueprint for Cort's life. Meredith was proud of Cort's accomplishments, and she refused to allow her father to manipulate their lives like they were pawns in his political chess matches.

Little did she know that he was masterfully setting the course of their lives from afar, creating opportunities for Cort without his knowledge. It was a roadmap for his son-in-law's life that had been set the day he married Trowbridge's only daughter. They were pawns, for now. Soon, their level of importance would jump exponentially.

CHAPTER 17

Pinecrest
East of Charlotte Airport

The Cortland family chattered away about the things they wanted to purchase at Walmart. Hannah focused on things to entertain themselves while at the Haven. Meredith reeled off a number of creature comforts and items that would make her job at the school easier. Cort focused on practical items such as food, first aid supplies, and ammunition for the guns he'd brought from home.

When he opted to take the back streets along Old Steele Creek Road toward Walmart rather than a more direct route to the Haven, he presumed any additional rioting or unrest would be absent until nighttime. He presumed incorrectly.

They had just approached the major intersection at Wilkinson Boulevard when a group of a dozen people stormed into a Church's Chicken restaurant to their left. Cort was stunned to see the attackers wielding clubs and baseball bats, mercilessly beating the few patrons before running out the side entrances carrying purses and trays of food.

Cort tried to remain calm as he looked for a way to avoid the men running across the parking lot toward their truck. "Meredith, crawl in the backseat and get down. If you can, reach for my handgun case. It's sitting underneath my duffle bag."

Their vehicle was surrounded by cars and Cort had no good options. He started to put the truck in reverse when the men ran past them, ignoring all the parked cars. They had another target in mind.

To Cort's right, a group of men came running out of the woods near the Walmart shopping center. They were screaming and hurling rocks at the attackers of the Church's restaurant.

"Gun," whispered Meredith as if she were trying to hide the weapon from the men battling one another in the middle of the intersection.

Cort reached back and took the case from her. He reached into his pocket to retrieve the key and unlocked the case. He pushed the magazine he'd loaded with bullets this morning into the bottom of the grip and readied the weapon.

The light changed to green, but none of the traffic moved. Cort had no intention of being stuck in the event the melee escalated to involve the motorists. He also gave up on the prospect of shopping at Walmart. His priorities changed to protecting his family and survival.

He put the truck in reverse and inched backward to create space between the Suburban and the pickup truck in front of him. He turned the wheel to the left and lurched into the other lane until he arrived in the restaurant's parking lot. Squealing the tires, Cort sped backwards, completing his one-hundred-eighty-degree turn around, and raced away from the intersection.

After checking his mirrors and noticing that only one other SUV had made a similar maneuver, he exhaled. "It's okay, honey. You can come back up here if you want."

Meredith's voice was barely above a whisper. "Um, no, thanks. I'm good. We're good."

Cort nodded, fully understanding how she felt. He looked for the next major cross street and turned right, systematically making his way toward the west until he ran into Billy Graham Parkway.

"Daddy, how much farther is it to our new place?"

"A little over an hour, Hannah," he replied, focused on the road in front of them.

She didn't immediately say anything, and then after a moment, she muttered, "Not too bad."

Cort closed his eyes momentarily as he turned on to US 321 and headed north toward Henry Mill River Village. He wanted to avoid exposing his daughter to the collapse he'd foreseen when he purchased property at the Haven. It was an investment that was low in cost, but high on commitment. They were required to leave their spacious, historic home that had been in the Cortland family for a century in exchange for a two-bedroom cabin about the size of their living room in Mobile.

It would've been easy for Cort to stay in his hometown under the presumption that a small Southern city was immune to big-city unrest. He'd just witnessed what societal collapse looks like, and he'd never felt better about his decision to purchase the cabin at the Haven than in that moment.

CHAPTER 18

Front Gate
The Haven

"I'm Delta."

Cort stared into the eyes of the man who greeted him at the front gate of the Haven. He chuckled and exchanged a knowing glance with Meredith, who had finally joined him in the front seat for the last twenty minutes of their ride. The name Delta would forever be etched in Cort's mind with his New Year's Eve flight from hell.

"Of course you are," said Cort with a smile as he extended his hand out the window to shake Delta's. "Michael Cortland, but everyone calls me Cort. This is my wife, Meredith, and my eleven-year-old is in the back. Her name's Hannah."

Hannah waved before her companion in the backseat made his presence known. "Woof!"

"Oh, yeah. Lest I forget, Handsome Dan, our English bulldog, is also pleased to make your acquaintance."

"It's nice to meet you guys," said Delta. "This won't take long, but if you don't mind stepping out of the vehicle, we have to do a quick security sweep. Also, I don't know how your handsome friend does with other dogs, but we have a German shepherd who'll be sniffing around the chassis. You know, just to be sure."

"Sure about what?" asked Meredith, who was leaning across the armrest.

"Bombs, ma'am. It's just a precaution."

Meredith scowled and whispered to Cort, "Really? Bombs?"

Cort shrugged and turned to Hannah. "Honey, we're gonna step

71

out of the truck for a moment while they make sure everything is safe. Will you put Handsome's collar back on and attach his leash?"

"Sure, Daddy."

The Cortlands stood to the side while Delta's security detail did their jobs. Delta struck up a conversation, starting with Hannah.

"I have a daughter who's about your age. Her name is Skylar. Trust me when I say she'll be excited to meet you."

"Sounds good," interjected Meredith. "Are there any other kids around elevenish?"

"Several," replied Delta. "However, everyone has been sticking to themselves, and Sky hasn't really met anyone. She'd love to have someone else to play with besides her brother."

"How old is he?" asked Cort.

"Fifteen going on three, at times, and thirty, at others," replied Delta with an eyeroll.

"Teenagers, gotta love 'em," Meredith quipped.

"Yeah, but that's only part of the story," said Delta.

One of the security team hollered over at Delta, "We're good, boss."

Delta smiled and gave Cort a thumbs-up.

Meredith asked another question. "Cort mentioned something about a school on the property."

"Yeah, as a matter of fact, it was just finished New Year's Eve before, well, you know. They call it the Little Red Schoolhouse."

This grabbed Hannah's attention, who'd been patiently waiting for Handsome to stop urinating on every bush nearby. "Wow, neat! Is it really red?"

Delta knelt down to her level. "It is fire-truck red."

"Cool."

"Say, Hannah, do you know why fire trucks are red?"

"No, sir?"

"Okay. Let's ask Siri."

"Who?"

"You know, Siri. On the Apple iPhone."

Meredith interrupted. "She doesn't have a cell phone yet. We were gonna wait until she turned twenty-one." The adults laughed at the suggestion.

"Well, let me tell you something, Hannah. Siri is a wealth of information. She is the brain of an iPhone, and if you ask her a question, she'll give you an answer. Do you wanna see?"

"Sure do!" exclaimed the child enthusiastically.

Delta reached into his pocket and retrieved his cell phone. He powered up the display and then smiled at Meredith with a wink. After the ding notification alerted him that Siri was waiting for him to speak, Delta asked, "Hey, Siri, why are fire trucks red?"

Delta held the phone out for everyone to hear the answer.

The robotic, female voice responded, *"Because they have eight wheels and four people on them, and four plus eight is twelve, and there are twelve inches in a foot, and one foot is a ruler, and Queen Elizabeth was a ruler, and Queen Elizabeth was also a ship, and the ship sailed the seas, and in the seas are fish, and fish have fins, and the Finns fought the Russians, and the Russians are red, and fire trucks are always Russian around."*

The group stared at Delta's phone in disbelief until, simultaneously, they broke out in uproarious laughter.

"This is a joke, right?" asked Cort, hardly able to contain himself. "I mean, you programmed that somehow."

Delta had a huge grin on his face. "Nope, all the iPhones do it. Try it sometime."

Meredith gave Hannah a high five. "Look at that, Hannah. You learn something every day."

Hannah, however, was still intrigued about the Little Red Schoolhouse.

"That is cool. Hey, Mom, you're a teacher. Can we go check out the schoolhouse later?"

"Um, honey, we'll need to—"

Delta raised his hand and smiled. "Say no more. I'll call Ryan and let him know you're here. I'm sure he'd love for you to get started if you're up for it.

Meredith smiled and nodded. "You know, I think all of us are ready to put the events of the last few days behind us and get started on our new adventure. So, yes, if it's okay, Hannah and I would love to invite Skylar to join us while we check out the school. We might even get things set up for the new school year so all the kids can have something to look forward to."

"Excellent," said Delta, who offered a fist bump to Hannah. "I'll make the calls. I assume you guys know where to go?"

"I do," replied Cort.

"Good. Our cabin is to the left. Once you go through the roundabout at the fountain up ahead, take a left, and we're down on the right. Our yard has a tire swing in the front."

"Cool!" exclaimed Hannah, who didn't hesitate to tug Handsome back toward the truck.

Meredith helped the stout pup into the backseat while Cort exchanged a few final words with Delta. "Is everybody here?"

"Not yet," replied Delta. "We have a regular meeting of the security team at the main barn in the mornings. Are you a part of our security?"

"Not likely," said Cort. "I mean, I can handle a weapon, but I'm not trained like you guys probably are. Are you ex-military?"

"Nah, cop," replied Delta. "Well, I'm sure Ryan has something in mind for you. I'll make the call, and you guys get settled in. He'll probably be around soon enough."

The men shook hands and the Cortlands entered the Haven, full of excitement.

CHAPTER 19

NBC Studios
Temporary Studio Set
Secaucus, New Jersey

MSNBC host Craig Melvin shuffled through the notes just handed to him by one of the production assistants. He listened to the instructions being given to him from his producer as he shuffled through the pages, reading the text message stream between their reporter and Chepe. The PA had also printed a map of the downtown Richmond area so Melvin could have a visual of the major roadways and points of interest.

He turned his attention to his producer. "They invited us to imbed with them?"

"That's right, Craig. As soon as Hallie closes out her segment, we're gonna go to breaking news and throw it over to you. It may very well cover the entire hour."

Melvin was happy to oblige. He'd covered societal unrest for the network as a reporter in years past before making the leap into the anchor's chair. When MSNBC approached its on-air talent about evacuating New York following the dirty bomb attacks at Times Square to a temporary studio setting across the Hudson River in Secaucus, New Jersey, Melvin was the first to volunteer.

He had a sense that the attacks were part of something bigger, more sinister. As the news reports came in from around the country, he gathered his personal effects and was the first to arrive at the former New Jersey Motor Vehicle Commission facility. Until his co-workers were located and brought across the river, he stood vigil as the sole news anchor available to the network as events unfolded.

Working with completely unedited, raw footage from news cameras and private cell phones, Melvin began to piece together a pattern to the attacks, one that troubled him deeply. He wasn't quite prepared to voice his opinion to his executive producer, opting instead to be a constant part of the news coverage, which enabled him to gather more information.

In his mind, the fact that Antifa was organizing to begin a series of protests and marches in Richmond, Virginia, of all places, was intriguing. He knew Antifa and their leadership. He also knew who pulled their strings. Melvin began to suspect something of a counterinsurgency operation. If he was right, all hell would be breaking loose very soon.

"Okay, Craig," said his producer into his earpiece. "You'll be live in thirty."

Melvin prepared himself and opened his segment as always. As instructed, he prepared himself to go live to Richmond, where an NBC news video team from their Washington, DC, bureau was in place to provide footage and a report.

After they dispensed with the preliminaries and set the scene for their viewers, the reporter relayed what he knew.

"Craig, when the march began, it seemed aimless. The group meandered through the streets of Richmond, stopping to chant and raise their fists in the air, but mostly gathering steam with random additions to their growing throng."

The reporter paused as he ran to keep up with the black-clad protesters, who began to move forward at a slow jog. Running backwards with a cordless mike, the reporter periodically glanced over his shoulder to avoid stumbling.

He continued. "However, all of that changed about ten minutes ago. The group seemed to coalesce around a goal as it became clear they were headed toward Interstate 95. As you know, I-95 is a major north-south thoroughfare that runs along the Atlantic Seaboard from Maine to Florida. The highway splits Richmond in two and is the most heavily traveled stretch of interstate in Virginia, especially now, as it's packed with motorists fleeing the carnage in the northeast."

Melvin interrupted, asking a question to allow the reporter to catch his breath. "Do they have a recognizable leader? And also, do you know why they're headed for the interstate?"

The reporter held his fingers to his earpiece and nodded. "Craig, I was invited by an anonymous text signed by Sabokitty. Because I've covered these types of organized protests in the past, I am familiar with the moniker. Sabokitty is the organizer, although I have no idea which of these individuals he or she is. I do know this, however. They intend to take the interstate."

"Wait. What was that? What do you mean by *take the interstate?*" asked Melvin.

"That's the exact question I asked when I was told why we'd changed direction. At first, I began laughing, trying to visualize what that meant. I imagined General Patton standing on top of a tank with his field glasses, surveying the French countryside. When the protestors didn't laugh along with me, and I could see the resolve in their eyes partially obscured by bandanas and masks, I realized they were serious."

Melvin interrupted again. "As we watch your footage, we can see people at the front of the pack begin to separate their rather large group into a series of smaller ones. What do they have in mind?"

"I'm told that this is the next step in their operation. They plan on crowding the on-off ramps and moving onto the overpasses. The goal is to disrupt traffic but spread out so the police can't contain them."

"How many protestors are there?" asked Melvin.

"Craig, it started with about a hundred. As the group passed Gilpin Court, a low-income housing project near the highway, its numbers swelled by more than double. The group includes men and women. Children, too. All ages are represented. Frankly, Craig, many of the new participants don't know why they're marching or what they're protesting. They just want to be a part of something."

Melvin leaned back in his chair as the producer indicated the camera was going to focus on him and pull away from the live feed. His facial expression became serious as he quickly transitioned from news anchor to opinion contributor.

"Well, I must say this is indicative of what we've been reporting to you from around the country. New Year's Eve created a night of fear for many as the terrorist attacks struck all walks of life. What we are seeing now are pure acts of defiance.

"None of these marchers appear afraid. To the contrary, they have a steely resolve to make their message heard. Their march may not change the world, or even the city of Richmond, but it will serve to put many on notice that this nation is about to undergo a radical transformation.

"New Year's Eve lit a spark in the hearts of many people. What we are seeing manifest itself in Richmond is a grassroots effort by the people to let their voices be heard."

Chapter 20

U.S. 301 at I-95
Near Richmond, Virginia

Hayden was making her way up the interstate on-ramp when her phone rang. The display read *Blair Smart*. She'd tried to call Blair an hour ago after she'd crossed the Potomac from Maryland into Virginia. The two exchanged pleasantries before getting down to business.

"Foxy, tell me you're on your way to the Haven," said Blair in a serious tone.

"Blair, I wish you guys wouldn't call me that," said Hayden half-jokingly. "I happened to be the sixth in line on the security team, but I honestly believe Alpha labeled me Foxtrot, or Foxy, on purpose."

"He's got the hots for you, Hayden."

"Yeah, yeah. Whatever. Not interested. We don't need that kind of soap-opera drama at the Haven."

Blair laughed. "Oh, girl, we've got drama. Don't you worry about causing more. You know, Ryan and I've talked about this. There are some pretty nice single guys roaming around the Haven. Why don't you consider—"

"No."

"But you haven't met—"

Hayden was emphatic. "Blair, no. I don't need the aggravation of a boyfriend."

"Don't you get lonely?" asked Blair.

"No, I have Prowler," replied Hayden.

"He's just a cat. You need someone to talk to. Share your day with."

Hayden shook her head vigorously. "Listen, I'm all about my career and I have Prowler to share my day with. I don't need some guy to monopolize my time or vie for my attention when I've got a lot going on."

The traffic slowed and then sped up in spurts as she continued the conversation. She changed the subject away from her love life, or lack thereof. "To answer your question. Yes, I'm on my way. I had to wait on the president to declare martial law."

Blair interrupted her. "I've been glued to the news today while dealing with other things. I haven't seen anything about his making it official. Oh, did you catch the scrap on CNN?"

Hayden chuckled. "Yeah. Prowler did too. He said it was lame."

Blair let out a hearty laugh. "I miss that cat, and so do my girls. Who knew they'd get along?"

"The three of them see each other as equals," replied Hayden.

"That's because they're about the same size, lol," added Blair before going back to the issue of martial law. "He hasn't officially declared martial law. Do you know something I don't?"

"Yeah, sort of. Let's just say it's in the works and an announcement will be made before the end of the day, most likely."

"Good to know," said Blair. "I'll pass it along to the guys. I'm glad to hear you're on your way. I tried to reach you after the attacks."

"Um, I know, and I apologize for not getting back to you. I had my own aggravations to deal with on the Metrorail. I'll tell you about it when I get there."

"Where are you?" asked Blair.

Hayden looked at her navigation screen on the Range Rover's dashboard and then glanced at an upcoming sign suspended across the six-lane highway. "I'm near the merge lanes of I-95 and I-64 just north of downtown Richmond. It's slow going, but steady. I expect it'll clear out on the other side of the city."

Blair hesitated before she spoke. "People are bailing out of New York and any parts of the northeast where their cars are still working. They all wanna come south. What makes them think we want them?"

"Beats me. I'm glad I found you guys and have a place—" Hayden stopped speaking as traffic came to an abrupt halt. She was underneath an overpass and glanced to her right. The same graffiti was painted on the concrete abutment holding up the road above her.

"Blair, what do you know about graffiti or artwork that looks like a fist holding up a black rose? I saw it in DC and now it's spray-painted here by the interstate."

"A black rose? I really don't know, Hayden. I can ask around. Describe it again."

Hayden put Blair on speaker and navigated through her iPhone to the camera app. She took several pictures of the graffiti with plans to compare this image to the one seen near her home.

"It's a fist held straight up, clenching the stem of a black rose. They've sprayed red paint to outline the image, almost like the color of blood."

"And it's the same in both places?" asked Blair.

Hayden took Blair off the speaker before responding, "Yeah, almost identical. Obviously, two different people did the work, but the design is nearly identical. It has to be related."

"I agree," said Blair. "I don't believe in coincidences. Hey, let me mention one more thing. Like I said, I've been monitoring the newscasts and going online to local news websites to get updates for people. You need to be careful going through—"

Hayden never heard Blair say the word *Richmond* as a cinder block came crashing down on the hood of her Range Rover, startling her and causing her to drop the phone.

This was just the beginning of the onslaught.

CHAPTER 21

Interstate 95
Richmond, Virginia

Hayden screamed, and Prowler angrily screeched as another large rock pelted her hood, which protruded just beyond the side of the bridge. Fortunately, her windshield wasn't exposed to the people throwing the heavy construction materials over the side. The same could not be said for the cars in front of her.

Windshields were shattered, rear windows were broken out, and one man emerged from his car with gashes in his face, causing his vision to be obscured with blood. Other drivers panicked, trying to force themselves forward to get out of harm's way, or backwards, to gain protection using the overpass as a shield.

The vehicle in front of her, a Mini Cooper, had been utterly destroyed by the blocks of concrete. All the windows, including the sunroof glass, were smashed. The back bumper of the Mini was only a few feet away from Hayden, so she could see the interior clearly. A woman was slumped over the steering wheel with a jagged piece of concrete embedded in her scalp.

Hayden frantically looked in all directions. She was in the far-right lane, having just entered the interstate. This gave her the opportunity to use the hard shoulder to move forward. However, there were several cars already scooting over to make their way past the bridge. Hayden inched backwards and received an angry blare of a horn for her efforts.

"Thanks a lot, buddy!" she shouted, waving her fist in her rearview mirror. She ignored his horn and relied upon the backup camera on her Range Rover's dashboard to avoid hitting the hostile driver.

She was able to create enough space between her truck and the Mini to turn her steering wheel and navigate toward the shoulder. Now she needed a little polite help from her fellow motorists. She kept inching the front of her truck into the traffic, hoping someone would allow her in. Just as a car slowed, the vehicle that passed by her suddenly veered left and careened into the Mini Cooper, adding insult to injury. The resulting crash caused the sedan to block most of the emergency lane and immediately subjected the driver to a barrage of concrete debris.

"Are they going to run out of crap to throw at us?" A frustrated Hayden yelled her question as she leaned forward to determine if there was sufficient room to squeeze by the wrecked truck. Another chunk of concrete came hurtling down from above and broke out her left headlight. Frustration grew to anger that quickly changed to fear.

Suddenly, a dozen people dressed in black clothing and wearing masks similar to the way the graffiti artists had been dressed the day before appeared at the chain-link fences guarding the interstate from pedestrians. They were using bolt cutters to create openings.

All of them were carrying aluminum baseball bats, tire irons, or large pieces of concrete. Hayden immediately reached into the back of the passenger seat and felt for her loaded handgun, which was stashed in a pouch behind the seat back.

"Prowler, backseat. Now!" The Maine coon sensed danger and jumped into the backseat on top of a duffle bag.

Hayden pulled the slide on her gun to load a round into the chamber but not before one of the attackers smashed the passenger side of her windshield with an aluminum bat. Another crawled onto her hood and jumped into the air, waving a club over his head like a lunatic.

With the cars ahead of her disabled, Hayden was cornered, and her attackers knew it.

CHAPTER 22

Interstate 95
Richmond, Virginia

Tom had sensed danger as he saw chunks of cinder blocks and concrete flying downward from the overpass in front of them. He instinctively looked up through the glass sunroof to determine if he and Donna were in danger of being struck, comforted by the span of steel beams and concrete above their heads. He checked his mirrors and turned in his seat to see if the vehicles behind him were being attacked. They were as well.

"We're trapped!" he shouted as the blaring of car horns reverberated off the steel and concrete that surrounded them. Tom quickly weighed his options. He didn't have any.

They were in the far-right lane, and the guardrail pinched the shoulder of the highway, so the oversized Yukon couldn't fit through. Vehicles succumbed to the debris both in front and in back of their position. In a frantic attempt to escape the barrage of debris, vehicles crashed into one another. Some drivers were badly injured as the rocky materials broke through windshields and sunroofs.

"Tom! There are people running down the hill over there!" Donna shouted and directed his attention to the right side of the overpass, where more than a dozen men raced down the hill, waving a variety of weapons. Tom wished he had one of his battle rifles. This assault would've been over in short order.

He glanced in the rearview mirror again beyond the small red KIA tucked under his bumper. He decided that backing out of the perfect choke point created by the bridge abutments and the stalled traffic was not an option. He looked forward again. "I'm gonna squeeze through!"

"Tom, we're too wide. You won't fit."

"We'll see." Tom turned the wheel to the right so that the Yukon barely scraped the guardrail.

"You're gonna tear up the side!" Donna warned him.

"Who cares?" he quickly responded as he forced himself between a Toyota Camry and the guardrail. The driver of the Camry began shaking her fist at him and beating on her horn out of anger as the bumper of the Yukon shoved her to the side. Tom gave the heavy truck gas, and gradually, a path was cleared, allowing him to scoot along the guardrail, with the KIA following his lead.

"Oh no!" shouted Donna, pointing at a masked man flailing away at the passenger window of the car in front of the Camry. The shiny black Range Rover was taking a beating until the man successfully broke out the glass.

In Tom's military career, he'd seen brutality. He'd seen the deadly toll of war and the bodies of the wounded when they returned home. They were visuals he'd never erase from his mind, nor did he want to. It was a constant reminder that war was hell, and regardless of the methods employed to wage it, the toll on humanity was the same.

The Range Rover shook violently as the attacker fell forward into the front seat. The darkened windows of the four-door sedan obscured his view of what was happening, but when the man freed himself from the passenger door, he fell backwards onto the pavement in a heap, his face ripped to shreds beyond recognition.

Donna screamed as she saw the man's mangled face.

"Unbelievable," muttered Tom, aghast at the grotesque appearance of the man's face.

"Tom, the driver is trying to get your attention." Donna had noticed as the chaos continued. The other attackers were mercilessly beating the vehicles and some of their passengers. The rear passenger window of the Range Rover rolled down, and a woman driver turned towards their truck, waving to get their attention.

Tom glanced around and then rolled down his window. "Are you okay?"

The driver shouted to be heard over the melee. "Yes! Can you scoot back so I can get in front of you? We can make it by the wreckage."

Tom pointed toward the attackers' reinforcements. "There are more coming!"

The woman glanced forward and then shouted to him, "I've got them. Please make room for me so I can get out."

Tom gave her a thumbs-up and placed the truck in reverse. The driver of the KIA immediately began to honk his horn at Tom, but he ignored the complaint. He slowly made contact with the KIA's front bumper and then pressed the gas pedal to the floor. The tires squealed at first, but then the KIA began to relent as it was pushed backwards into other cars that were trying to follow them along the shoulder.

"That's enough, Tom," said Donna. "She's clear. Oh my god!"

CHAPTER 23

Interstate 95
Richmond, Virginia

Hayden winced and forced herself against the driver's side door as her attacker released a guttural scream. Another blow of the baseball bat caused the passenger glass to explode inward, forcing her to cover her face with her arm and protect herself. The next thing she heard was Prowler.

"Rrrreeeeeer!"

With lightning quickness, Prowler leapt from the backseat onto the console as the attacker stuck his head through the window to reach for Hayden. The large house cat became a vicious animal, drawing upon his instincts to protect Hayden.

First, Prowler clawed at the man's hand to force him to withdraw from Hayden's arm. This caused the man to fall forward slightly so that he was half in and half out of the Range Rover. This was a fatal mistake that resulted in a brutal beatdown that only could be imagined in a horror movie.

With a continuous roar of earsplitting screeches, Prowler ripped into the man's face. The first couple of blows pulled the bandana-style mask away, exposing his skin. The next several clawing motions came so fast that Hayden, whose body remained pressed against the driver's door, couldn't attempt to count. She'd never seen Prowler act like this before.

Scratch after scratch, he clawed at the man's face, ripping into his skin until pieces of flesh began to fly about the truck. The attacker was screaming in agony as Prowler's last blow found the man's eyelid, ripping it away from his eyeball. It was a gruesome sight, sickening to anyone who might've witnessed the scene.

But not to Prowler. It was the beginning of the end for his mommy's attacker. He growled again, a deep guttural sound that caused the hair to stand up on the back of Hayden's neck. While all around her, motorists were being terrorized by people dressed in black, smashing their weapons against windshields and car hoods, her cat was viciously mauling one of their comrades.

Hayden readied her weapon, prepared to shoot the poor, hapless marauder who had become limp from Prowler's ruthless and barbaric mutilation of the man's face. She raised her weapon, but the man's body weight finally pulled him backwards onto the highway.

Prowler jumped up onto the window opening, disregarding the bits of broken glass under his feet. Hayden feared he'd jump out after the man, who was likely unconscious from the beatdown the Maine coon had put on him.

"No! Prowler, stay!" She gave him orders as she would a dog. Prowler was trained that way and understood. He stood alert but didn't chase after the attacker. He continued, however, to bitch about it, emitting a series of growls and yowls to express how pissed off he was.

Hayden had to stay alert. The assault was not over. She glanced to her left and saw two men with spray-paint cans drawing the black rose symbol on the hood of an SUV while a woman pounded on the driver's window with a tire iron.

"Prowler, we're getting out of here!"

Hayden looked to her right and got the attention of an older couple who'd fortunately been spared from the onrush of rioters. She took a chance and rolled down her rear passenger window. She waved at the driver to get his attention.

The driver, an older man wearing a white sweater and a baseball cap with a U.S. Navy insignia, checked around his car and rolled down his window.

"Are you okay?" he yelled to her amidst the screams and shouts of the attackers.

"Yes!" replied Hayden. "Can you scoot back so I can get in front of you? We can make it by the wreckage."

The man looked forward and pointed. "There are more coming!"

"I've got them. Please make room for me so I can get out."

The man hung his arm out the window and gave her a thumbs-up. He was driving a GMC Yukon that was more than strong enough to force the red Kia parked against his rear bumper out of the way. The Kia driver slammed on his high-pitched horn, but it was no match for the brutish, three-ton Yukon.

The driver squealed the tires, shoving the offended Kia out of the way to make room for Hayden to get in front of the Yukon. As she did, the attacker was awakened by her right rear tire running over his arm, snapping it in several places.

"Sorry, jerkoff!" shouted Hayden, who wheeled her truck onto the emergency lane, only to be met by half a dozen screaming banshees racing toward her, carrying buckets of paint and bricks.

CHAPTER 24

Interstate 95
Richmond, Virginia

"Really?" asked Hayden as she gritted her teeth and set her jaw. "What is their problem?" She inched forward so that the front end of her smashed-up truck was able to get around the wrecked vehicles blocking the road. She periodically glanced in her rearview mirror to make sure the Yukon was behind her.

Hayden had learned to shoot as a young girl on her family farm. Although most of her practice was with long guns, primarily while hunting, she'd taken the time to learn how to use a sidearm by practicing extensively with her father. She was naturally right-handed, but she'd learn to throw darts left-handed and had transferred her ambidextrous skills to shooting as well.

Hayden rolled down her window and glanced over at Prowler, who was still loaded for bear. "Hold on, buddy, and watch your ears." The fur on the tip of the Maine coon's distinctive ears wiggled slightly as he hunkered down in the passenger seat.

Hayden eased her way onto the shoulder so that the truck would barely fit between the guardrail and the wrecked vehicle. The Yukon was wider than her Range Rover and would experience a tighter squeeze, but should be able to clear the narrow opening.

She hung her left arm out the window. The fresh set of assailants was upon her when she fired the first warning shots over their heads. Two rounds exploded out of her weapon, causing the group to scatter and jump for cover. This also had the effect of attracting the attention of the first group, who immediately stopped their assaults on other motorists and looked in Hayden's direction. She was now the focus of the entire group's ire.

They began hurling expletives in her direction, together with anything at their disposal. Rocks bounced off the rear hatch of her truck, and a quart-sized can of paint sailed over her roof, nailing the Yukon on the hood and exploding in a spray of red. The driver immediately turned on his windshield washers and smeared the red paint until it began to dissolve.

Hayden had cleared the opening but didn't immediately take off, opting instead to ensure the driver of the Yukon could make his way through the opening. She could hear the high-pitched, squeaking sound of metal on metal as the Yukon bulled its way past the wreckage.

Another can of paint pelted her truck, soaking the hood in blood-red stain. A man jumped from behind the wreckage and raced toward her door. Although Hayden didn't want to shoot anyone unless she absolutely had to, she took aim at the aluminum bat he was wielding and quickly fired three rounds until she found the barrel.

The sting the man experienced from the bullet ricocheting off the hard aluminum caused him to yell in pain, and he dropped the bat. Once again, the attackers sought cover, giving Hayden the time necessary to accelerate down the shoulder of the road. Because traffic had been stopped by the attack, all of the southbound lanes had opened up and she was able to speed away.

Hayden managed a smile as she noticed the driver of the Yukon was behind her, with nothing more than a poorly painted red hood to go with the gold factory paint of his truck. She slowed to pull over and assess the damage to her truck. The Yukon pulled alongside and an older woman shouted to Hayden, "Thank you! Godspeed!"

CHAPTER 25

Interstate 95
Richmond, Virginia

Tom reacted to Donna's outburst by gripping the wheel and jamming on the brakes. It wasn't her intention to startle or warn him, but it was a genuine expression of astonishment.

"What?" he asked.

"That woman ran over the guy," she replied.

"Good," said Tom as he focused his attention and followed the Range Rover forward. They made slow progress through the gap between a wrecked vehicle and the guardrail, scraping the side of the Yukon with a high-pitched squeal.

Suddenly, a can of paint struck the hood and emptied a splash of gooey red paint all over the truck. The windshield was also covered in red, so Tom turned on his windshield wipers in an attempt to wash it away.

That was when gunshots could be heard. "Get down, Donna. Now!"

Donna slumped down and crammed herself between the seat and the glove box. Tom also slid down in his seat to lower his profile. He felt this would protect him from gunfire and more debris being thrown off the overpass.

The Range Rover was past the wreckage, but the driver paused as if to wait for Tom to follow. He set his jaw, gritted his teeth, and forced the beast of a truck past the debris.

"Is it safe?" asked Donna as she slowly rose out of her crouch.

Tom glanced around one last time as he raced to keep up with the Range Rover. "Yeah, come on up. That woman just saved us."

"Was she firing the gun?"

"I believe so. She did a good job, too. She only used a few rounds to send those thugs scrambling for cover. Hold on. I wanna catch up to her and say thanks."

Tom accelerated so that he was next to the driver's side door. Donna rolled down the window, causing the cold wind to blow throughout the truck. She leaned her head out the window, and the female driver responded by rolling down her window as well. She smiled at Donna and gave a casual, polite wave.

Donna shouted to the driver of the Range Rover, "Thank you! Godspeed!"

The woman suddenly slowed and the Sheltons never heard her response. Seconds later, they were taking advantage of the now deserted interstate. Full of apprehension, Tom focused his attention on the highway in front of them while Donna kept the black Range Rover in her side-view mirror for as long as she could, concerned about the fate of the young woman who'd probably saved their lives.

CHAPTER 26

Interstate 95
Richmond, Virginia

Hayden was puzzled. Did she hear correctly? She slowed down suddenly to attempt to speak to the passenger of the Yukon. She hung her head out the window and shouted, "What? What does that mean?"

The driver took off at a high rate of speed and probably never heard her ask the questions. Hayden couldn't blame him. She wanted to get as far from Richmond as she could, but first she needed to make sure her truck could continue.

While she inspected the exterior and found everything to be safe, she continuously mumbled the word *Godspeed* to herself.

"Come on, people. Where is this coming from? *Godspeed.*"

She urged Prowler to sit in the driver's seat while she hurriedly removed bits of glass from his seat onto the floor mat. When the center console and seat were cleared of the debris, she dumped all of it onto the side of the road.

Still puzzled, she continued to talk out loud. "I've gone nearly my entire life and never heard anyone say that except in some old Charles Dickens movie or some such. Godspeed? Safe travels? Good luck? What's the context?"

She rolled her eyes and shook her head as she walked around the Range Rover to the driver's door. A couple of cars sped past, apparently following through the gap she and the Yukon had created. Hayden was more troubled by the use of the term *Godspeed* in the text messages and from the passenger in the Yukon than she was about the condition of her Range Rover. After all, she had insurance, she thought to herself with a chuckle. *Big whoop.*

As she got back under way and traveled through Richmond, she saw fires burning out of control in the vicinity of the state capitol. Traffic slowed on I-95, allowing her the opportunity to view the historic colonial-style structure as she passed. She recalled from her history studies that the building had been conceived by Thomas Jefferson and had managed to endure centuries of political turmoil and bloodshed.

Now, sitting high atop a hill in the center of Richmond, the capitol once again appeared to be surrounded by turmoil.

Hayden laughed to herself and then said, "Godspeed, Richmond. Looks like you'll need it."

She glanced one last time at the historic structure; then the voice of her former boss, Justice Samuel Alito, came into her head.

"That's it, Prowler!" she exclaimed, stirring the cat out of his curled position. "Justice Alito said that to me once. I was traveling back to the farm and he said, *Godspeed, Miss Blount.* I wonder…"

Her voice trailed off as she immediately began to process the events of the last few days and the mysterious texts she'd received. Was there a connection between them and a Supreme Court justice? And why would he reach out to her like that?

CHAPTER 27

Haven House
The Haven

Ryan entered the kitchen and hugged Blair around the waist. He kissed her on the back of the neck and whispered, in his best Hank Williams voice, "Hey, good-lookin'. Whatcha got cookin'?"

Blair smiled and allowed Ryan to snuggle her before she playfully turned on him. "Get off me. I've got hungry children who are demanding breakfast."

"Breakfast? It's almost noon o'clock!" Ryan laughed as he turned around to find the girls sitting side by side like statues, waiting for their yummies. He addressed his four-legged daughters. "Don't you two have school today? Have you cleaned your rooms or done any kinds of chores? Ever?"

The English bulldog sisters simply stared back at him, Chubby's lower jaw protruding outward with her tongue half out of her mouth while The Roo was more closed-mouth, opting instead to study Ryan. *She's a thinker.*

"Pffft."

Blair snapped her head around and looked at Ryan.

"Shew, Chubby!" exclaimed Ryan as he pulled his sweatshirt up over his nose.

"Don't blame the child," interjected Blair.

"What? It wasn't me!" Ryan's voice rose several octaves as he pointed down at Chubby, who appeared to be laughing at him. "Look at the smile on her face. She did it!"

Blair pushed past him with two bowls of yummies for the girls.

"What kind of father blames his gassiness on the children. So rude, right, girls?"

The girls were less interested in the debate over the guilty gasser and chased after Blair, who placed their breakfast down at the end of the kitchen island.

Ryan feigned a pout. "Whatevs. Hey, I don't have much time. Can we get caught up before I spend the day with the guys?"

"Yeah, me first," responded Blair. She fixed them both salads topped with canned chicken and the last of the raw vegetables in their refrigerator. She'd prepared cut celery, carrots, and broccoli to be served with egg dip for New Year's Eve, but needless to say, the party never got off the ground.

Ryan added some cornbread croutons and doused the salad with low-fat bleu cheese dressing. He often joked about how salads are supposed to be good for you, especially for dieters. But by the time you add shredded cheese, maybe a boiled egg, and your favorite dressing, you might as well have swung through the Chick-fil-A drive-thru window.

"Talk to me," he said as he shoved a forkful of lettuce into his mouth.

"Well, I heard from Hayden. The good news is that she's on her way. The bad news is that I lost contact with her in the middle of the conversation. I'm not sure what happened, but it sounded like she dropped her phone."

"Has she called back?"

"No, and I've tried a few times to reach her. She was on the road somewhere. I was just about to warn her about the problems in Richmond when I lost contact."

Ryan continued eating and nodded his head. "Foxy will be fine. She's like a younger version of you. You don't tangle with a wildcat." Ryan allowed a sly grin and looked up over his forkful of salad to wait for his wife's response. He loved to tease her and she took great pleasure in giving it back to him.

She closed her eyes slightly and gave him the look. "Shut up."

That drew a big smile from her husband. "Speaking of wildcats, is she bringing that beast, Prowler?"

"I'm sure she is. I miss our cats from home. I really think they would've enjoyed living in the boonies."

"Lord knows there are plenty of mice to catch," added Ryan. "Besides, they seem to prefer tropical climates. Whadya have planned for this afternoon?"

"With the new arrivals, I'm gonna do a quick orientation after lunch. I'll assign jobs to those you haven't already recruited for your stuff. Also, with the Cortlands' arrival, our kid population is almost maxed out except for the Rankins. They're supposedly heading this way too after Tyler and Angela get their jobs squared away."

"Can they get the school ready for Monday? I want everyone settling into a routine and not getting complacent. You know?"

"Yeah. The school will be ready. Let me just tell you where I think we are on several things. Besides school, I think our weapons and ammo numbers are excellent. I'm sure Hayden will add to that significantly. The Sheltons and Rankins, not so much."

Ryan asked about food and supplies. "Are you gonna send out another shopping team this afternoon?"

Blair nodded. "I think I will. As long as it's safe and the stores have things we need on their shelves, we'll snatch it up. Also, I had Echo make a bank withdrawal and sent him into Hickory to the gold dealers. I checked spot gold this morning, and prices are starting to rise."

"Is the dollar still crashing?" asked Ryan.

"They halted trading, so it's bottomed out. As soon as I saw the reports this morning, I sent him to buy all he could find before the locals figure out what's happening."

"Junk silver, too?"

Blair grimaced. "I doubt it. We buy all they get as soon as it comes in."

Ryan finished his lunch and cleared their plates into the kitchen. He refilled his water bottle and washed his hands. Blair joined him to wash hers. She rolled her head around, causing a noticeable series of crackles.

"Darling, is there something else bothering you?" he asked.

"No, not really," she replied. "People are asking a lot of questions. Naturally, they're concerned about their futures and they're also starved for information."

"Yeah, I'm getting the same thing."

Blair washed her hands as she spoke. "They're looking to us for leadership, and I think it's important that everyone is on the same page with what we believe is going on out there."

"What are you thinkin'?"

Blair wiped her hands and wandered out of the kitchen toward the family room. She stopped to stare at the news reports of riots in major cities around the country. "Your security team is top notch. But you also need advisors and people to act as your right arm. Ryan, you can't spread yourself too thin because if the Haven gets challenged, you'll be overwhelmed trying to wear too many hats."

Ryan took her by the hand and encouraged her to sit on the hearth with him. They stared into the spacious family room while the fire warmed their backs. He squeezed her hand. "I'm listening."

"Cort is a levelheaded guy and a politician. I like your idea of making him your right arm from an administrative aspect. He can play bad cop to your good cop role."

"I can be the bad cop when necessary."

Blair chuckled. "No, honey. You can't. You're too nice. I'm a better bad cop than you are. Talk to Cort. He's a real asset because he's fought in the trenches of DC's swamp."

"I will. What else?"

"Tom Shelton will be here this afternoon, too. He's a general, for Pete's sake."

"Commander," Ryan corrected. "But virtually the same thing."

"Okay, a commander. Let him be more involved in the defense strategies of the Haven. I trust Alpha, don't get me wrong. But he also has a tendency to be very rah-rah, gung ho Marine with his security details. That works well with Bravo, Charlie, and maybe even Delta, but your civilians-turned-security team members may not get it. Tom has experience dealing with all levels of the military. He can handle a direct crisis and the day-to-day security without wearing out our people."

Ryan smiled. This was just one more reason why he loved his wife. She offered another set of eyes, a different perspective, from which to manage the operations of the Haven. "I agree a hundred percent."

Blair pushed off her husband's knees and stood. She reached for his hands and hoisted him upward. They weren't getting any younger.

"The Sheltons and the Cortlands will both be here before suppertime. Let's have them and the Echols over to talk about things. Okay?"

"Book it, Danno," he replied, using one of his favorite sayings from the original *Hawaii Five-O* television series.

CHAPTER 28

Delta's Cabin
The Haven

Delta arrived back at his cabin with a sack full of barbecue sandwiches under his arm. He was in a jovial mood after speaking with Ryan about involving the kids in some of the Haven's activities. He could only imagine what it was like for Ethan and Skylar. They'd been taken away from their home and their things. There wasn't any television in his cabin, and in the dead of the damp, North Carolina winter, there wasn't much for them to do outside. Hopefully, the new activities would lift Ethan's spirits, too.

"Hey, guys! I've got some news. Barbecue for lunch, too."

Ethan emerged from the bedroom looking as if he'd been asleep. "Did you find me a phone charger?"

"Um, not yet," replied Delta. He wouldn't be able to hold his son off much longer. "But I have something else cool to tell you about."

"What is it, Daddy?" asked Skylar, who emerged from the kitchen area. Her hands were covered in multiple colors of paint. Delta frowned for a moment, wondering if the commissioned artwork required a brush, or if she was finger painting. He shrugged it off and motioned for them to join him at the dining table as he unpacked the sandwiches.

"What's this, Daddy?" asked Skylar.

"Venison barbecue with homemade sauce. Wait'll you taste it!" Delta unwrapped the foil and slid a sandwich in front of each of them. Both kids settled in and took big bites. A good sign. "And look what else I have."

"What?" muttered Ethan with a mouthful of sandwich.

Delta pulled out a sixteen-ounce bottle of Mountain Dew. "Do the Dew!"

Ethan chuckled and then snidely remarked, "Very Southern, Dad."

"Yeah, it is, and I like it," said Delta. "Okay, let me tell you the news. First, for you, Sky."

"All right!"

"Yeah, first thing is this. Another family just arrived from Alabama. They have an eleven-year-old daughter."

"I'm eleven," she added.

"I know, and guess what, her mom is a teacher. She'll be one of the ladies who'll be teaching at the Little Red Schoolhouse."

"Neat."

"Sooo, they wondered if you'd like to help them set up the classrooms? School starts in a week, just like it would at home. Miss Meredith and Hannah, that's their daughter, plan on working on it this afternoon."

"When did they get here, Dad?" asked Ethan as he continued to eat.

"About an hour ago, but they want to hit the ground running. I met Mr. Cortland and he's a really nice guy."

Ethan never took his gaze off his barbecue sandwich. "Does he have an Android phone charger?"

"Ethan, I don't know, but you can bet I'll find out." Delta showed his aggravation, and Ethan's reaction by raising his eyebrows and dropping his sandwich spoke volumes. Both Hightower men were over the cell phone issue, for different reasons.

"Daddy, when do I get started?"

"Right after lunch, Sky," replied Delta, who then turned to Ethan. "You'll have a new job, too, son."

"Doing what? Scrubbing the blackboards?" His sarcastic tone threatened to put a downer on Delta's upbeat outlook for his kids' afternoon.

"No. Actually, it's something very important for our safety. It requires a lot of responsibility and a good attitude."

"Are they gonna make me carry a gun? I don't want a gun, Dad."

Will finished his sandwich and gathered up the trash to take to the kitchen area. "It's a job doing security, but not carrying a gun. You'll be part of the drone surveillance team."

"Drones?" Ethan's interest perked up. "Like the kind that fly?"

"That's exactly right, son. You guys grab your jackets and let's head out. I promised to deliver you both right after lunch."

"Come on, Ethan! We've got jobs to do!" Skylar scurried off and put on her imitation UGG boots and her overcoat.

Ethan slowly made his way to the bedroom, where he donned his black trench coat. Delta loved his son, even though he was trying at times. But first impressions were not good. He wondered if the boy had any clothes that weren't jet black to match his hair.

The trio loaded up in the truck and headed off to the school. While Ethan waited in the front seat, Delta escorted Skylar inside and made the introductions. The two young girls hit it off immediately, and they set about exploring the schoolhouse and all of the supplies the Smarts had acquired over time.

When Delta returned to the truck, he noticed that his cell phone's display was illuminated. He suspected his son had attempted to access the phone and found it to be locked by the face-recognition app.

He chose not to say anything to Ethan about the intrusion, opting instead to see how the rest of the day played out. Delta assumed any fifteen-year-old boy would jump at the chance to operate a camera-equipped drone all day. Sure, monitoring the Haven's perimeter might not be as much fun for a teen as snooping in people's windows, but it was a start.

In any event, Delta hoped it would be sufficient to distract Ethan from the never-ending quest for a cell phone charger and access to his mother. He also expected a turnaround in Ethan's attitude.

Turned out, he was wrong.

CHAPTER 29

HB-1
The Haven

The main barn at the Haven, designated HB-1, had been a central gathering spot from the first day Blair and Ryan Smart had purchased the property. During the filming of the *Hunger Games*, the existing buildings were left in their original state in order to lend authenticity to the movie. Only the large barn had been updated with modern plumbing and electrical wiring, together with a large meeting room that was now used as a conference room for Alpha's team.

Initially, the Smarts used the space to meet with prospective contractors and their subs. Now it had a variety of uses, from storage to a meeting place. This was Alpha's domain, as Blair and Ryan spent a considerable amount of time at the main house or on the property overseeing renovations.

The morning started at HB-1 with a meeting of security personnel in the conference room. Throughout the day, Alpha and members of his team would gather for meals together, plan their activities, or retrieve equipment based upon the project they were working on.

One of those projects was an addition to their security program that Alpha had concocted many months ago. It employed the use of mini-drone quadcopters to act as eye-in-the-sky surveillance of the Haven's perimeter. Although Ryan had told him that money was no object, Alpha was cost-conscious in choosing the right machine to do the job.

The Haven was parceled together with hundreds of acres of land that was bordered by a county road for a long stretch, as well as the Henry River for the entirety of its southern perimeter. The entire boundary totaled several miles.

He chose a midrange quadcopter to perform the surveillance task—a DJI Spark Ultimate model. At five hundred dollars, it was definitely on the high side of mini-drone options, but its video capabilities suited their needs perfectly.

The alpine-white quadcopter was equipped with a dual-axis gimbal camera capable of taking both twelve-megapixel still photos as well as 1080p video technology. The features Alpha liked the most were its GPS and night-vision capabilities, its thirty-one mile per hour speed, and a range in excess of a mile. By deploying three of the quadcopters—one at the center of the Haven and one at each end of the oblong-shaped tract—he could cover the entire property from the sky.

The quadcopter, like all devices of its kind, had a negative. The operator could only use it for fifteen minutes at a time before it needed to be recharged. In a time of crisis, this would limit their capabilities. So, at Alpha's request, Ryan doubled the fleet to six. Besides, as Ryan accurately pointed out, if one broke down, they'd have backups.

"*Three is two, two is one, one is none,*" Ryan had reminded Alpha at the time. Alpha was not a prepper. He was more of a survivalist, as many ex-military veterans were. But he saw the logic in many of the preparedness concepts Ryan had taught him, and embraced the lifestyle completely. After the events of New Year's Eve, he was glad he did.

"Alpha? Are you around?"

Delta led his son into the barn, where Alpha waited by a long workbench. The quadcopters had their own storage shelf built. Each one was labeled from H-Quad-1 through H-Quad-6. Thus far, due to lack of operators, none of them had been deployed. Ethan would be the first operator to patrol the perimeter.

"Back here, Delta." Alpha's voice boomed through the empty barn. "I've got H-Quad-1 ready to deploy."

"Sounds official, Dad," whispered Ethan.

"It is, son. Listen, this is a very important job and I hope you don't take it lightly. Security is the number one priority around here."

"You must be Ethan," greeted Alpha as he extended his right hand to shake with the teen. He held the quadcopter remote in his other hand.

"Um, yes." Ethan appeared intimidated by Alpha, whose large stature and booming voice immediately commanded the respect of anyone he came in contact with.

"Glad to have you on the team, Ethan. You'll be the first member of our drone air force. Take a look."

Alpha fiddled with the remote controller, and suddenly a low hum could be heard from the back of the barn. Red and green lights could be seen rising into the tall rafters before coming slowly in their direction.

Alpha maneuvered the drone closer to the group. "Smile, gentlemen. You're on camera."

"Hey, that's pretty cool," said Ethan as he genuinely seemed to enjoy the moment. He managed a smile for the first time, causing Delta to smile as well.

"Watch this," said Alpha as he made a couple of adjustments on the controller. The quadcopter's rotors revved up and the drone raced through the barn doors at a high rate of speed until it was out of sight.

"Wow! Where did it go?" asked Ethan as he chased after the device and stood in the opening.

Off in the distance, the high-pitched whine of the rotors could be heard. Alpha walked next to Ethan and showed him the controller. "Check out the display."

"Is that the main house?" asked Ethan.

"It is," replied Alpha.

Delta joined their side and put his hand on Ethan's shoulder so he could see as well. Ethan didn't pull away this time, a good sign. Delta and Alpha exchanged imperceptible nods at one another. In full disclosure, Delta had told Ryan and Alpha about the difficulties he'd been having with Ethan. He also told them that Ethan needed something to be a part of, or he'd be a handful to control.

Apparently, the Haven's drone air force piqued the teen's interest.

Ethan was impressed. "The camera is amazing."

"Yeah, it is. The new model allows us to record directly into a computer at the main house. All the footage can be reviewed until it is erased, or in the event of an attack, it can be monitored from one central location so we can address our vulnerabilities."

"Attacked?" asked Ethan.

"Son, we don't know what to expect," started Delta, who'd planned on downplaying Alpha's choice of words. Then he thought better of it. Perhaps his son needed to know how dangerous this world could become. "There will come a point in time that outsiders will want what we have here at the Haven."

"That's right," interjected Alpha. "By having eyes on the ground as well as in the air, we can react quicker to someone trying to infiltrate our perimeter."

"You have a wall, right?" asked Ethan.

"True, but not along the river," replied Alpha. "Boats, rafts, and swimmers could cross and make their way inside the Haven. One of your primary duties will be to patrol the shoreline until we get our own boats ready for deployment."

"We've got a navy?" asked Delta, who was unaware of the boats.

"We have boats," replied Delta. "We'd prefer not to use them to patrol because of the anticipated shortage of fuel, and the noise will attract curious neighbors. They'll be deployed as a reactionary force. That's why the drone patrols are so important. A quadcopter can buzz up and down the riverbanks and search for intruders much faster than a boat can."

"I like it," said Ethan. "You can count me in, sir."

Delta couldn't suppress the grin on his face.

CHAPTER 30

Schwartz Estate
Katonah, New York

"The sell-off started with a mysterious plunge that immediately caused the exchange to halt trading. Foreign exchange markets intervened with multiple ten-second pauses to prevent steeper declines in the U.S. dollar. Abroad, futures trading was halted within minutes thereafter."

CNBC's morning market-analysis program, *Squawk Box*, was playing on one of the television monitors in the Schwartz conference room. Jonathan Schwartz had rejoined his father to watch the aftermath of their currency manipulations. Joe Kernen, reporting from NBC's London offices due to the evacuation of Midtown New York, appeared disheveled as he caught his breath and continued.

"Traders also speculated that the selling could be attributed to a large fund, or group of funds, liquidating its position in the dollar. The dollar index has fallen to a level well below its lows of 2008, and it appears that there is no end in sight. With Washington in disarray due to the terrorist attacks of New Year's Eve and speculation running rampant that the president will be announcing the implementation of the U.S. continuity-of-government contingencies, there is little to soften the blow of this free fall as investors are more than jittery. They are downright terrorized at the prospects of a collapsing dollar."

Schwartz chuckled as he lowered the volume on the set. "As well they should be. After the forex markets halted trading on the dollar around the world, they will test the waters by reopening the futures market. At first, there will be nervous investors looking to buy in at the bottom of the decline. Others will continue to dump the dollar before it crashes further."

Jonathan pulled up a chair next to his father and sat down. "In the meantime, we'll step back in. There will be a whipsaw effect in dollar futures that will cause a wild market swing upward. We will profit from that, and then in the morning, the Treasury Secretary will announce that all is right with the world as the mighty dollar regains strength and—"

His father finished the sentence. "We'll crash it all over again. Son, markets like stability. There's a reason we developed the concept of *velocity logic*. Our computer programs can instantaneously detect market movement over time in relation to all indices. As a result, we can overcome the built-in safeguards by Wall Street and London. Our trades happen much faster than their reactions."

"It's ingenious and nearly undetectable," his son added.

"That's why we use it sparingly. Some have weapons of mass destruction. We have weapons of financial devastation. We can destroy businesses, banks, and now, my son, empires, using the power our wealth affords us."

The two men sipped their tea in silence as they monitored the frenzied trading activity shown on the various news programs. Live feeds from around the globe—including London, Chicago, Tokyo, and Hong Kong—revealed the same images.

Schwartz finished his tea before pushing his cup and saucer to the side. He leaned forward on the conference table and folded his hands in front of him. "Son, this president has always had tyrannical tendencies, in my opinion," he began.

Jonathan nodded his agreement.

"Our actions will hasten his incentive to declare martial law. I believe despite his physical stature, he has a bit of a Napoleon complex. His overly aggressive, domineering behavior on social media and in his approach to the news media compensates for his inadequacies as a leader. I believe he relishes the opportunity to wield power through the military. He has probably dreamt of the opportunity to consolidate control over the government within the executive branch."

"My sources tell me that will happen today," interjected Jonathan.

Schwartz continued. "Yes. I bring this up for a reason. The president has longed for an attorney general within his control and loyal only to him. One that is not accountable to the Congress or the media. By declaring martial law, his Department of Justice will have unfettered powers to investigate, arrest, and stall prosecutions."

"Undoubtedly, habeas corpus will be suspended."

"Those placed under arrest can potentially be held indefinitely without any rights to protest their detention."

"Dad, why are you bringing this up now?"

Schwartz took a deep breath and pushed his tired body out of his chair. He wandered around the conference room, pausing to look at each of the monitors. He stopped at the screen that displayed the CNBC reporting. He tapped on it with his knuckles before turning back to his son.

"They all know who's responsible for this. Every one of these so-called experts are whispering around their respective water coolers. As I close my eyes, I can hear the Schwartz name being bantered about."

Jonathan tried to reassure his father. "It's a natural assumption, but it cannot be proven. Frankly, there are any number of world financiers who could've pulled this off."

"Son, not true, and you know it. Plus, we've accomplished this before. To be sure, we've been caught, as in 2018 when the Hong Kong exchange fined one of our funds for compliance failures during the series of shorting trades on Great Wall Motors. The fine was miniscule compared to the profits gained, and in China's autonomous region, there were no criminal charges to be filed. The U.S. is different."

"Yes, I understand. Still, Father, there would have to be investigations, court hearings, SEC and Treasury hearings. The process is long and drawn out. The Hong Kong matter took nearly four years to come to a conclusion."

Schwartz began to wander the room. He looked down at the elaborately designed Persian rug and raised his arm, finger waggling as he walked. "Ahh, but therein lies the rub, as Hamlet said. The declaration of martial law and the corresponding suspension of habeas corpus sets aside the normal rules. Americans love to lie to themselves with their often-used phrase *innocent until proven guilty*. That is an absolute farce. In this country, a seasoned federal prosecutor can indict a ham sandwich, as they say, and under martial law, said ham sandwich can be arrested and detained indefinitely."

"In other words, trumped-up charges," said Jonathan, grinning at his intentional play on words.

Schwartz smiled and shrugged. "*Тайга.*" He used the Esperanto term for *appropriate*.

"What do you suggest?" his son asked.

"Perhaps it would be an appropriate time for a trip to our New Zealand home. The weather is much more favorable this time of year."

"As is the jurisdiction," added Jonathan as he rose from his chair to make the arrangements.

CHAPTER 31

VCU Medical Center
Critical Care Hospital
Richmond, Virginia

It had been a trying morning for Angela, beginning with her usual trek near the grounds of the Virginia State Capitol, which lay between their house on one end of Clay Street and the VCU Medical Center Critical Care Hospital on the other. As she made her way past the Richmond Coliseum, she began to notice a crowd of fifty or more people walking from the VCU campus toward the capitol building. They seemed to be on a mission, not interacting with onlookers, but clearly moving toward the antebellum building with a purpose.

Angela had experienced something similar just a couple of years prior. Hundreds of protestors had descended upon the state capitol building one day in November, carrying signs and chanting *down with hate*. The focus of their anger was the state attorney general's opinion that Virginia's colleges could not include sexual orientation as part of its discrimination policies.

The protest was intended to be peaceful. Nonetheless, a police escort, including horse-mounted officers, escorted the group to the capitol so they could yell at a building that was largely empty at the time.

However, that night, things began to turn ugly as the protestors, frustrated that they weren't getting a response or any form of interaction with state officials, began to cause damage to storefronts and offices along East Broad Street. Reports indicated that the VCU students were joined by outsider groups who were largely responsible for the destruction and near-riot conditions. Angela recalled how they could hear the ruckus that evening from their home eight blocks away.

The scene this morning was reminiscent of that protest, only this time, there was no police escort, and instead of holding signs, the protestors were carrying clubs and rocks.

Angela paused and found a side street to further her progress to the Critical Care Hospital without running head-on into the mob. She was shaken at first, and then her resolve strengthened as she became more convinced that she and Tyler were making the smart move.

Cornering the administrator of the residency program was a more difficult task than avoiding the angry mob. The night before, while the Rankins were trying to survive the attack in the tunnel, parts of Richmond exploded into what the media was calling *anarchy*. Neighborhoods and businesses were under siege from hoodlums and vandals.

People were randomly attacked walking down sidewalks or were pulled from their cars while stopped at intersections. Flash mobs stormed convenience stores and small businesses, ransacking shelves and robbing employees. Fires were randomly set throughout the town, and not in the usual neighborhoods associated with social unrest. Rather, the affluent seemed to be the brunt of the attacks, with one neighborhood being evacuated as the SWAT team was called in to restore order.

Dr. Jennifer Mason, the administrator, spent her days managing the program and creating the daily schedules of those under her wing, but she was still a highly skilled doctor. Pinning her down that morning was near impossible, and Angela, despite the fact she was not supposed to be on the schedule for several more days, pitched in to help.

The Critical Care Hospital at VCU housed many intensive care units for patients who were critically injured or ill. Trauma patients ranging from gunshot victims to burn patients were constantly being treated at the hospital on East Clay Street. However, Angela had never experienced anything like the chaos in the emergency room this morning.

She'd been a fan of television shows like *Grey's Anatomy* and *ER* when she was growing up, getting a thrill and an adrenaline rush when the emergency rooms portrayed on television dealt with a mass casualty event. Whether it be a plane crash or a building collapse, the television doctors and nurses sprang into action to save the day.

In reality, however, the mad rush and a chaotic ER rarely occurred. At least not in Angela's experience, until today. This moment was what she dreamed of. The opportunity to bounce from gurney to gurney, assessing a patient's condition and then diving in to save lives and limbs.

Angela had donned a set of scrubs from her locker and got to work. Patients had been arriving throughout the night from the relentless beatings being administered around the city. Burn victims had pushed the hospital to the brink, with some minor cases being sent to other hospitals in the area.

She'd just finished treating one of the burn victims when Dr. Mason grabbed her attention. "Rankin! Get over here!"

Angela joined her administrator's side as the women stood out of the way to allow a gurney to be pushed into the room. Two uniformed officers of the Richmond Police Department accompanied the patient, who was handcuffed to the rails of the bed.

"What've we got?" asked Dr. Mason. An EMT from the ambulance service that accompanied the patient provided her the vitals.

"The patient was transported from I-95 after being taken into custody. He was involved in an armed assault of motorists when one of them fought back."

"How long has he been unconscious?" asked Dr. Mason.

The EMT replied, "He was in and out when we loaded him into the wagon. After he was cuffed to the gurney, he became violent and began thrashing around. Per the RPD policy, because he was officially in custody, we sedated him."

Following the Freddie Gray incident in Baltimore years ago in which a young man taken into custody flailed about in the back of a police paddy wagon, resulting in his death, the Richmond Police

Department authorized emergency medical technicians to sedate injured patients taken into custody to avoid further complications from their injuries.

Angela carefully examined the unconscious man's face. It had been horribly mangled, and a gauze patch was strapped to one of the man's eyes.

"What did this?" she asked.

The EMT shrugged. "We really don't know. It had to be a bobcat or something like that. His eyeball was hanging out of the socket by the optic nerve. After he was sedated and calmed down, we held open his eyelid and gently replaced it into the socket."

Angela carefully removed the bandaging and pulled her flashlight from her jacket pocket. She pried the patient's eyelids open and ran a beam of light over them. The patient was still unresponsive, but his pupils instinctively reacted to the bright light.

"Well, good work," she began. "His pupils responded, so you most likely saved his eye. His face is another matter. We're gonna need plastics paged on this one."

A nurse acknowledged Angela's request and picked up the phone near the door to page a plastic surgeon.

Dr. Mason examined the man's hand and forearm. "There are tire marks embedded in his skin. Who ran over him?" She glanced over at the police officers.

"Have no idea. Probably the same person who clawed his face off. This guy was one of a dozen who attacked motorists from an overpass. Once we arrived on the scene, they'd beaten most everybody they could get their hands on."

Dr. Mason continued to study the patient's face. "Start him on fluids. Rankin, let's clean up the wound and—wait. Forceps!"

A nurse scrambled to her side and slapped the scissorlike tool with pincers at the end into her gloved hand.

Angela leaned in to get a better look. "I see it."

Dr. Mason carefully spread the gash in the man's jaw open and expertly inserted the forceps into the wound. "Got it. It was embedded in the jawbone."

Angela leaned back to provide Dr. Mason additional light. "That's a deep gash."

"It's a cat claw. Look, it's not broken off. It pulled out of the animal's phalanges and even brought some of the elastic ligaments."

Angela took a closer look. "That cat must have been enraged to do this. And look how big the claw is. I had a cat as a kid and it looked nothing like this."

Dr. Mason shook her head in amazement. She instructed one of the nurses to preserve the claw in case it was needed for medical study or evidence. She stepped aside, allowing the nurses to clean the man's wounds and watch over him until the plastic surgeon arrived.

Angela broke out in a nervous sweat, as she finally had Dr. Mason alone. They stood in the hallway watching the activity for a moment, and then she broached the subject of leaving. She'd barely gotten started into the conversation when Dr. Mason stopped her.

Another ambulance had arrived, and two stabbing victims were being unloaded into the ER. The conversation would have to wait, much to the chagrin of Angela.

CHAPTER 32

Cortlands' Cabin
The Haven

"Daddy, somebody's here," shouted Hannah from the front porch of the Cortlands' cabin. She was enjoying the light snow that had fallen overnight. It was only the second time she'd seen measurable snowfall, the first being on her one and only visit to meet her grandfather in Connecticut.

Cort emerged from the cabin and immediately recognized Ryan as he emerged from his heated four-wheeler. Cort shook his head and laughed as he pointed toward the Ranger. "Nice ride," he quipped as he shook Ryan's hand.

"Good to see ya, Cort," said Ryan before turning his attention to Hannah, who was standing as tall as she could to get noticed by the two men, who stood six feet three and six feet five, respectively. "You must be Hannah."

"Yes, sir," she replied, extending her arm to shake hands.

Ryan laughed and gave her a hearty shake. "Well, it's nice to meet you, Hannah." Ryan paused as he noticed Meredith emerge from the cabin as well. He smiled and waved. "Hi, I'm Ryan."

"I'm Meredith, one of your new schoolteachers."

"So I hear. I also understand you wanna get started right away?"

"If it's okay."

"Well, the doors to the Little Red Schoolhouse are always open, and we've just hung the sign to finish off the construction. Any time you want to have a look, by all means."

Hannah waved to Ryan and then joined her mother on the porch.

Cort turned to the founder of the Haven. "We have a lot to discuss, not only about what's happened, but what comes next."

"I agree, Cort. I'm really glad you're here. Now that the purpose for which Blair and I designed the Haven has come to pass, I need a right arm, somebody with good organizational skills and, more importantly, somebody I can trust with my inner thoughts. The security team is set as soon as one other person arrives. There's somebody else supposedly due to arrive later who will help you and me as well."

"I'm glad to do anything you need, Ryan."

"Also, Cort, there will be times that I need to separate myself from disciplinary actions because I'm the developer of the Haven. You know, I can't be heavy-handed sometimes."

Cort laughed. "Listen, I'm chief of staff to one of the most influential senators in Washington. I know how to play the bad guy."

"Perfect. You guys get settled and maybe take your girls over to the school. Head over to the house when you get a chance."

Cort slapped Ryan on the back and they said their goodbyes. He returned to the cabin, where Meredith and Hannah were getting a few things together.

"I wish we could've gone to Walmart like we'd planned," Meredith said.

Cort hugged his wife and rubbed his daughter's cold cheeks. "Ryan and Blair are detail-oriented people, and they've put equal emphasis on all aspects of the Haven. I'll bet you'll be pleasantly surprised."

"Good," said Meredith. "Well, Hannah, are you ready to check it out?"

"Yeah! Can we pick up Skylar, too? The more the merrier, I always say."

Her parents laughed at their daughter's enthusiasm. Cort nodded in agreement and then he whispered to Meredith, "Ryan wants me to work directly with him, you know, on the administrative side. I guess I've gone from chief of staff to a senator to the chief of staff for, um, king of the Haven."

"Good grief," said Meredith with a chuckle. "Enjoy your first day as *Hand of the King*."

Cort stood a little taller. "Hand. I like that. Like the *Game of Thrones* Hands."

"No, Cort. Not like those Hands. They always get stabbed in the back or beheaded."

"Good point. I don't want my head on a pike."

They kissed, and Meredith was on her way. "Let's go, Hannah. Skylar Hightower is supposed to meet us at school. I think you'll like her. We'll see about setting up the classrooms together."

The Cortland women arrived at the Little Red School House where Skylar greeted them at the door. She and Hannah immediately hit it off, and the two became inseparable as the day progressed. Meredith was impressed with the amount of supplies and school materials the Smarts had accumulated for the new school, which still smelled of fresh paint.

Each of the three classrooms were divided into age groups—toddler through third grade, fourth through sixth, and seventh through ninth. A larger assembly room was designed for chairs to be brought in for large presentations. There were no classrooms for high schoolers. Those kids were expected to work around the Haven and continue their educations at home under the supervision of their parents.

"Skylar, your dad said you have an older brother," began Meredith as she coordinated distribution of materials to individual cubbies in each classroom. She was unsure how many students there were at the Haven, so she simply spread out what was available to her.

"His name is Ethan and he's fifteen," replied Skylar. "He's in high school and he doesn't like it very much. My mom doesn't know it, but he skips class most days."

"He does?" asked Meredith.

"Yes, ma'am," she replied politely. "Um, well, my parents got a divorce, and Daddy moved to Atlanta. My brother has been angry ever since."

"Oh, I'm sorry to hear that. Divorce can be hard on kids."

"Yeah, I'm kinda okay with it except I don't like how my dad lives so far away. I would never tell my mom this 'cause it would hurt her feelings, but I really like it here. You know, just being with my dad."

Meredith walked next to the young girl and put her arm around her. She knelt down onto one knee and looked her in the eye. "It's tough being away from a parent. I understand what that's like. But listen, if you ever feel the need to have a girl talk, you can always come to me, okay?"

"Okay," she replied sheepishly.

"And me too," added Hannah. "We could be BFFs."

"Yeah, besties."

The three continued setting up the classrooms. As they did, Meredith overheard Skylar talking to Hannah in another room.

"My brother has run away before. Mom didn't even go after him. She said if he didn't want to live at home, that was okay by her."

Hannah chimed in. "I can't imagine running away. I wouldn't have any place to go."

"Neither did he," said Skylar. "He has friends from high school, bad friends, my mom says. He never brings them to the house, so I don't know what they're like."

"Is he mad about something?" asked Hannah.

There was a break in the conversation and Meredith strained to listen, thinking the kids had lowered their voice to avoid being heard. Finally, Skylar replied in a quiet, heart-breaking tone of voice. Her response spoke volumes about the mindset of Ethan Hightower.

"He's mad about everything."

CHAPTER 33

Rankin Residence
East Clay Street
Richmond, Virginia

"Home alone, Peanut!" J.C. yelled after Tyler pulled out of the driveway. "Let's make mac and cheese. Maybe hot dogs too."

Kaycee started laughing. "There's no way Mom has that stuff in the house. I bet there's plenty of quinoa and Dad's oatmeal."

"Hey, what kind of food do you think we'll eat at the cabin?" asked J.C. It had been a year since the family went there together. They had stocked the place with some outdoor clothing and camping supplies, but not food.

"Last year, we went out to eat every night. Do you remember that Mexican restaurant? That was pretty good."

The two kids stared into the refrigerator, waiting for Oscar Mayer beef franks to magically appear, but they eventually closed the door, disappointed. Kaycee reminded her younger brother they had chores to do or their mom would be upset, so they started on the laundry first before going to their respective rooms to pack.

"All my summer clothes are clean," said J.C. to his sister, whose room was across the hallway.

"Same here. I'm gonna pack my swimsuit in case we're there in the summer. Do you remember the river that was by our cabin?"

"It was muddy," J.C. recalled.

Kaycee said, "That's because it was springtime and it had been raining a lot. It's not always like that."

The two moved around their rooms, loading up their suitcases first except the clothes that were being washed. Kaycee retrieved the grocery totes, and they carefully selected toys and games to play with. The family loved board games and playing cards together, so those options were a priority.

After a break for peanut butter and jelly sandwiches with milk, Kaycee rolled the last load of wash into the dryer. "Mom and Dad's clothes will be dry by the time they get home, and now we can—"

The sound of glass breaking outside caused her to stop speaking.

"What was that?" asked J.C. as he rushed to the bay window in their living room. He crawled onto the cushioned bench seat and parted the sheers to look outside. Kaycee quickly joined him.

"Where did all of those people come from?" asked Kaycee as she pressed her face against the glass and looked to the west along Clay Street.

"Kaycee, they're breaking things. Look at the car windows."

Vehicles that were parked on the street in front of the residences were being beaten with metal pipes and baseball bats. On both sides of the road, the group would stop and indiscriminately pound on the hood, fenders, and windows of each car or truck until it was destroyed. Then they'd move on to the next one.

"Look!" shouted Kaycee as she pointed to their left. Drivers who'd entered their street were frantically trying to back off of East Clay Street to avoid the mobs making their way toward downtown.

A woman screamed, causing the kids to snap their heads back toward the west. The group had rushed onto the front porch of a home like theirs and were threatening a woman who was sitting in a rocking chair.

"What should we do?" asked J.C.

"We've gotta call Dad," Kaycee replied as she scrambled for the phone. Just as she reached the kitchen, she remembered. "He doesn't have a cell phone!"

"Should we call the police?" asked J.C.

Kaycee hesitated. "Um, I don't know. They haven't done anything to us."

J.C. suddenly backed off the bench seat and allowed the sheer curtains to close. "Not yet, you mean. They're coming to our house!"

"Why? We didn't do anything!"

The two kids ran into the middle of the living room and began frantically searching for answers to their questions.

"Should we hide?" asked J.C.

Kaycee ran to the back door and looked into their yard. There was activity in the house behind them, and she saw a woman race off her porch onto the lawn. She gathered her wits and turned to her brother.

"Dad's guns! Come on!"

"Do you know how to use them?" asked J.C.

"Yeah, he taught me last summer," she replied as she raced down the hallway to her parents' bedroom.

J.C. followed behind, quizzing her as she ran. "When? Why didn't he teach me?"

"You're too young."

"No, I'm not. I am older than—" J.C. froze, the rest of his sentence floating in a state of suspended animation as the windowpanes flanking their front door were broken inward.

The two kids stared at each other, eyes wide in fright, as they could hear the voices of a man and a woman on their porch. When the sound of the dead-bolt lock snapping open hit their ears, they rushed into J.C.'s bedroom to hide.

Kaycee gently closed the door behind them.

"Lock it," whispered J.C.

"No, they'll know we're here for sure," she countered. "Do you remember that space in your closet where the old furnace used to be?"

J.C. nodded his head.

"Can we both fit in there?"

"No, just me."

Kaycee furrowed her brow as she considered her options. "I have to get to Dad's shotgun, but I need to make sure you're safe. Hurry, get in the crawl space and stay there until I come for you. Can you do that?"

"Um-hum."

J.C. opened the bifold doors to his closet and moved some toys and a few stored pillows out of the way. The panel to the closet pushed inward and he made his way inside the dark, dank space. Kaycee quickly covered up the access point and closed the doors behind her.

She made her way back to the bedroom door and cracked it slightly to look down the hallway. The man and woman were milling about the living room, picking up the family's home décor and tossing it aside, as it wasn't of interest to them.

Kaycee knew they'd turn their attention to the bedrooms next, so she decided to make her move. She slowly opened the door to avoid detection, and as soon as the two intruders turned their backs to her, she dashed into the master bedroom. This time, however, she closed and locked the door behind her. Kaycee knew she'd be trapped in there whether the door was open or locked shut. If she forced the intruders to break in, she'd have the precious seconds she needed to respond.

Tyler had purchased a bed that contained a hidden compartment in the headboard for his weapons. A key lock was installed at the top of the headboard with a spring-tensioned access door. Kaycee knew her dad kept the key in the nightstand drawer. She scrambled across the bed and retrieved the key. She stood on the bed and pressed down on the access door, which popped open. She quickly inserted the key and turned it.

Nothing happened.

Then she walked backward and studied the headboard. *Why isn't it opening?*

She grabbed the top of the headboard and gave it a slight shake, hoping the gun would suddenly reveal itself.

"Let's check the rest of this place out," said a woman's voice from the hallway.

"I'm guessin' they just left, 'cause there ain't no car and the dryer's runnin'," her male partner added.

Kaycee began to shake as panic set in. She dropped to her knees and flung the pillows out of the way. She ran her hands along the decorative panel inserts along the headboard. Then she felt the upper part of the panel give way. She pushed it a little harder and her dad's Mossberg 590 shotgun fell into her hands.

Yes! Let's go! she shouted in her head. Kaycee stood on the bed and glanced out the bedroom windows.

The mob was moving past their house and down the street toward the city. She quickly slid off the bed and made her way to the window, cautiously glancing outside. To her right, the streets were empty, although signs of the *locusts* were evident. To her left, the marauders were antagonizing a wayward motorist and breaking out windows of homes as they went.

Kaycee swung around and steadied her nerves. It was still very quiet in the house except for the gentle tumbling sound of the dryer. She knew the moment she pulled the slide of the shotgun to load a shell into the chamber, as her dad had taught her, the loud metallic click would draw the attention of the intruders. Tyler had once told her that nothing frightens a burglar more than the sound of a shotgun racking a round.

Kaycee decided to test his theory, but she'd wait until the people entered the room. With the gun in her hand, the lanky eleven-year-old gained confidence and stood defiantly waiting for them to enter. The only question she hadn't asked herself was whether she was capable of pulling the trigger.

CHAPTER 34

Rankin Residence
East Clay Street
Richmond, Virginia

Kaycee heard them breathing before she saw the door handle begin to turn. When the lock stopped the handle's progress, the intruder turned it the other way. Kaycee's hands turned clammy and the barrel of the rifle began to shake as her nerves started to fail her. The handle shook violently as the person on the other side grew frustrated.

"Open up, dammit!" the woman screamed as her partner began to pound the six-panel door with the back of his fist. Blow after blow evidenced their anger and their violent intentions.

"Go away!" shouted Kaycee.

She heard the two whisper to one another. They were plotting.

"Open up, kid!" the man shouted. "Or we'll huff and we'll puff and we'll blow the door down. Then we'll make you pay for the trouble you caused us."

"I've got a gun! I'll shoot!"

Kaycee was certain this would back off the duo of intruders. The response she got surprised her.

They paused for a moment, and then the two thugs began laughing uproariously. It was an evil cackle combined with genuine delight at terrorizing the young girl.

"You aren't gonna shoot anyone!" shouted the woman. "Open this door, or we'll burn the place down with you in it!"

Kaycee instantly grew afraid that they meant what they said. She'd heard her parents talk about the fires around Richmond earlier and knew it was bad guys like these two responsible for them. She thought of her brother huddled in the dark space in his closet. She knew he could hear them shouting at her. There wasn't much time.

The first kick at the door almost broke it off its hinges. The flimsy bedroom door lock wasn't designed to keep members of a crazed mob out. One of the marauders kicked again, and the door almost gave way.

Kaycee didn't hesitate. She squeezed the trigger and the Mossberg blasted a load of #10 birdshot into the center of the door, blasting a hole in the hollow door with over eight hundred lead pellets. The recoil knocked her backwards onto the bed while the shotgun flew over her head onto the floor by the wall.

"Arrggggh!" the man screamed as the lead shot found its way through the opening. To be sure, the hollow door slowed the impact of half the shot, but the other half performed admirably, scattering into the hallway and ripping into the faces and exposed skin of the assailants.

Kaycee flung herself over the back of the bed to retrieve the gun. Pain seared through her right shoulder, which was now partially dislocated. Yet she found an inner strength. She scowled as she picked up the rifle and loaded another shell into the chamber.

In position to fire again, she could see into the hallway. Blood splatter was all over the wall that was adjacent to J.C.'s bedroom. The drywall was littered with pellets, some of which fell out periodically as the young girl waited for the attackers to make their next move. She listened.

Nothing.

Had she killed them? Both, with one shot?

Her mind raced as she took a step around the bed and cautiously approached the door. She steadied the shotgun's barrel on the opening, planning to shoot again if she saw movement. The pain in her shoulder became worse, but she was able to block out the distraction. Kaycee peeked through the opening.

It's easier the second time, she thought to herself.

Then she heard a dragging sound. Crawling noises across the

wood floor and down the hall near their kitchen.

Kaycee moved to the side of the bedroom door to view the hall from a better angle. There wasn't anyone outside the door, and then she noticed a bloody handprint near the doorjamb of J.C.'s room.

"Help me!" groaned the man from the area of their living room.

"I'm trying," whispered the woman. "We've got to go before she kills us."

"My shoulder," the man was crying. "It's… it's… it's gone."

Kaycee was emboldened. The young girl sensed fear in her adult attackers, and a killer instinct overcame her. She'd never felt this exhilarated in her life, even at the top of Kingda Ka. She pulled what was left of the door open and ran into the hallway.

"You'd better run!" she screamed.

The terrified woman screamed back, begging for their lives. "Okay! Okay! We're leaving! Don't shoot!"

Kaycee moved slowly down the hallway, steadily pointing the shotgun in front of her. The shoulder pain was worsening, but she wanted to finish the job. She arrived in the living room and swung the gun back and forth. Then she turned her attention to the front door.

The knob and door were covered in bloody handprints. A pool of blood had accumulated on the stoop. Kaycee ran to the bay window and slowly parted the sheers to look outside. The intruders were hobbling down the sidewalk, not looking back. The man was putting all his weight on his partner by draping his left arm over her while his right arm dangled from a mess of tendons and bone. A trail of blood marked their path out into the street.

Instantly, Kaycee became overwhelmed with emotion. She gently set the gun down on the bench seat and buried her face in her left hand. The pain caused by the shotgun's recoil, coupled with the realization that she'd shot someone, took a hold of her, causing tears to flow.

Then she remembered J.C. Confident that they were alone, she gathered herself and went to his room. She opened the louvered doors to his closet, expecting him to still be barricaded in the old furnace compartment.

She was wrong. He gave her a start as light filled the closet, and there he was, crouched and ready to spring out. As soon as the opening was sufficient, J.C. jumped up and hugged his sister.

"Are you okay, Peanut?"

"Yes, but easy on my shoulder."

"Okay." He let go of her and looked past her. Some of the pellets had created holes in the drywall near his nightstand. "Um, did you kill them?"

"No, almost," she replied sadly.

J.C., on the other hand, was intrigued by it all. He pushed past her and ran into the hallway. "Cool!" he exclaimed as he examined the blood and gore dripping down the hallway wall. For a moment, he stood in the hallway looking back and forth, surveying the scene.

Kaycee walked past him and headed toward the foyer. "Come on," she began. "We have to barricade the front door with the sofa or something in case they come back."

"I can do it," proclaimed the eight-year-old muscleman. This didn't surprise Kaycee because she'd seen her younger brother slide the furniture across the hardwood floors when it came time to help their mom clean house. "Do you think they'll come back?"

Kaycee glanced at the shotgun that rested peacefully on the padded window seat. "If they do, they won't get inside next time."

CHAPTER 35

East Clay Street
Richmond, Virginia

Richmond, Virginia, was no stranger to civil war or civil unrest. During the dark days of the first American Civil War, the city served as the capital of the Confederacy. Its strategic location made it a logical choice as several major railways terminated there, allowing the Confederate army to move weapons and supplies to the battlefield.

During the Civil War, the Union forces made several attempts to invade Richmond. It wasn't until the final campaigns of General Ulysses S. Grant that residents of Richmond evacuated, and the city was captured. It was a momentous time for many reasons. A week after General Grant visited with President Lincoln at the Virginia State Capitol, he was assassinated in Washington by a Confederate sympathizer, John Wilkes Booth.

Also, during the Civil War, residents of Richmond fought one another. The Richmond Bread Riot took place in 1863 as the Confederate economy began to buckle under the strain of war. A series of laws passed by the Confederate's Congress resulted in confiscatory taxes, leading to hoarding and inflation.

A group of Richmond's women took their complaints to Virginia's governor, who refused to meet with them. Their anger turned into hostilities as a mob assembled outside the state house. The crowd grew larger and began to destroy businesses around the capitol in protest. The governor called upon the Confederate army to disperse the angry mob, a heavy-handed response that quelled the uprising.

Now, more than a century and a half later, another angry mob was descending upon the Virginia Capitol. Like their predecessors, they destroyed property and viciously attacked anyone who stood in their way. This time, however, the Virginia governor did not call upon local law enforcement or the National Guard to shut down the mob. They were spread too thin dealing with unrest throughout Northern Virginia. Instead, a local group stepped up and quickly mobilized to meet the mob head-on, at the intersection of East Clay and North First Streets.

The Richmond Guardian Angels were established in June of 2011 as an offshoot of the Guardian Angels of New York City. The Guardian Angels were a nonprofit volunteer organization of vigilantes formed in the late 1970s by Curtis Silwa, a New Yorker fed up with rampant crime in his neighborhood. Working with his friends and family, he began patrolling the streets of their neighborhood and quickly gained national notoriety for stopping crime.

Today, over a hundred chapters of the Guardian Angels have been formed around the world, training their members to make citizen's arrests for violent crimes. The Richmond Chapter of the Guardian Angels had been credited for reducing crime and cleaning up neighborhoods with horrible reputations, such as Oak Grove, Hillside Court, and Broad Rock.

Thirty-seven members of the Richmond chapter descended upon East Clay Street after one of their members heard the 9-1-1 dispatch reports over their police scanners. Dressed in their white, hooded sweatshirts bearing the red Guardian Angels logo, eagles wings with a shield bearing the Eye of Providence in the center, they descended upon East Clay Street to confront the angry mob.

Tyler had been sitting in traffic, frustrated that he was unable to get through the intersection of East Clay and First. A box delivery truck in front of him obscured his view, leading to his aggravation.

He checked his new cell phone again to see if service had been established. He'd purchased the phones at a nearby Verizon store as it was closing unexpectedly. The mob descending upon the capitol earlier in the day had forced downtown businesses to send employees home early. The salesclerk gave Tyler their new phones as they were locking up, together with his personal assurance that he'd follow up and activate the phones after the store was closed.

He powered on the display again and tried to call the house, but his service was still not available. He slapped the steering wheel out of frustration. Suddenly, two cars parked on the side of the street pulled out of the way, and Tyler decided to fill the gap. He'd purchased a *gently used* pickup, as the salesman had called it. Tyler didn't care, as the truck had four doors and was strong enough to tow a trailer with his Bronco strapped down on top of it.

The rig was long, making maneuvering in traffic difficult, but when the box truck moved up slightly, Tyler pulled onto the side of the street to park. It was only a block to his house and he could always return to pull the truck and trailer in front of their sidewalk when it was time to load up.

He exited the truck and locked it. After a quick glance to make sure the Bronco was properly secured, he began walking toward the house. After a minute, he saw what the trouble was.

A large group of rioters was harassing motorists, dragging them from their cars and beating them on the street. Tyler frantically looked around for a police response, but there wasn't one. Suddenly, from both sides of First Street, the Guardian Angels entered the intersection. The groups clashed in a melee of fisticuffs and clubs swinging at one another.

Tyler was awestruck as he watched the battle unfold. "This is madness," he murmured as he looked around to determine if he was in immediate danger. The red berets of the Guardian Angels stood out among the crowd as the two groups created a forty-person scrum in the middle of the street.

Over the screams and shouts of the two groups doing battle, Tyler couldn't hear the shotgun blast emanating from his home. But he sensed his kids were in danger.

Tyler wanted the handgun that he'd purchased earlier to replace the one taken into evidence by the Virginia state troopers. He turned to run back toward his truck, but a crowd of onlookers had emerged on the sidewalk, blocking his path backwards.

He focused on getting to the kids instead. There wasn't a way to go forward unless he wanted to become a part of the battle. So he looked down the driveway of the house he stood in front of and noticed they didn't have a fence in their backyard.

Without hesitation, he pushed past the owners, who stood in their driveway, and ran between the houses. At the rear of the property, a short scrubby hedgerow blocked his progress, but with his adrenaline racing, he easily hurdled the bushes. The sounds of the melee were behind him, and he began to feel confident that he could circle around the intersection and get to his home through the backyards.

He sped along the driveway between the houses, becoming

increasingly concerned about Kaycee and J.C. He turned left to run down the sidewalk, but in his frantic state, he didn't see the person who raced toward him from his right. The two bodies collided, knocking them both into the grass part of the lawn between the sidewalk and the street.

Stunned by the collision, Tyler shook the dizzy spell out of his eyes and searched for the Mack truck that had crashed into him.

It was Angela.

CHAPTER 36

East Clay Street
Rankin Residence
Richmond, Virginia

Angela dusted the grass and dirt off her leggings before turning her attention to Tyler. When she saw it was him, she managed to laugh despite the tense situation. "Hey, watch where you're going! I had the right of way!"

Tyler was still doubled over in pain as he rose to his knees to make eye contact. When he saw it was Angela, he simply waved his hand at her and began to cough in an effort to catch his breath.

She walked to his side and helped him stand. "Are you okay?"

Tyler nodded and inhaled. He mustered a few words. "Yeah. Kids. Fighting."

"I know. Can you keep up?"

Tyler nodded and pushed her ahead of him. "Go."

Angela didn't wait for him and ran down the sidewalk, dodging stopped cars and pedestrians headed toward the fighting on First Street. With Tyler in close pursuit, the parents rushed toward the homes located behind theirs. After they reached the fourth house, they turned down the driveway and found the gate to the family's wooden privacy fence left ajar.

Angela hesitated until Tyler arrived, and then held her index finger to her lips, advising him to be quiet. She stuck her head through the fence and saw the yard was empty. She cautiously pushed the gate open and they eased into the yard.

Tyler reached for the sleeve of her jacket and stopped her. "We've got to get over the fence somehow."

They both glanced around and looked for options. Tyler backed through the fence gate and a large galvanized trash can caught his eye. He hustled over to the trash can and emptied the garbage onto the driveway. Trying not to clank the galvanized steel on the fenced gate, he showed Angela their makeshift stepping stool.

With one final look around, they raced toward the privacy fence that separated their yard from this one. They'd rounded a neatly stacked cord of firewood when Angela abruptly stopped. She pointed toward the ground and then her head turned on a swivel, looking for danger. A woman's body was lying half-dressed on the wet mulch between the fence and the firewood.

She knelt next to the body and felt for a pulse. The woman's head had been bashed in by a piece of firewood that lay on the ground nearby.

"Tyler, what's wrong with people?" asked Angela as she pulled the woman's clothes over her partially exposed body. Then Angela removed her track jacket to cover the victim's bloody face.

Tyler had finally caught his breath and had recovered from their collision. Seeing the woman's dead body gave him a renewed sense of urgency. He reached down and urged Angela to take his hand.

He was trying to urge her on but was also respectful of her feelings for the victim at the same time. "Come on, babe. We've gotta get to the kids."

Angela nodded, leapt on top of the trash can, and hoisted herself over the fence. She waited for Tyler to do the same and they ran hand in hand to the back door. Before they could ascend the steps into the kitchen, Kaycee opened the top half of the Dutch door and waved to them. J.C.'s head popped up into the opening as well.

He couldn't wait to break the news. "Mom! Dad! Peanut shot somebody! It's so cool!"

Tyler looked at Angela, who sprinted ahead to see what their kids had faced.

Kaycee opened the door as Angela took the steps two at a time. She dropped to her knees and hugged her kids so hard that both begged for her to let go. J.C. wanted to pull her inside to show her the bloody mess, but Kaycee told her mom about her shoulder injury first.

Tyler arrived and hugged his kids, then turned to Kaycee. "What happened?"

"Dad, these two guys broke in, and I had J.C. hide in the closet. Then I ran into your bedroom and found your shotgun. Um, I knew how to open the lock. I'm sorry." She hung her head.

Tyler pulled her chin up and asked, "Are you guys okay?"

"Yeah, it's my shoulder. It hurts really bad from the gun. It's stronger than the one you taught me to use."

Tyler closed his eyes and shook his head side to side. He glanced up at Angela, who returned the look of shock. Their daughter had found their gun and shot somebody.

"Honey, let me see your shoulder," said Angela. She examined Kaycee's right shoulder and addressed Tyler. "She's got a shoulder subluxation."

"The kickback on the Mossberg isn't as bad as most shotguns, but it's a lot for her size and frame," offered Tyler. "Is it partial?"

Angela nodded. "The humerus was partially kicked out of the glenoid socket. If it was knocked out totally, she wouldn't be calmly standing here."

The recoil of the shotgun had partially dislocated Kaycee's shoulder. The shoulder is one of the most mobile joints in the body. It contains many bones, ligaments, and muscles that work together to keep it stable. Because the shoulder is so mobile, it is very susceptible to dislocation. The shotgun's kick had weakened the arm muscles and forced the upper arm bone out of the socket.

"Do we need to get her to the hospital?" asked Tyler.

Angela studied Kaycee's shoulder for evidence of swelling and trouble moving the joint. After a moment, she shook her head. "I can take care of it here. Why don't you go see what happened and take J.C. with you? I don't want him to see me fix his sister."

"Closed reduction?" asked Tyler, whose EMT training had provided him with advanced first aid techniques like treating partial dislocations of the shoulder.

"Yeah."

"Come on, buddy. You show me around while your mom gets Peanut fixed up."

J.C. didn't hesitate, grabbing his dad by the arm and pulling him toward the foyer first to show him how the intruders had broken in. While their son gave the blow-by-blow details of the attack and subsequent shooting, Angela addressed Kaycee.

"Honey, I know it hurts. What I'm about to do is gonna hurt for a brief moment, and then it'll be good as new. Afterwards, we'll fix you up with an ice pack and I'll strap it onto your shoulder with an ACE bandage. Okay?"

"Sure, Mom. No problem. Should I bite down on a wooden spoon or something?"

Angela laughed and kissed her daughter on the forehead. "I don't think that will be necessary. I'll give you fair warning so that you can be ready, okay?"

"Sure."

"Okay, you relax and I'm gonna count to five. After five, I'm gonna pop your shoulder back into place. Ready?"

Kaycee smiled and nodded, opting to stare out the back door into the yard. Angela began the countdown.

"One. Two. Three."

Snap!

Angela expertly replaced the humerus into the shoulder joint while Kaycee's body was relaxed.

"Hey, you said five!" said Kaycee as she rolled her arm around as if it had never been dislocated.

Angela smiled as she gently rubbed her daughter's shoulder. "Did I? Oops, sorry."

Tyler and J.C. emerged in the kitchen. Tyler smiled as he saw that his daughter had regained mobility of her shoulder. "Are we okay?"

"Piece of cake, Dad," replied Kaycee.

Tyler pulled two chairs away from the dinette set in the kitchen and motioned for the kids to take a seat. He reached into the top of the pantry and pulled out a bag of cookies. "Guys, munch on this for a minute while I talk to your mom, okay?"

"Okay!" the kids said in unison as he set a package of Nutter Butters on the table.

"I've been saving these for a special occasion," he said with a wink.

Tyler took Angela by the hand and led her into the hallway. When she saw the carnage and blood, she covered her mouth with her hand.

"My god, Tyler."

"Yeah, no kidding. It seems they were trying to break into our bedroom, where Kaycee was hiding. She shot them through the door."

Angela walked closer to the wall full of shotgun pellets and bloody flesh. "She hit at least one of them."

"Maybe both, based on what J.C. told us," added Tyler. He took a deep breath and exhaled. "Listen, we've got to get out of here. These two may have friends and might come back looking for revenge. But it's not just that."

"What else?" asked Angela.

Tyler sighed. "You've fixed our daughter's shoulder. It may take some time to fix her memories of what happened here today."

CHAPTER 37

The Haven

Blair walked along with the newest additions to the Haven, conducting an orientation for those who hadn't been assigned a job or who were generally unfamiliar with the many changes they'd made to the property in the last year.

"Our goal, first and foremost, was to create a community in which residents could feel safe from the madness that might be happening around the country. Naturally, all of you share an interest in preparedness and we're all like-minded thinkers. We understand that the threats our nation faced were real, and lo and behold, our worst fears were realized."

"Blair," interrupted one of the women on the tour, "I'm going to be very up front about something. We are the only African-Americans in the Haven. That just seems a little bit, um…" Her voice trailed off as if she was sorry she'd broached the subject.

Blair stopped, smiled at the woman, and put her arm around her shoulder, a sincere, comforting gesture. "Listen, every decision we've made here is color-blind. The Haven is not intended to be exclusionary, nor is it a social experiment in which we check all of the boxes to cover every nationality and race. We live in dangerous times, as we've seen. Our goal was to bring together a group of people who share a common interest—the survival and protection of their family."

The woman nodded, and Blair gave her an extra hug of encouragement before continuing. "What's important to us, as well as y'all, is the fact that everyone has an important skill, a certain level of expertise, that will play an important role in the sustainability and longevity of our community. Ryan and I have developed the Haven with the capability of living here for decades if necessary.

"Keep in mind, this is where we live, too. We have a vested interest in your safety, as well as ours. Your strengths overcome our weaknesses. If we pull together, we can keep the madness at a safe distance while we find some semblance of normalcy in our lives."

Several of the people on the tour added their opinions, and Blair continued the casual stroll, making conversation. They stopped at the Armageddon hospital, where she assigned one of the women who'd been a pediatric physician's assistant for years.

Later, they struck up a conversation with Charlotte, Echo's wife, who was logging in the newly received food and supplies into one of the Haven's secured supply depots. Ryan had built several of these around the Haven. They were all block and brick structures designed to store food under cool, dry conditions. He'd constructed six of them, with a seventh in progress, in order to, as he would say, *prevent all of their eggs from being in one basket.*

One couple had experience with canning and growing a garden, so they were placed on Echo's team. Blair talked about their sustainability program. "Throughout the Haven, we have many gardens and greenhouses that take advantage of the varied soils, hillsides, and shade trees that make up the landscape.

"Growing your own food is like growing your own money. And in a post-collapse world where grocery stores' shelves are barren, the maintenance of these sustainable gardens becomes very important."

One of the attendees raised his hand. "Do you think it will come to that? I mean, empty grocery stores."

"It already has," replied Blair. "We're sending out teams twice a day, scouring the neighboring towns for any food and supplies that we will need for the future. Not everyone out there believes the events of New Year's Eve will have a measurable impact on grocery deliveries. We disagree, as Echo's teams can attest. Each run yields less."

"Will the sustainable gardening harvests last?" asked one of the women.

"Forever, if we maintain them properly," replied Blair. "There are several aspects to our program, but the most important has to do with the heirloom seeds we have stored and our harvesting procedures at the end of a growing season. We have sufficient seed packets in a wide variety of fruits and vegetables to last a decade. However, properly harvested, the heirloom seeds from the plant material can be reused the next season. The crops those seeds produce will produce new seeds to be used later."

A young boy raised his hand. "Why do you call the seeds heirloom?"

Blair looked down to the boy and mussed his hair. "You're here with your parents and grandma, right?"

"Yes, ma'am."

"Well, that means there are three generations of your family at the Haven. Your grandma had a baby, then your mom had a baby, and one day you'll meet a nice girl and you two might have a baby. Heirloom seeds work the same way. They're grown in a tomato, for example. After we pluck it off the vine, we remove the seeds, dry them, and then store them for next year. Then we plant them and grow another crop of tomatoes. We do it over and over and over again, for years if necessary."

"That's pretty neat," said the boy with a grin, as he enjoyed the attention from the boss lady.

"You know what, this is the type of thing you'll learn in our new school," added Blair. She pointed ahead toward the Little Red Schoolhouse. "Of course, you'll learn the basics. You know, the three R's—reading, 'riting, and 'rithmetic. However, you'll also learn about practical, real-life things like growing food, basic first aid, and when you're older, how to handle a weapon."

Blair continued their walk and then paused as some of the famous buildings featured in the *Hunger Games* movies came into view. Thus far, the new arrivals, to their credit, hadn't bugged her about the movie set. As a result, she decided to reward them and spend some time explaining the background.

She showed them the country store that had served as Mellark's

Bakery, and the Katniss Everdeen home, both of which had been restored and left intact. When she and Ryan purchased the property, they agreed that the history of Henry River Mill Village should be respected, and the prominence it received from the *Hunger Games* movies should not be forgotten. Several of the structures were renovated and put into use, but the exterior facades were left in their original state.

Blair pointed out several wells that had been dug to ensure that fresh water was available and also the solar arrays that had been installed to take the Haven off the grid. A tour of a large greenhouse and a look inside the school finished off the walking tour.

By the end of the two hours, everyone was enthusiastic about the jobs they'd been assigned, and any trepidation they had regarding life in a confined area disappeared.

Blair and Ryan had adopted a survival mindset years ago. It was one thing to buy supplies and fill up their closets. However, to survive for years during the apocalypse, they had to adopt a preparedness lifestyle, one in which sacrifices were made and approaches to everyday living changed.

Now their task was to instill this mindset into everyone who lived at the Haven. Their collective survival would depend upon it.

CHAPTER 38

The Haven

Ethan had spent an hour that afternoon learning all of the features and operation requirements of the quadcopters. Alpha was a very patient teacher, offering encouragement to the young man, who soaked in the knowledge. Eventually, he was left alone with the controller, and he practiced flying the drone around the Haven until he'd mastered its capabilities.

Toward the end of his training session, something was said that puzzled Ethan at first, and then angered him. As Alpha was leaving, Ethan's attitude changed, and he successfully hid his aggravation from Alpha. As he flew the drone along the perimeter of the Haven, his mind recalled the exchange.

He'd asked Alpha if he'd been able to find a charger for his Android cell phone. He explained that he'd left his behind in Atlanta and that his dad would ask about one. Alpha knew nothing about it. To the contrary, he immediately offered one up out of an electronics cabinet in HB-1 that contained a variety of electronic devices and their accessories.

Ethan instantly became mad at his father for lying about the availability of the charger. After Alpha left him alone, Ethan took the charger from the storage and raced back to the Hightowers' cabin to retrieve his phone. While he operated the drone, he charged his phone with plans to call his mother as soon as he could.

Once the phone was charged, he repeatedly tried to contact his mom or her boyfriend, Frankie, to no avail. This simply added to Ethan's frustration, and the anger swelled inside him. As he stewed over his father's lack of candor, he recalled the seriousness of the situation outside the Haven. His mind conjured up several horrific scenarios that could apply to his mom's safety. He reminded himself that his father hated his mom, and that he'd be just fine without her in their lives.

All of these things compounded the teen's anger until he decided he'd take matters into his own hands. He returned to HB-1 and shelved the quadcopter. He chose another one out of its cubby in the barn and took it for a flight. This time, rather than patrolling the Haven, he ventured beyond the property's borders in search of other homes and businesses.

It was more than idle curiosity. Ethan Hightower had a plan.

He'd picked up on the operation of the quadcopter quickly and now was highly confident in his ability to fly it around any number of obstacles. He'd also figured out how to adjust its programming. The first thing he did as he flew H-Quad-4 across the eastern perimeter of the Haven was to turn off its recording capabilities. He didn't want anyone to come back later and see what he'd been up to.

Secondly, he slowed down his flight speed. Before, he'd enjoyed buzzing about at high rates of speed, caring little about the surveillance aspect of his job. He was playing, but now he was all business.

He began to surveil adjacent farms. There were only a few homes in the area, as this part of North Carolina was very rural. Ethan thought that might work to his advantage for what he had in mind.

It took him almost an hour, and several different quadcopters, until he found what he was looking for. Just past the bend in the Henry River, at the edge of the Haven's property, there was an isolated farmhouse. A white, four-door sedan was driving slowly up the driveway from the road.

Ethan hovered high above the car and slowly followed it toward the garage. The driver pulled up short and stepped out. Ethan used the zoom function on the camera to get a closer look. An older man slowly exited the vehicle and walked around the trunk to the passenger side. He opened the door and helped an elderly woman get out. They leaned on each other as they made their way inside.

"Perfect!" Ethan exclaimed before he caught himself and stifled his exuberance. He looked around to see if anyone had heard him, but he'd been left to his own devices for hours.

He lifted the drone to a higher elevation and flew it back to HB-1, diligently making mental notes of the farmhouse's location in relation to the barn.

Minutes later, the drone was stored on its shelf and Ethan meticulously put everything away so as not to draw attention. Then he thought about his next step.

He didn't want to go back to their cabin, as he was afraid he might get trapped by his dad or sister. There was really nothing there that he needed. He had his favorite clothes on and he had his phone.

Ethan took a minute and walked around the barn. He tried the door handle to the conference room, but it was locked. He began to open up some wooden lockers on the wall adjacent to the conference room. Each locker had a backpack stored in it.

Ethan pulled one out and rifled through it. It contained some camping equipment, meal replacement bars, water purification supplies, and two bottles of water. *Works for me*, he thought to himself.

He put his arms through the backpack straps, took another look around, and began making his way through the thick woods toward the location of the farmhouse.

Yes, Ethan Hightower had a plan. It was not a good one. But he'd made up his mind. He was going to Philadelphia to get his mom, and he was gonna need a ride.

CHAPTER 39

Duke Homestead
Durham, North Carolina

"This is getting ridiculous," Tom lamented as he tried one exit after another in search of gasoline. He didn't want to wait until the fuel gauge hit empty, but despite his best efforts, he found gas stations closed or out of gasoline.

"This next exit seems to be an option," added Donna, who pointed ahead toward the Guess Road exit off the interstate. Tom craned his neck and saw the Popeye's Chicken sign across the street from an Exxon station. As he slowed to take the ramp, a Home Depot appeared on their right, and then several other familiar businesses could be seen.

"We'll give it a try," he said as he waited for the light to change.

Traffic was light, and he noticed that some of the businesses were closed despite being the middle of the day. He turned right onto Guess Road and smiled at the thought of a Quarter Pounder with cheese from McDonald's. His hopes were dashed upon a closer look. The restaurant had closed, and a maintenance crew was in the process of boarding up the building's windows.

"Do you think they're having the same trouble that Richmond is?" asked Donna. Her nose was pressed against the glass as she watched the men work to secure the restaurant.

Tom was rubbernecking the activity as well, so when he pulled into the Exxon station, he didn't notice that plastic bags covered all the pumps.

"Dammit!" he exclaimed out of frustration. The store had a single clerk inside and a couple of customers, but clearly, they'd sold out of gasoline. Tom pulled through the pumps and glanced in both directions on the four-lane road. Several businesses were closed, but Popeye's and Bojangles' seemed to be operating on all cylinders.

Donna leaned forward and turned the radio back on. They'd given up on listening to national news, as the networks had no definitive answers and instead supplied a variety of commentators who voiced their opinions via speculation.

Tom had avoided telling Donna about his morning conversation with Tommie. The fracas in Richmond had interrupted their talk and she never brought up the subject again. As they drove south, mostly in silence, the pundits raised all kinds of possible culprits for the terrorist attacks, but none of them suggested an inside job, as Tom considered it to be. The ramifications of Tommie's revelations were enormous. He suspected the intelligence agencies would leak the information to the media at an opportune moment, depending upon the leaker's agenda.

"I see a BP station a little farther down the road. Might as well give it a try."

Donna didn't respond, instead focusing her efforts on finding a local Durham news station to determine why the businesses were closing. Tom pulled into the BP station and beamed when he saw motorists pumping gas.

"Jackpot!" he exclaimed as he drove between a pickup truck and an old Buick in order to access the center pump. He was so ecstatic to be able to fill up, he shrugged off the price tag, which exceeded eight dollars per gallon.

He frowned, however, when he saw a cardboard sign taped on the pump that read CASH ONLY. He had no idea how many gallons the Yukon held, but he guessed at least twenty-five. Based on the yellow warning light on the truck's fuel gauge, he calculated he'd need two hundred dollars' worth. A record fuel purchase in his lifetime.

As he walked inside to pay, he pulled out his wallet. He only had a few twenties, so he dug into his emergency stash. When he was young, his father had taken him aside and taught him some of the basics to becoming a man. Some of the tips had to do with carrying a wallet.

First and foremost, his father had told him, always carry your wallet in your front pocket when in a crowd to avoid being pickpocketed. He rarely followed his father's advice on that point. His father also said don't stuff your wallet with anything unnecessary. A fat wallet was considered a prime target for thieves.

He was told to carry a condom at all times—*just in case*. This was old-school fatherly advice that Tom didn't follow either. He was a rare young man growing up, opting to wait until he and Donna were married before he took the plunge into sexual activity. He laughed to himself as he wondered if there were any more like him today.

The other important thing he learned was to keep a *secret stash of emergency cash*, as his father called it. Back then, a twenty-dollar bill was sufficient. Over time with inflation, he had increased the amount he carried to two hundred-dollar bills.

He recalled explaining the logic to his son-in-law, Willa's husband, one day. "I look at it this way. I think about what I paid for my first house. Then I compare that to what I paid for my new car. I paid more for my car than I paid for our first house. Twenty bucks barely gets you a number one at McDonald's nowadays."

Tom reached into his wallet and retrieved the crisply folded hundred-dollar bills and handed them to the clerk. She took his cash and told him to come back for change when he was finished.

He didn't bother.

Tom was mesmerized by the fuel pump as the dollars and cents ticked away until he'd spent over a hundred dollars.

"Thirteen gallons so far," he muttered, amusing himself over the outrageous price per gallon. He shrugged it off as he considered that Europeans had been paying these prices for years.

As the pump continued to dispense gas into the truck, Tom heard shouting from the direction of the interstate. On the other side of the adjacent Family Dollar, people were marching down Duke Homestead Road, shouting and yelling. They weren't in trouble but were clearly agitated.

Expletives were hurled, and soon a hundred people or more had spilled out into the intersection of Guess Road and Duke Homestead Road. Donna turned in her seat and waved to get Tom's attention. He rushed to the driver's door and opened it.

"The president is declaring martial law!"

"When?"

Donna was quick to reply. "Right now. I just found it on the radio. Listen."

Tom backed out of the truck and looked down the street just as the gas nozzle clicked, indicating the tank was full. He had thirteen dollars to spare on his prepaid amount, but he didn't wait to squeeze a few more drops out. He returned the nozzle to the pump and climbed into the driver's seat.

Tom wheeled the Yukon around two vehicles blocking the exit and jumped a curb in order to get back onto Guess Road. He pressed the pedal all the way to the floor, and the heavy truck roared to life, speeding toward the intersection, where a large group of people had gathered. Many were carrying signs and waving banners.

"Tom! You can't run over them!"

"Hold on!" Tom kept his speed, and some of the group noticed him racing toward them. They didn't yield and instead faced him down defiantly.

"Tom!"

"Here we go!" he shouted as he whipped the steering wheel to the right and raced through an office building's parking lot. He bounced over a sidewalk and slid across the grass in front of the entrance to an adjacent church.

Donna turned to watch as several people in the crowd began to shout and throw rocks at them. Tom plowed through the wet grass and steered back onto the road, where his tires grabbed the pavement, causing the top-heavy Yukon to shake back and forth as it gained traction.

"Are we clear?" He shouted his question.

"Yes! Slow down, please!"

"Not until we're on the highway," he responded under his breath.

He weaved past several slow-moving cars and raced up the ramp on to I-85, looking in his rearview mirror the entire time. After a mile, he exhaled and removed his hands from the steering wheel, one at a time, to wipe the sweat off his palms.

"Tom, do you think they were protesting the martial law announcement?" asked Donna, who was remarkably calm.

Out of breath from the anxious moment, he replied, "Maybe, but that's not what concerned me."

"What was it?"

"Did you notice what was on the sheets they turned into signs?"

"No, what?" asked Donna in reply.

"A black rose held by a fist."

CHAPTER 40

George Trowbridge's Residence
Near Pine Orchard, Connecticut

Trowbridge was philosophical as he watched the events unfold from Mar-a-Lago. The president had formally declared martial law and, with a significant military presence protecting him, lifted off in *Marine One*, which had been transported from Washington to the *Southern White House* in Palm Beach, Florida. The fighter jets overhead were escorting the president and members of his family to Patrick Air Force Base in nearby Brevard, just north of Palm Beach.

"Harris, when you're the leader of the free world, you're bestowed with a tremendous amount of power. This president has been besieged from the day he was elected in 2016. The constant attacks by the media and the opposition party may have bruised him, but it strengthened his resolve. It also created a martyr, of sorts."

"How so, sir?" asked Harris before adding, "Martyrs are typically deceased."

Trowbridge managed a slight laugh. "Well, if you believe the media reports, this presidency was dead on arrival in Washington. That proved to be a continuous false narrative. His reelection confirmed that."

"Sir, if the media couldn't bring him down, either the Twenty-Fifth Amendment actions or promised impeachment proceedings will."

"Maybe, maybe not. At least a third of the country, if not more, believe those political machinations are nothing more than revenge and sour grapes. Some have outright called these efforts a coup against the president."

Harris pointed to the television. "Yet there he is. Still in charge."

"Taking actions to safeguard the ideals he believes in," said Trowbridge before taking a deep breath. "What we have initiated is not different, although many will question our methods. It's been said that if there's something wrong, those who are capable of taking action should take action. That's what we have done. History may condemn our efforts, but the results will be warranted."

Harris's cell phone vibrated, and he quickly powered on the display to read a series of text messages. "Sir, there's been a development."

"Go ahead," grumbled Trowbridge. He was in no mood for surprises.

"The Schwartz jet has been readied for takeoff."

"Have they submitted a flight plan?"

"Not yet," replied Harris. "However, they have circumvented FAA policy in the past when it suited Schwartz. His unexpected appearance at Davos the year you couldn't attend is one such example. It enabled him to avoid media scrutiny and, frankly, was a blatant attempt to take advantage of your health issues."

Trowbridge nodded. The World Economic Forum in Davos, Switzerland, was attended by world leaders, entrepreneurs, and wealthy financiers. Many deals were made, and alliances confirmed. It was during that January in 2019 that Trowbridge's health took a turn for the worse, forcing him to ultimately be bedridden in his home.

When Trowbridge didn't verbally respond, Harris tried to get his attention. "Sir? Is there anything you'd like me to do?"

Trowbridge rubbed his temples. If Schwartz fled the jurisdiction, the opportunity to use the martial law declaration to take him into custody would be lost. Once in custody, the Department of Justice could create any number of charges to hold him indefinitely, and well after martial law was lifted.

"Ground him!" he blurted out louder than either man expected. "This might work to our advantage. He is showing himself to be a flight risk in the eyes of a court. Attempting to leave the country without a filed flight plan is ample evidence of that. Between the inability to get bond and the suspension of habeas corpus, Schwartz may spend the rest of his life confined to a prison holding cell."

"I'll call our FBI contacts now," said Harris as he scurried out of the bedroom.

Trowbridge leaned his head against his pillow and closed his eyes, but not to nap. The safety of his daughter and Cort wore heavily on his mind. He desperately wanted to make arrangements for military assets to surround the Haven.

But if he did, it would raise unnecessary suspicion and put them in danger. If he sent someone to pull them out and take them to a location he perceived to be safer, he ran the risk of alienating his daughter, which might also serve to push Cort away.

And that couldn't happen, as Trowbridge had big plans for his son-in-law.

CHAPTER 41

Outside the Haven

Ethan was not an athletic kid, but fueled by adrenaline and excitement, he hustled through the woods of the Haven undetected and scaled the perimeter wall with the aid of a fallen tree. He cautiously made his way toward the farmhouse, using large oak trees and several outbuildings for cover. By the time he reached the side of the farmhouse, he was winded, but exhilarated.

He had been part of a car theft before. Well, in his mind, it wasn't really something as dramatic as grand theft auto or anything like that. It was more of a joyride. He and some of his buddies from high school had been running around, smoking weed, when they came upon a van parked behind a strip center near their neighborhood.

The Sherwin-Williams paint store had used the van for delivering paint to contractors in the area during home construction and remodeling. It wasn't fancy, but for the kids high on marijuana, it was that perfect storm in which stupidity and opportunity crossed paths.

The driver had forgotten to remove the keys from the Ford Econoline van, and much to the delight of the high teenage boys, the vehicle was unlocked. For the next three hours, they drove around town, visiting the favorite hangouts of their classmates and doing donuts in the front yards of some kids they disliked.

As their high wore off, reality sank in, and they thought it best to return the van to where they'd found it. In their mind, no harm, no foul. Ethan and the other boys didn't get caught, so their success emboldened them to try more daring adventures.

Soon, breaking and entering became part of their nightly activities. Once they found several pawnshops that happily accepted certain types of stolen goods in exchange for cash, no questions asked, Ethan and his pals decided to form their own criminal enterprise.

All of which led to this moment that encouraged Ethan to return to his criminal roots and steal the old couple's car. Now, as most criminals often do, Ethan rationalized his theft. It was necessary to protect his mom. They could drive the car back to the owners with a full tank of gas and maybe an anonymous thank-you note. Besides, old people shouldn't be driving around in the middle of the apocalypse anyway. It was too dangerous. In his mind, he had the best of intentions. All he had to do was get the keys and he'd be on his way.

Ethan ran to the side of the car. Most people didn't leave their keys in their vehicles, but neither did most paint store employees. Ethan had learned early in life that if something happened once, it could happen again.

And indeed it did. He eased his head over the passenger door to avoid being seen by the old couple inside their house. He grinned as he saw the keys dangling from the ignition of the gold 2004 Oldsmobile Alero sedan. It wasn't a sports car like he'd hoped for, but it wasn't a Ford Econoline van full of paint buckets either.

Ethan quickly opened the door and slid into the passenger side of the Olds. He tossed the backpack in the backseat and then sat deathly still, waiting to see if he'd been noticed. When no one approached, he let out his breath and wiped the sweat off his brow.

He sat up and slid across the bench seat behind the steering wheel. Ethan was only fifteen, but his mom and Frankie had taught him the basics of driving. Ethan had enrolled in the Pennsylvania Graduated Driver Licensing program, having obtained his learner's permit several months before.

He looked around and studied his surroundings. He didn't have a map and wasn't sure where to go. His first priority was to get off the farm undetected, and then he could make a run for it. The dirty gold sedan would easily blend in with traffic, and he'd be away from this backwoods hideout before anyone noticed.

Ethan fired the ignition and calmly backed the vehicle around the side of the house until he was pointed out toward the driveway. He glanced at the fuel gauge, which showed the fourteen-gallon tank of the Olds was full. Ethan smiled, thinking to himself that old people were responsible like that, although a little too trusting.

Back to the task at hand. He was careful not to gun the engine, hoping that the old people were hard of hearing or otherwise preoccupied. He gripped the wheel, ignoring his sweaty palms, which made it slippery. This was the moment of truth.

The Olds moved forward and he casually drove down the tree-canopied driveway as if he were going on a quick trip to the store. He kept his eye fixed on the rearview mirror, fully expecting the old guy to come chasing after him with a shovel or a gun.

None of those things materialized.

Ethan found his way to Costner Road and then followed it in an easterly direction, per the dash-mounted Ritchie compass. Before he knew it, he found another cross street that pointed him north and in view of a sign marking the entrance to Interstate 40.

His body awash with relief, Ethan began hootin' and hollerin' inside the Oldsmobile. He slapped his hands on the dashboard and picked up speed as he was eastbound and down on I-40. He fiddled with the radio and searched for some tunes.

Ethan Hightower was about to have the time of his short life. He was free and on a mission. And he'd be gone five hundred miles when his day was done.

CHAPTER 42

Front Gate
The Haven

Tom and Donna were filled with apprehension and excitement as they approached the front gate of the Haven. The sinister branches of the leafless trees hung over the dark entrance like guardians of an asylum. Beyond the iron gates, the main house could barely be seen, slightly obscured by the mist that filled the air. Prior to this time, the Sheltons had driven to the Haven on sunny days, intent on spending a rustic weekend away from their beloved Charleston, with the secondary intention of stocking up for the apocalypse that they feared would be upon them.

Tom had learned long ago to never underestimate the depravity of man. In a way, that was why he'd joined the Navy in the first place— to protect America from those who'd do her harm. The last few days had shown him that there were enemies within the nation's borders as well. Combatants who'd stop at nothing to change the course of a nation's history. The question he wrestled with was whether it was for the greater good.

He pulled the busted-up Yukon to a stop, immediately garnering the attention of several men, who took up defensive positions behind the HESCO barriers installed behind the gate. Their reaction alarmed Donna, who'd been on edge since Richmond.

They took nothing for granted as they made their way south toward Henry River Mill Village and the Haven. Every overpass was a cause for closer scrutiny. Each stranded motorist might have a weapon to ambush you. *You just never know where the bend in the road might take you.*

"Tom?" she asked uneasily.

"I'm not surprised, dear. I've felt like they do for hundreds of miles."

Donna managed a laugh and nodded her head. "What should we do?"

"Let me reintroduce myself. Wait here."

Tom stepped out of the Yukon and immediately raised his hands high over his head. He was still wearing his Navy cap. "I'm Commander Tom Shelton, U.S. Navy Retired. My wife and I—"

"Welcome home, Commander!" Alpha's booming baritone voice was unmistakable.

"Alpha, I never thought I'd say it's good to hear your voice."

"I'll take that as a compliment, Commander. Please, sir, lower your arms." Alpha turned to his men and instructed them to lower their weapons and open the gates. He and Tom shook hands and shared a bro-hug, a friendly gesture signaling to Donna that it was safe to join them.

"Hello, Alpha," she began. "You are a sight for sore eyes."

"Well, two nice compliments in one day," Alpha said with a laugh. "My sizable head might swell up a couple more notches."

"We've had an interesting, but rough journey," said Donna. She glanced back at the front of the Yukon. She hadn't seen it from that perspective yet. The red paint on the hood looked like they'd plowed over half a dozen zombies on a country road.

"Apparently," said Alpha. He took a moment to apologize and explain that his men needed to inspect their vehicle as part of the check-in process. While they did their due diligence, the conversation continued.

"How are things here?" asked Tom.

"Hittin' on all cylinders," Alpha replied. "People are still arriving, and we've added some new residents since you were here last. They're all a nice fit for the Haven."

"Are you keeping Ryan straight?" asked Tom.

"Oh, yeah. You know Mr. Smart, he's all work and no play. I'll say this, his due diligence and planning has paid off. From the moment they sensed trouble, every aspect of what we'd worked towards was set into motion. We established our security and had reached out to almost all of the property owners before dawn on New Year's Day."

Donna yawned and wrapped her arm through her husband's to support her tired body. She addressed a concern of hers. "That's good. Say, you mentioned some new folks. Are any of them medical personnel? I took a nasty tumble and hurt my ankle."

"Yes, ma'am. Blair recruited a top-notch ER doc and her husband, a firefighter who's also an EMT. They can fix you up."

"Great," said Donna. "Listen, where is their cabin located? I'd like to see her about something."

Tom glanced over at his wife's face and gave her a puzzled look. It appeared she was talking about something more than a simple sprained ankle.

Alpha responded, "Well, they're actually not that far from you guys, but they're not here yet."

"Oh. Are they on their way?"

"I don't know, honestly. I've been on the front gate for a few hours, and as of this morning, Blair hadn't heard from them."

"Okay," said a dejected Donna. She turned to go back to the truck and then she stopped to ask, "Where are they coming from?"

"Richmond, I think," replied Alpha.

The Sheltons exchanged looks and shook their heads. Alpha noticed the odd reaction, so he asked, "Is that bad?"

Tom kicked at the gravel and then stepped closer to Alpha. "Richmond is FUBAR. If they haven't left yet, they're probably up to their eyeballs."

CHAPTER 43

X-Ray's Cabin
The Haven

Ryan and Cort toured the entire perimeter of the Haven, reviewed several of the newer buildings, and discussed Cort's role going forward. Cort was more than happy to stay out of Ryan's relationship with the security team. Ryan had an excellent rapport with Alpha and the others, while Cort was not really a military type. Cort said that if anyone wanted to have a discussion about international diplomacy, he was their guy. Otherwise, he'd leave the nuts and bolts of perimeter security to Ryan.

The two men strengthened their rapport, and by the end of the afternoon, they were discussing the residents. Ryan told Cort a little bit about their newest addition to the community, as well as the intrigue surrounding his background.

"Cort, I can tell you now that Blair and I didn't just accept every applicant into the Haven, including your family. Most of the folks here don't realize that we surreptitiously recruited them. When we developed the concept, we sat down and identified all our needs. Then we set about finding people who could fill them, and who were likely open to the concept. Frankly, you were one of the rare exceptions to that process. When you contacted us about the Haven, I was a little shocked considering your position in government. I thought you'd have contingency plans using military protection."

Cort laughed a little. "Well, unfortunately, I'm one ladder rung below the top. If I were chief of staff to a cabinet member, then Meredith and I would be hunkered down in a bunker somewhere."

"Or unemployed, right?" asked Ryan with a chuckle.

"That's true. The bloodletting opened a lot of eyes, to be sure. Here's the thing that everyone was reminded of after the president cleaned house. We all serve at the pleasure of the President of the United States. Cabinet members. Top military brass. Department heads. Even chiefs of staff, to an extent. The day of the bloodletting, I phoned Meredith and told her I was glad my boss didn't take the Defense Secretary position he was offered after General Mad Dog Mattis resigned. Senator McNeil seriously considered the offer, but as chairman of the Senate Intelligence Committee, he was already one of the most influential politicians in Washington."

Ryan was curious. "Why did you reach out to us?"

Cort sighed. "It was based upon a conversation I had with my father-in-law some time back. It was a good idea, especially considering what I know about the nation-states that hate us. However, my wife was going through a period in which she didn't want her father, quote, *meddling*, unquote, in our lives." Cort gestured with both hands to create air quotes.

"Daughters can be like that, I guess," added Ryan.

Cort shrugged and continued. "One day when I found myself stuck in an airport waiting on a delayed flight, I was bouncing around Facebook, looking at preparedness groups, and I saw someone mention the Haven. They provided a link to another page that discussed the concept in general terms, but never disclosed the location. I liked the idea, and based upon my father-in-law's suggestion, I followed up with a direct message. I never heard anything again for weeks and had frankly forgotten about it."

Ryan hesitated and then smiled. He leaned over and lowered his voice. "Well, we didn't forget about you. Please don't be offended at this, but, Cort, after your inquiry, Blair began to conduct some research on you and your family. We vet everyone that shows an interest for the reasons I said a minute ago and to make sure you'll coalesce with the group as a whole. By the time she reached out to you to pursue your inquiry, we'd compiled a pretty extensive file on you guys and determined you'd be a great fit for the Haven."

Cort leaned against the passenger seat and studied Ryan. "What did you say you did before you started this project? Counterintelligence?"

Ryan laughed. "Yeah, right. I'd never pass their vetting process. No, Blair and I are students of reality television. The best way to learn about your fellow man is to take them out of their comfort zone and place them under the microscope of a camera. Pretty soon, you learn what they're all about. We kinda do the same thing with our recruits."

Cort adjusted his seat and nodded. "Yeah, I see."

"Ryan, our process was intrusive and an invasion of privacy. But lives are at stake, including ours. If we bring the wrong person through those gates for an interview and reject them, they might come back with a larger group and try to take what we have. We've only rejected a few families, most recently on New Year's Eve. It's the kind of thing that keeps me up at night. Concealment is our friend."

Ryan wheeled the Ranger down the hill toward the banks of the Henry River. He pointed ahead to X-Ray's cabin. Seconds later, he pulled up to the front door and X-Ray emerged onto the porch.

"Come on, Cort. I want you to meet our newest addition."

X-ray waved and motioned for them to come inside. "Hey, guys! It's a lot warmer in here. I'm working on that barbed-wire phone project I was telling you about."

"Barbed-wire phone?" asked Cort with a puzzled look on his face.

Ryan laughed and motioned for Cort to lead the way. "Yeah, X-Ray is our resident tech nerd. Is that fair to say?"

X-Ray shrugged and laughed. "Well, I guess if you call an old-school, wild-wild-west telephone system technology, then you're right."

Once they were inside, Cort marveled at the extensive spread of electronics, monitors and computer systems that filled the cabin. X-Ray began the introductions by shaking Cort's hand.

X-Ray was in a jovial mood. "My name is Eugene O'Reilly, but everybody calls me X-Ray, even before I arrived at the Haven."

"Like the corporal on *M*A*S*H*?" asked Cort. "I used to watch that show as a kid."

"That's right. It's kind of a long story. It's a nickname my grandfather gave me, and I guess I grew into it, sorta."

"X-ray, this is Michael Cortland. He's from Mobile but works in Washington for a senator."

Cort towered over X-Ray. "Everyone calls me Cort. It's a nickname I've been stuck with for a long time."

X-ray's demeanor suddenly changed. He turned tense and began rubbing his fingers on his palms. Neither Cort nor Ryan noticed his nervousness.

"Nice to meet you, Cort," said X-ray as he quickly turned his back to his guests. "Um, let me show you what I've got going on with the, um, phone design."

He sat down in a chair at his computer and powered up a screen that contained a schematic of the Haven's perimeter. It identified the river boundary as well as the existing block walls. Just as X-Ray was about to explain, Ryan's phone rang.

"Excuse me, guys. I need to take this."

"Okay," mumbled X-Ray.

Ryan politely stepped away from the computers and wandered toward the fire. "Go ahead, Bravo."

He began to pace. "Why?"

"How many? Six? That's overkill, don't you think?"

"Does he have a—?

"No, hell no. Don't let him in. Tell him... You know what, hang on. I'll be there in a minute and tell him myself."

Ryan disconnected the call and turned to a curious Cort. "Cort, we need to head over to the front gate. X-Ray, I'm sorry, but this'll have to wait."

X-Ray spun around in his chair and held both hands in the air. "Hey, no problem. You know where to find me. Um, nice to meet you, Cort."

Cort waved goodbye and darted out the door to catch up with Ryan, who was already getting into the Ranger.

*****

X-Ray followed Cort to the door and quickly closed it behind him. Then he made his way to the edge of the window frame and peered around the corner, watching the Ranger make its way up the hill and under the tree canopy that covered the gravel trail.

He exhaled, breathing normally for the first time in several minutes. He furiously rubbed his hands on his jeans to dry his sweaty palms. After wiping his brow on his sleeve, he began pacing the floor.

After a minute, he took a deep breath and made his way to the fireplace. He stood on the hearth and wiggled the fireplace mantel until it loosened on its brackets. X-Ray glanced once more toward the front window, and satisfied Ryan hadn't returned, he took the mantel off the stone wall, revealing a missing river rock the size of his fist.

Another deep breath later, he set the mantel aside and retrieved a ZTE flip phone from the small space. The Tracphone was one of several in his possession that he'd purchased from a Walmart on the way to the Haven. The untraceable burner phones, as they were called, allowed him to create an anonymous phone account with a number from anywhere in the world. This particular phone was assigned a 307 area code that was somewhere in Wyoming.

X-Ray ran his thumb across the numbers of the flip phone. He closed his eyes and steadied his nerves. He opened the text message app and began to type. He had to choose his words carefully so they weren't misconstrued.

The eagle's mark is in sight.

X-Ray set the phone down on his dining table as if it had shocked him with ten thousand volts. The device spun around in a circle for a moment before stopping.

Now he waited. *Will they respond? I've done what I was supposed to do, right?*

He paced the floor again, waiting for a response. He was hovering nervously near the front window, fearful that Ryan and Cort would return unexpectedly. He contemplated replacing the hearth and simply hiding the burner phone somewhere more accessible. Or perhaps he'd just throw it in the Henry River, never to be seen again. That would be an easy solution.

Except he'd already sent the text. The door was open. You couldn't delete a sent text.

The eagle's mark...

Buzzzz.

A response. X-Ray hesitated at first; then he walked to the table. He didn't touch the phone, as if somehow his fingerprints would implicate him in something sinister. He turned his head sideways in order to look at the display head-on.

Tell no one.
Will advise.
Godspeed, Patriot.
MM

CHAPTER 44

Front Gate
The Haven

"Do you want me to handle this so you don't have to get your hands dirty?" asked Cort. "I'd hate to see my Yale law degree go to waste just because of the apocalypse."

Ryan smiled. "Nah, I know this guy. Sheriff Bragg has been pretty nosy from the day we started building the block walls around our perimeter. It seemed the more we closed off our property, the more he felt he had a right to know what's going on."

"It's kinda like driving down a country road and you suddenly come across the iron gate and you wanna know what's behind it," added Cort.

"Exactly. Nobody needs to know the extent of our preps, even the local sheriff. What puzzles me is why he felt the need to bring two carloads of deputies with him."

"Intimidation," Cort quickly responded. "It's a classic technique when law enforcement investigators are trying to bull their way into a place they don't belong. He doesn't have a warrant, and mere speculation is insufficient to enter your private property. By bringing a show of force, he hopes you'll be afraid to back down."

Ryan laughed as they approached the gate. "Wrongo." He parked the Ranger, and the two men quickly exited to join the standoff between Bravo, Charlie, and Burke County's finest.

"Good afternoon, Sheriff," Ryan greeted in a monotone voice.

"Mr. Smart," the sheriff responded, together with a tip of his hat. "This doesn't have to turn into a big production. We're conducting an investigation of a crime in the area, and we'd like to take a look around."

"My people said you wouldn't be specific about what it is you expect to find here."

"Well, it's an ongoing investigation," the sheriff replied.

"I understand, but what does that have to do with us?" asked Ryan. "We've not reported anything to the sheriff's office."

The sheriff pressed on. "We have reason to believe that someone from your—" he hesitated before continuing "—your *community*, um, might have some knowledge of a reported theft on an adjacent farm."

Cort detected the sheriff's hesitancy and the way he spoke the word *community*. He decided to step in. "Sheriff, I'm an attorney. I understand you don't have a warrant, am I correct?"

"Yes, for now, but—"

Cort cut him off. "Do you have someone that you'd specifically like to speak with?"

"Well, no."

"And do you have anyone that is a specific target of your investigation?"

"No, not yet. But we would like to take a look around and speak—"

Cort was unafraid to challenge the sheriff's authority. He turned and swung his left arm around behind him, prompting the sheriff and his deputies to look past where Cort and Ryan were standing.

"Is there anything visible to you that constitutes evidence or might be associated with the crime you're investigating."

"No, of course not," he replied sheepishly.

The sheriff backed down and his shoulders slumped. Cort inwardly smiled as he recognized the sheriff's look of defeat.

Ryan tried to pry out the purpose of the sheriff's intrusion. "Look, Sheriff Bragg, I don't want to appear unreasonable, but these are trying times, and we'd like to maintain our privacy. If you'll just let me know what happened, we'd both be glad to look into it and report anything we find."

The sheriff kicked at some loose gravel and then slowly approached the gate. He lowered his voice, forcing Ryan and Cort to come closer.

"Okay, here's the deal," he began. "An old couple who owns the farm immediately adjacent to your property reported a stolen vehicle a little while ago. We wanted to canvass the area quickly in the event we could locate it and the thief before they got away. I, um, understand that you've got a lot of new faces around here, and I thought, well, maybe somebody knew something."

"Sheriff, I can assure you that none of these fine people are car thieves," said Ryan reassuringly. "In fact, we have more cars than we need. Heck, with the gas shortages being reported, all of our cars may be replaced by the horse and buggy soon."

Ryan's folksy approach and humor helped defuse the unnecessarily tense situation. The sheriff saw an opening.

"So you'll let us come in and take a look around?"

Ryan chuckled. "Um, no. I didn't say that. But I promise you we'll conduct our own investigation, and if anything comes of it, we'll gladly turn over any car thieves to law enforcement."

"You can't ask for much more than that, right, Sheriff?" Cort encouraged the sheriff to see it their way.

"I suppose you're right." The sheriff tipped his hat and raised his arm in the air, circling his index finger, indicating to his deputies they should load up and leave.

After they pulled away, Ryan gave instructions to Bravo and Charlie before pulling Cort aside. "Do you think there's any truth to that? I mean, was he just making up a reported theft to get his foot in the door?"

Cort grimaced and shrugged. "I don't know. I kinda doubt it. I mean, was there a car theft? Probably. But I got the sense he wanted to snoop more than he wanted to investigate a theft."

Ryan nodded. "Yeah, me too."

CHAPTER 45

Sheltons' Cabin
The Haven

"Tom! Tom!" Donna emerged from the bedroom, still groggy from a fitful two-hour nap. Sleep came easily, initially; then the dreams began. One's personality and their interaction with the world typically determines the contents of the dreams. For Donna, her dreams were used by her brain to subconsciously organize and compartmentalize her memories, thoughts, and interactions. This time, her dreams were more creative. They took bits and pieces of the day's events, from the attack in Richmond to the angry mob chasing them through Durham. Only, in her dreams, she and Tom weren't successful in avoiding the attackers.

When she awoke and found Tom missing from the cabin, she immediately became concerned. It was a small space consisting of a single bedroom filled with two full-size beds and a variety of furniture to hold their belongings. The simple bathroom included a toilet, a pedestal sink, and a stand-up shower. The remainder of the space was open with the kitchen, dining, and living areas part of a single room.

Tom had started a fire as soon as they arrived, and the wood-burning stove generated so much heat that Donna considered slightly opening the windows. Instead, she found her way to the front door to look for her husband.

Tom was returning from the front yard as a vehicle was pulling away. When he saw her standing in the doorway, he hustled up the steps of the porch to join his wife.

"Hey, I thought you'd still be sleeping."

"No, um. I had a dream. Who was that?"

"That was Echo and his wife. Do you remember—?"

"Of course," replied Donna. "Very nice people. In fact, they were the only ones that were close to our age, not that it seems to matter to anyone here."

Tom laughed as he escorted his wife back into their cabin. She'd left the door ajar, allowing some of the cold air in, or the heat to escape, whichever the laws of thermodynamics allowed.

"I remember when I broached the subject of age with Ryan," began Tom as he backed his fanny to the woodstove and warmed his backside. "By the way, did you know he's sixty?"

"Really? You can't tell."

"Yeah, lucky guy. Anyway, he quoted Mark Twain, of all people. He said age is an issue of mind over matter. If you don't mind, it doesn't matter."

Donna laughed. "Men can think like that. You guys look better with age. Women see it differently. We see our glory years slipping away."

Tom shook his head and approached his wife. He wrapped his arms around her and kissed her. "Glory years?"

Donna shyly looked down. "You know, when I was healthy and had smooth skin and, um, all my teeth."

Tom burst out in laughter. "Good Lord, Mrs. Shelton. You act like you've got one foot in the grave. We've already cheated death. Let's not welcome it back in based upon a few wrinkles and a couple of missing molars."

A few tears streamed down her cheeks and she held her husband close to hide her angst. He felt like something was wrong inside her, but she didn't want to unduly concern him. They'd been through a lot since New Year's Eve. She felt responsible for it all.

She was the one who insisted they take the ill-fated trip to New York at that time of year. She knew better than to put them in such a position considering the times they lived in. And to top it off, she inwardly chastised herself, she'd dragged her husband down to Times Square, ground zero for the terrorist attack on the city.

"Hey, hey. Don't be sad, dear. Is there something else?"

She wiped her cheeks with the sleeves of her sweater and patted him gently on the chest. "No, not at all. It's just, um, I'm glad we're safe. And, Tom, I really do feel safe here."

"That's good. These are good people."

Donna pulled away and yanked a Kleenex out of the box sitting on a side table. "I look forward to seeing Echo and his wife tomorrow. I hope the—"

"Well, let me mention this," Tom interrupted. "Now, you may not be up for it, but they were on their way over to the main house. Ryan and Blair have been having some casual get-togethers at suppertime. You know, potluck type of stuff. She knows we're tired and by no means would be expected to bring anything, but we are invited to join them."

"When?" she asked.

Tom began to take off his jacket as he replied, "Anytime. I suspect Ryan opens up the bar for cocktails beforehand."

Donna didn't hesitate. "I'm there. Let me grab my coat."

Maybe a drink was just what the doctor would order for her melancholy mood.

CHAPTER 46

Haven House
The Haven

Echo and his wife, Charlotte, were the first to arrive, as always. Charlotte loved to cook and enjoyed playing the role of the grandmother figure at the Haven. She and Blair had a close relationship, often having long conversations about what life would look like after a collapse event. They both agreed the Haven offered them the best chance to have a normal life.

After Echo and Ryan set out the alcohol and mixers, the Cortlands arrived. Ryan provided them a quick tour of Haven House while Blair got Hannah settled in with videos and games. Hannah immediately asked whether Skylar was coming, and Blair responded that her dad was invited, so naturally Skylar was as well.

The three couples were hanging out by the fire when Delta arrived alone. They encouraged him to fetch his children, but he declined, saying they were most likely tired from a full day of activities around the Haven.

The conversation turned to events around the country, and everyone was sharing their opinions as more guests arrived. Ryan greeted Tom and Donna Shelton at the front door. He started by giving Donna a hug.

"You guys have been through a lot," said Ryan, feeling genuine compassion for the retired couple. His mother and father had been frequent travelers, unafraid to tackle any challenges associated with visiting unique destinations around the world.

His mom had been born in Berlin, Germany, and grew up there during World War II. She'd experienced firsthand what the collapse of a nation looked like. Moreover, his mom had known hunger, fear, and isolation. She'd become a survivor during those difficult years as a young girl, foraging for food while avoiding the demented clutches of Russian soldiers as they invaded Berlin. Ryan was grateful to his mom for passing on those survival genes to him.

Donna chuckled as she removed her coat. "Going to New York and Times Square had always been a dream of mine. Tom indulged me and tried to make it a trip of a lifetime. I could've done without the theatrics, however."

Tom laughed and joined his wife. He accepted a hug and gave her a peck on the cheek in return. They were every bit in love today as the day they were married.

Tom began to remove his coat as Meredith approached to meet them. Ryan made the introductions. "I'd like you to meet Commander Tom Shelton and his wife, Donna. They're from Charleston, but they took a roundabout way of getting here, am I right, Tom?"

The older man laughed. "Boy, that's an understatement. Over the river and through the woods doesn't begin to describe the route we took to get here."

He extended his hand to shake Meredith's. Instead, she moved in to hug them both. "I'm a hugger, if that's okay."

Donna smiled and a tear appeared on her cheek as she accepted the hug. "Of course, dear."

"Donna, I'm so sorry. I didn't mean to overstep—"

Donna patted her on the cheek and shook her head from side to side. "No, it's fine. It's just. Well, we've got two daughters your age and I worry for them. They're in the military and I'm sure they're safe, but, well, you know." Her voice trailed off.

"I totally understand, Donna. And you're right, I'm sure they're safe, and most importantly, I bet they're relieved that their parents have found a safe haven as well."

"Meredith, did you make this nice woman cry?" asked Cort laughingly as he approached the group with a glass of wine.

"No, silly man," replied Meredith. "I guess, um, we were just having a moment, right, Donna?"

Donna laughed, wiped off her wet cheeks, and hugged Meredith again.

Cort moved closer and shook hands with Tom. "I'm Michael Cortland, but my friends call me Cort."

"It's nice to meet you, Cort. I'm Tom and this—"

Tom Shelton froze. A chill ran up his spine and he began to blink rapidly. Everyone noticed his sudden change in demeanor, and Donna let go of Meredith to reach for her husband.

"Dear, are you okay? Tom?"

Tom forcibly shook his body. His eyes darted from Ryan to Cort and then over to Meredith. He returned his attention to Cort. "Son, I'm sorry. Did you say your name is Cortland?"

"Yes, sir."

He and Donna exchanged knowing glances as the light bulb went off in her head as well. Tom addressed Meredith. "And you're Meredith? Meredith Cortland?"

A look of bewilderment overcame Meredith. "Um, yes. Cort and I've been married for nearly ten years."

Tom patted his jacket and reached inside to confirm the envelope was still there. He turned to Ryan. "Is there a place where I might have some privacy with these folks?"

Ryan shrugged. "Sure. You can use my study. Tom, is there something I can help you with?"

Tom furrowed his brow and thought for a moment. "No. Not just yet. I just need a quick moment with the Cortlands, and then we'll speak with you if they deem it appropriate."

Meredith looked at Cort and then said, "Tom, I'm sorry, but what's going on? This is all so mysterious."

Ryan took the lead and answered for Tom. "Let me show you guys some privacy where you can talk. Take as long as you need and then come out when you're ready. Dinner can wait for a little while."

He escorted the group into his study and excused himself, gently closing the door as he backed out. Once they were alone, Tom pulled the envelope out of his pocket and fumbled with it nervously. Before he turned it over, he took a moment to explain. "I take it you both know George Trowbridge."

Meredith and Cort looked at one another. "Yes, of course. He's my father."

Tom handed her the letter. "I have known your father for many years. Our relationship was, well, out of the ordinary. Let's leave it at that."

"He has a lot of business associates like that," said Meredith. She turned the envelope over and over again in her hands. "He gave you this? To give to me?"

"Yes. When we evacuated from the city, we had several options that would get us to an airport that was still open. New Haven was one of those options. I'd been to your home on one other occasion, many years ago. I took a chance that your father was there and would agree to help us get back to Charleston, or here. He was very accommodating."

Donna interjected, "He booked us passage on a nuclear submarine. Can you imagine?"

Cort grinned. "Yes, actually we can."

"Anyway, just as we were about to leave his bedside, he handed me this envelope. He didn't tell me who you were or how I would even cross paths with you. Yet here we are. Standing across from one another."

"My father has a way of knowing things, I suppose," said Meredith, who still appeared to be stunned by the developments. She looked to Donna for support. "You were at his bedside?"

Donna picked up on the fact that Meredith might not be fully informed of her father's medical condition. "Yes, but keep in mind, we arrived unannounced. He looked well and seemed to be getting excellent care."

All Meredith could do was nod her head as she studied the envelope. She picked at the sealed flap with her thumbnail as an inner debate raged within her. She'd quarreled with her father far too often. Most times, she regretted their exchanges, as a stubborn old man who claimed he only wanted the best for his daughter butted heads with a young woman desperately trying to find her own way with the man she loved. Meredith was completely unaware of the fact that Cort had a close, secretive relationship with Trowbridge.

She looked at Cort. "Should I open it now?"

Tom offered to leave and made his way toward the door. "Donna, let's step out and give them some privacy."

Meredith quickly stopped him. "No. I mean, please stay. Obviously, my father held you in high enough regard to trust you with this letter. Plus, we both might have more questions regarding his, um, health."

Tom nodded and returned to Cort's side. He patted the younger, much taller man on the back to offer his encouragement. "We're here for you both."

Meredith carefully opened the envelope and retrieved the two-page letter. As she read, tears streamed out of her eyes and she fought back sniffles. She finished reading the letter and handed it to Cort, who quickly glanced at it.

Donna broke the silence. "I hope this isn't bad news."

Meredith shook her head. "No, it's actually a very sweet letter. I love my daddy and always will. He just has a way. Well, you know."

Tom chuckled, and he reached out to take Meredith's hands. "Listen, young lady. I'm a retired Naval commander. I treated my daughters as if they were under my command more times than I care to remember. But, at the end of the day, we're still a loving family. It's that love that pushes all those *Commander Shelton moments* out of their memories."

Meredith nodded and smiled. The waterworks turned from sadness to tears of joy. "I can see why he wrote the last paragraph."

"What did it say, dear?" asked Donna.

"It read that we can absolutely trust Tom Shelton, but no one else."

CHAPTER 47

Haven House
The Haven

The Sheltons and Cortlands emerged from Ryan's study in a jovial mood. Their timing was perfect, as Blair and Charlotte had begun bringing food from the kitchen for a family-style dinner of beans, rice, and ground beef. Mundane as the options might sound, Blair had had the foresight to include a variety of sauces, spices, and toppings to make the post-collapse staples tasty.

Hannah was enjoying a Disney movie from Blair's extensive collection, settled in on the sofa with Chubby and The Roo. She'd promised the girls that tomorrow she'd be back with Handsome Dan so the three English bulldogs could have a playdate. Hannah was impressed with the number of toys the girls had from their favorite online store—*Bark Shop*. Even Hannah recognized that the pups were spoiled with every imaginable toy.

Ryan approached Tom and Cort briefly before everyone took a seat, and confirmed that all was well. They promised to fill him in on the details after dinner. In fact, the brief conversation led to a promise to have daily meetings between the three as they fostered the residents of the Haven through a post-collapse world.

"Kudos to the chef," exclaimed Delta, who was the only guest without a partner. He'd become accustomed to dining alone since his divorce, and this was the first family-style meal he'd had. "I never thought beans and rice could taste so good."

"How'd you fix yours?" asked Blair.

Delta finished his generous spoonful and picked up a thirty-ounce jar of red sweet pepper relish. He turned the jar so everyone could view the label. "I used this relish. It's made by the Amish."

"That's good stuff," added Ryan. "We bought a couple of dozen cases of it when we took a trip to Sarasota before moving here. I think we've got enough to last several years."

"Not with Delta around," joked Blair as Delta scooped another tablespoon into his bowl.

Everyone had a good laugh and continued their conversation, which turned to media reports from Richmond.

"Tom, you were in the middle of the melee," began Ryan. "Do you think it was orchestrated or spontaneous like the news reports are saying?"

"I have to say orchestrated," he replied. "It's almost as if they had a plan of attack. Their first goal was to stop traffic, and they did so by assaulting the vehicles from the bridge overpass. Once vehicles were neutralized, dozens of thugs came out of nowhere to attack cars and motorists."

"Were they protestors?" asked Meredith. "I mean, what could they possibly hope to accomplish?"

Tom furrowed his brow and shook his head. "No, they weren't protestors as the media has portrayed them. They had a goal and that was to hurt, or even kill, people indiscriminately."

"Interesting choice of words," said Delta. "Indiscriminately."

Tom shrugged, then explained. "Certainly not intentionally, Delta. However, it fits. In today's age, our polarized society seems to be divided by race in many instances. While the people in the mob that attacked our cars were predominately black, there were whites in the group too. Moreover, at least from our limited perspective, the motorists being attacked were from all races and walks of life."

Delta shrugged and muttered, "That's indiscriminate."

Meredith added what she'd picked up on from news reports in Charlotte. "The media is blaming the president and his supporters for creating a climate of rage and hate. Basically, they're excusing the actions of the mobs in Richmond as being frustrated students and disadvantaged residents who decided to take out their anger on anyone in their path."

Ryan took a deep breath and gave his opinion. "That's predictable, and we all see the media's agenda coming out. Let's be honest, a lot of Americans have had a lot to be angry about for a long time. Blacks struggled for a long time to get their freedom and continue to struggle for equality and opportunity. There are also working-class Americans who feel like a mouse on a wheel, living paycheck to paycheck, hoping for a better economic opportunity at some point."

"These issues have been ongoing for half a century," interjected Cort. "The point, at least from my perspective, is that the anger started many decades before the president was elected. It dates back to the sixties and the civil rights movement and the Vietnam War."

"Exactly," added Ryan. "I'm comfortable in saying this, however. Over the last dozen years, an us-versus-them narrative has risen to the forefront. Name-calling—including the labels racist, misogynist, dregs of society, and deplorables—is far too common. Eventually, when a large group of any people, especially proud Americans, continue to be called names and be disparaged by the media, whether it be news or entertainment, then hostilities can boil over."

Echo sat up in his chair and pushed his plate forward. "Ryan, are you saying that all of this social unrest is partly our side's fault? And listen, by our side, I'm referring to conservatives. I make no bones about where I stand politically."

"You and I've had this conversation before," Ryan began his reply. "To an extent, there's plenty of blame to go around. I've been warning for years, albeit privately, that if the rhetoric and rancor didn't get tamped down, we'd end up shooting at each other."

"But that's not our fault," said Echo.

Ryan took a deep breath. "Okay, let me tell you a story."

Blair groaned. "Here we go. We're about to get one of Ryan's famous analogies or theories."

Most of the group chuckled, but both Delta and Echo were intently listening to Ryan.

Ryan squeezed his wife's hand and smiled. "You'll survive. For the benefit of our new friends, I have a habit of making analogies so that they are relatable. Let me give you this example. How many of you have seen the Stephen King movie *Needful Things?*"

Everyone raised their hand.

"Okay, good. Now, you know there is this evil guy, Leland Gaunt, who shows up in this small town, Castle Rock, in Maine, of course, and opens up a shop. He calls it Needful Things. But Gaunt is more than a shop owner. He's the devil incarnate. Now, he knows what makes the people of Castle Rock tick. He knows what they're hiding, what their fears are, and how to stir up their angers."

"Yeah, my favorite scene was where the kid was throwing chicken poop and mud on crazy Wilma's sheets," said Charlotte before continuing, "I would've taken a switch to that boy if I caught up with him."

"See, that's the point," said Ryan, who had command of the room. "Wilma didn't know it was young Brian who ruined her sheets. She thought it was Nettie. Gaunt played those two against each other to the point a crazed Wilma and a grief-stricken Nettie duked it out in the middle of the street with a knife and a meat cleaver."

"Gaunt pitted everyone against each other by playing on their emotions," interjected Cort.

Ryan smiled and nodded. "The same thing has been happening in America for decades. One side of the political spectrum has effectively convinced their constituents that our side is full of racists, misogynists, and is guilty of every *ism* created in the social-justice-warrior handbook."

"But we're not saints either," added Blair.

"I agree. Our side has convinced us that everything related to government is bad. Washington is out to get us so that all of our tax dollars can be squandered on social programs and freeloaders and illegal aliens."

Echo agreed. "I have to say it's hard to argue with that. All I've ever heard from people who think like me is that the government needs to get out of our lives and the downtrodden need to get a job."

"Here's what I'm saying," continued Ryan. "Many of us have lost the ability to step back and look at the situation from an independent, detached perspective. Why? Because the media and politicians, the real-life *Leland Gaunts*, keep us stirred up in a fit of anger against the other side. That's called polarization, and we haven't experienced levels of division this great since the sixties. Both the 1960s and the 1860s."

The group grew quiet as they allowed Ryan's words to soak in.

"That's an interesting analogy to the Civil War," said Delta, breaking the silence. "Do you think our country is headed toward a second civil war?"

Echo started laughing and then apologized for his outburst. "Trust me, Ryan and I have discussed this topic since the day we met. I say yes. He says no."

Ryan smiled and pushed his chair away from the table slightly so he could cross his legs. "I can imagine that conversations like this were had around dinner tables over drinks in places like Washington, Georgia, or Charleston, South Carolina, in the late 1850s. Gentlemen, plantation owners, and slaveholders all vowed that the North could never be allowed to force their Yankee ways on the gentile Southerners."

"I'm a Yankee." Delta laughed. "Pennsylvania born and raised."

Ryan pointed at Delta. "Again, his statement will help make my point. In the eighteen hundreds, America was divided culturally by geography and economics. The South was primarily agricultural, requiring large amounts of inexpensive labor to tend to crops and cotton. The North was primarily industrial, requiring machinery and more skilled workers to work in the factories or coal mines.

"Make no mistake, slavery was a horrible practice and needed to be abolished. But Northerners had their own form of slave labor, too. The men they sent into those unsafe coal mines and unregulated industrial manufacturing plants were paid, and they were free, but they were put at great risk. History has shown that more people died in the industrialized North, working a regular job, than slaves died in the fields of Southern plantations. That doesn't make slavery good, but it adds context to the struggle for equality."

Delta persisted. "Setting aside the basis for the Civil War, can it happen again?"

"Back then, it was easy to define your opponent, the enemy. Southerners spoke in a distinctive dialect, and their cultural mannerisms were far different from those in the North. They lived in states like Virginia, Georgia, and others across the Southeast. As the conflict deepened, it was easy for certain states to secede because the vast majority of its citizens were like-minded thinkers."

"That wasn't necessarily true west of the Mississippi," interjected Cort, who was also a student of history. "States like Kansas and Nebraska were brutally divided as people were forced to take sides."

"The same is true today, Cort," said Ryan. "Our nation is homogenized."

"There's a hundred-dollar word," said Blair sarcastically. She was always teasing Ryan, her *author-wannabe*, about his use of big words.

"Do you mean like the milk?" asked Meredith, who decided to play along and tease her host.

"Yes, and it's not a hundred-dollar word," replied Ryan with a wink. "Onomatopoeia is a hundred-dollar word. That means—"

Blair interrupted him and raised her palm toward Ryan. "Hold up. You need to explain *homogenized* first."

Ryan grinned and playfully wagged his finger at his wife. "To homogenize something is to take two normally insoluble liquids, like fat and cream, and integrate them into something that works—milk.

"Our society has become integrated since the sixties, supposedly into something that works. America is no longer divided geographically by culture or political thinking. North Carolina used to be a traditionally red state that has turned purple by the influx of liberals into areas like Charlotte and Raleigh-Durham. Virginia is similar, as left-leaning federal government employees moved into the northern part of the state, but commute to DC."

Cort was enjoying the conversation. "So, because the nation doesn't have defined geographic boundaries, like whole states during the first Civil War, a division, or secession, couldn't take place."

Ryan sighed. "No. Not in my opinion."

"Then how do we resolve the continued division between us?" asked Meredith.

Ryan grimaced and then answered, "Sadly, I think it'll happen the same way that Nettie and Wilma resolved it in *Needful Things*—with a butcher knife and a meat cleaver in the middle of the street."

CHAPTER 48

Delta's Cabin
The Haven

Skylar was having so much fun with her new friend, Hannah, and her mom that she'd completely lost track of time, although there was no set schedule for her. At home, her mom worked, and she was used to fending for herself after school. In fact, it wasn't unusual for her to stop at a friend's house to play and even eat dinner before her mom got home around six in the evening.

She'd said her goodbyes earlier and declined the offer by Meredith to escort her inside. Despite the fact she was in a new place, under mysterious circumstances, Skylar was comfortable in her surroundings. The day at the Little Red Schoolhouse had helped give her a sense of normalcy.

So when Ethan wasn't at the cabin, and her dad was still busy, the isolation didn't feel unusual. In fact, she immediately embraced it. Back home in Philadelphia, she'd probably turn on some brainless television show and get a snack.

She wasn't into video games like her brother had been when he was eleven. Skylar was a painter, and, on this evening, she was excited about being alone to focus on the artwork requested by Miss Blair.

She retrieved her sketches from her bed and spread everything out on the dining table. Feeling a chill, she opened up the wood-burning stove's door and stoked the coals like her dad had taught her. They kept a stack of firewood and kindling in the cabin to stay dry, so it didn't take long for Skylar to get the heat going again.

"I'm a pioneer woman," she said to herself as she retrieved the last of the Mountain Dew her dad had brought home for lunch.

She sat at the table and became immersed in her artwork. Time flew by, and Skylar stopped just once to use the restroom. She didn't have a watch, but since it was dark outside, she assumed it was after six o'clock. Skylar found her dad's laptop and opened it. Although the display was locked by a passcode, she could see the time.

"Seven!" she said aloud as she instinctively looked around the nine-hundred-square-foot cabin to see if anyone heard her.

Consumed by her project, Skylar had lost track of time and considered that neither her father nor Ethan had come back to the cabin. For the first time since their arrival at the Haven, she became concerned. She didn't have a phone, and her father had a two-way radio, but he carried it with him everywhere.

For the next fifteen minutes, Skylar paced around the cabin, stepping onto the front porch several times to look and listen for any signs of life. The Haven was like no other place she'd ever seen before. It was completely quiet and dark. Standing in the dim light emanating through the open front door, she *blew smoke* into the cold air as the water vapor in her breath condensed into tiny droplets of water and ice.

Skylar grimaced, looked up and down the deserted gravel road one more time, and decided to go find somebody. She scurried back inside, gave the fire a final look-see to make sure it was safe, and bundled up for a walk.

She ambled along the gravel road, kicking at rocks and blowing smoke, trying to make the most out of a frightening situation for a young girl. She expected to come across a moving car or a cabin with a light on, but neither materialized.

An eastern owl screeched to her right, startling her. Skylar picked up the pace as she made her way toward the fountain in the middle of the circle between the main house and the front gate.

She'd begun to jog toward the fountain when she came to an abrupt stop, causing her to slip on the gravel and fall to her hands and knees. Skylar wanted to scream in pain, but her voice betrayed her. A primal fear had overcome her as she froze on all fours, eye level to a ghostly creature that stared directly at her and hissed.

Then it began to utter a low growl followed by a chattering sound. Skylar's eyes grew wide as the all-white animal approached her. Mouth agape, she tried to find the strength to yell for help but couldn't. She backed up, tearing the knees in her jeans on the gravel road, causing her hand to bleed on a sharp stone.

The moonlight illuminated the animal, so Skylar could see it better. She stopped her retreat and, in total bewilderment, studied her adversary. She was face-to-face with one of the rarest creatures in existence—an albino raccoon.

Albino raccoons, weighing twenty-five to thirty pounds, live naturally in the Eastern United States but rarely make it to adulthood. Because they weren't born with natural camouflage like their counterparts, they spent the vast majority of their lives avoiding predators.

The probability of Skylar encountering this unusual critter was similar to the odds of winning the lottery. Yet, there they were, in a standoff as the two tested each other's will.

Skylar was relieved to see that the ghost was in fact a raccoon. She was aware of the rabies threat from her classes in school, so she knew better than to reach out to the rare raccoon. At this point, she was happy for the experience and would like to be on her way, as she suspected was the case for her adversary.

"Shoo! Go away, pretty girl!" Skylar had no idea how to determine the gender of the raccoon, but the animal was cute in its all-white fur, so she presumed it to be a girl.

Skylar started to stand, and the raccoon rose slightly to mimic her actions. The standoff continued, as neither was willing to give ground. As Skylar found her footing, she inadvertently kicked a rock in the albino's direction, causing it to react with a subtle hiss before moseying back into the woods.

Skylar brushed the leaves and stones off her pants before letting the albino raccoon know she hoped to see her again sometime. The fear had left her, and she remembered the reason for being out in the dark alone in the first place. She picked up the pace and trekked up the hill to Haven House, where only a faint orange glow could be seen from the windows.

CHAPTER 49

Danbury Municipal Airport
Danbury, Connecticut

Jonathan Schwartz stood on the tarmac outside the Bombardier Global 6000 jet as the final preparations were being made for their departure. He wanted to personally supervise the loading of their luggage and nearly two dozen crates hastily put together by the estate's staff. Under the circumstances, he and his father would not be traveling light for their trip to New Zealand. Computers, some family heirlooms, and precious metals would also accompany them out of the country. Jonathan surmised that their self-imposed exile from the United States would be long-lasting.

The pilots were readying the aircraft as the final boxes were loaded in the baggage compartment. Jonathan paused to check his cell phone for any final messages or phone calls before he removed the SIM card. SIM, an acronym for *subscriber identity module*, was a small circuit board that, practically speaking, acted as a middleman between the phone and the carrier's cell tower, allowing the two pieces of hardware to communicate.

Each SIM card had a unique identifier that was engraved on the body of the card and communicated to the cell phone tower. Once it was removed from the phone, it didn't have the necessary hardware to connect with a cell phone tower, rendering the phone useless, but untraceable.

Jonathan was in the process of dismantling the device when a black Chevy Suburban came roaring around the side of the airport hangar. Several other vehicles could be seen at another entrance to the airport runway.

He had to make a decision. They were caught by surprise and it was too late for the jet to take off. The baggage handlers were frozen like a deer in headlights, mesmerized by the sudden activity. Jonathan wanted to protect his father, but he knew there wasn't a way to avoid his own capture.

He glanced up at the porthole windows of the Bombardier. His father's sullen face looked back at him. With an imperceptible nod and a wink, he received the blessing he needed to run. In a flash, Jonathan ran toward one of the baggage cars and grabbed a blue Danbury Airport uniform jacket. He quickly slipped his arms through the oversized jacket and scampered under the nose of the aircraft.

The airport was dark except for the blinking runway lights. Jonathan had to hope that the approaching vehicles would be focusing their attention on the aircraft and the prospect of arresting its passengers.

He raced across the concrete runway as fast as his leather Ferragamo slip-ons could carry him. His hopes of escape lifted when he hit the tall unmowed grasses between the runway, until he slipped and fell, falling forward. He tumbled over and over into a drainage ditch, ripping open his pants. Blood began to ooze out of his knee.

Out of breath and scared, Jonathan lay in the cold grass, listening. Sirens were approaching, but he dared not look up to see how close they were to him. He rolled over onto his belly and began to crawl through the ditch. Now soaked and shivering, he came to a thirty-six-inch corrugated-steel culvert.

He needed to get his bearings, so he risked popping his head out of the grass despite the closeness of voices carrying across the runway. The culvert led away from the aircraft. *To where?* Jonathan didn't know. All he knew was he'd be caught if he remained where he was.

A gentle trickle of icy water poured out of the culvert. He took a deep breath, put aside his fear of the dark, and entered the pipe. Crawling, slowly at first, Jonathan focused on a faint light off in the distance.

He'd traveled for three hundred feet when he finally reached the other side of the culvert. He crawled up a slight incline and found himself next to another runway. He could no longer hear conversations, so he raised his body onto his knees to look back toward the terminal. At least a dozen FBI agents could be seen in the headlights of their vehicles, milling about the jet.

His father was being led away in handcuffs and was thrown into the backseat of an unmarked car like a common criminal. Anger built up inside Jonathan before a tear rolled down his cheek. It saddened him to his core to see his father being treated that way.

The sadness turned to fury when he began to assign blame for what was happening. Ultimately, it was the President of the United States who'd have to approve a hastily made arrest like this one. However, Jonathan Schwartz was also astute enough to know that revenge against his family would not be foremost on the president's mind during this time of crisis. Someone else. A powerful individual who had both the contacts and the motives to settle old scores was behind this.

Jonathan clasped his hands together and then extended his index fingers forward to emulate a gun barrel. He pointed toward the east. Toward New Haven. Toward George Trowbridge. Then he muttered the words, "It's time for you to die, old man."

CHAPTER 50

Haven House
The Haven

Everyone helped clear the dishes from the table, and Ryan poured a final round of after-dinner drinks. He didn't want it to appear that there was an unlimited supply of alcohol at the Haven. As part of their vetting process, they tried to learn about the personal habits and activities of their residents. If someone appeared to visit Cancun on a regular basis, constantly photographed with a Corona in hand, they were most likely excluded from the start. The Smarts were interested in a community of responsible adults, not partiers.

The group assembled in Ryan's study following dinner except for Charlotte, who insisted on cleaning up the kitchen and watching over Hannah. She really enjoyed the company of the young girl and wanted to allow the Cortlands the opportunity to participate in the discussions without feeling like they were pushing their child on their hosts.

"Ryan, this is an impressive room," began Tom as everyone walked around and admired his mix of historic collectibles and books. "I'm sure there's a story behind every one of these pieces."

"Like this?" asked Cort, holding up a hardbound book depicting a colonial soldier holding a musket. "It's from the Boys of Liberty Library. *The Minute Men of Massachusetts* by John Morgan."

"Yeah, that's an old one," added Ryan. "Published in 1892, if I remember correctly. It was part of a collection of school books taught in history classes before they started rewriting history."

Everyone passed the book around before Cort placed it back on the shelf. After he did, Tom scooted up next to Cort.

"May I see that again?" he asked.

Cort used his basketball-player frame to easily retrieve the book from the upper shelf. He handed it to Tom, who studied the cover and then thumbed through the pages before returning it to Cort.

"Hmm," he mumbled and then turned to the rest of the group.

Ryan slid several wood panels to the side, revealing multiple concealed whiteboards. "Guys, I have a theory, but I need the help of different perspectives. And, let me say, a very important voice in all of this hasn't arrived yet. Her name is Hayden Blount."

"I know of Hayden," interrupted Cort. "She's a real up-and-comer. She's one of the attorneys representing the president in front of the Supreme Court."

"That's right, Cort. She'll have some interesting insight into all of this, which is why our conversation tonight will probably extend into tomorrow after she has arrived, hopefully."

"Hopefully?" asked Meredith.

"Naturally, Hayden lives in Washington," replied Ryan. "And, because she had to wait and see what happened with the Court's calendar, she got a late start to the Haven."

"She'll have to travel through Richmond like we did," added Tom. "Is she aware of the problems we had?"

"We don't know for certain," replied Blair. "I was talking on the phone with her when the call was suddenly disconnected. I wasn't able to reach her after that."

Donna shook her head, seeming to recall their own ordeal on the highway. "I'll pray for her and her safe arrival."

Ryan turned back to the whiteboard. "Bear with me as I lay out what I'm calling the *Leland Gaunt Theory*."

"I told you," lamented Blair, who laughed along with Meredith.

"Cort does the same stuff," she whispered.

"All men think they're Einstein," Blair quipped.

"Or Sigmund Freud," added Meredith.

"I heard that, and I'm ignoring you both," said Ryan as he continued to use the specialized markers to write on the whiteboard. Applying different colors, he wrote down the locations of the major cities that were attacked, and the means. He also included the concert chaos in Atlanta and the downing of Delta 322, Cort's aircraft.

"Delta, let me ask you first," Ryan continued. "At the stadium, the power was lost, but also, didn't you say there was some kind of gas released through the ventilation system?"

"Yes. Naturally, security treated it like a bioterror weapon. You know, some type of noxious gas or even anthrax. It turned out it was from smoke grenades."

Ryan thought for a moment. "Would it be safe to say the goal of the attackers, terrorists, or whatever was to create a mass panic situation but not necessarily kill anyone?"

Delta shrugged. "Yeah. There were deaths, but they resulted from people trampled in the panic."

"What kind of concert was it again?" asked Ryan.

"Beyoncé and Jay-Z."

Ryan stuck out his lower lip and nodded. He wrote this on the whiteboard under Atlanta. He then turned to Cort. "I know that you're probably in no mood to talk about the plane crash, but can you remember anything about the moments before the plane lost power or immediately thereafter?"

Cort exhaled. Interestingly, during dinner, the stimulating conversation, coupled with the adult beverages, was the first time he hadn't been replaying the events of forty-eight hours ago in his head.

"Honey, you don't have to—" Meredith began, trying to protect her husband from the memories of the crash.

"No, it's fine. Actually, it helps. Two things stand out. One, we were on final approach into Mobile. You could see the lights of Pensacola on the right side of the aircraft and the oil rig platforms on the left side where I was sitting. Second, the power loss was total. I mean everything. Emergency lighting, cell phones, and anything electronic."

"EMP," offered Blair.

"More specifically, an RFW," added Tom. "That's short for radio frequency weapon. The military, and not just ours, has been targeting a variety of advanced weaponry that can be used to disable the electronics of specific targets using a directed burst of energy—an electromagnetic pulse, as Blair suggested."

Ryan asked Cort, "How far was the aircraft from these oil platforms? Close enough to be hit with an RFW?"

"Absolutely, but I don't recall seeing any flash of light or traces of a high-energy beam," he replied.

"You wouldn't necessarily," interrupted Tom. "Plus, the burst occurs so quickly, it would be barely perceptible to the naked eye."

Ryan wrote this information in the column designated *Mobile*. "Tom, is it safe to assume that a civilian couldn't get access to a weapon like this?"

"True, and not only that, most terrorist organizations, from al-Qaeda to ISIS to Hamas, couldn't obtain one either. North Korea, maybe, but doubtful. This kind of technology is in its infancy, relatively speaking. The Russians and Chinese are working on it, but we're way ahead of them."

Tom sat backwards into one of Ryan's leather chairs. Meredith addressed him directly. "Are you suggesting that our own military might have shot down my husband's plane?"

"No, not necessarily. All I'm saying is that we've got the technology and it works. I can't say the same for the technology of our adversaries."

Ryan wrote the word *military* with a question mark after it under Mobile. He then walked in front of the column designated *Philly*.

"This couldn't have been an RFW," he began. "The outage was too widespread. Only a nuclear-driven EMP could kill the power from Baltimore northward into New Jersey. Yet it was isolated."

Tom leaned back in his chair and spread his arms with his palms facing upward. "I hate to say this, but once again, I must point to our military capabilities. We've successfully tested submarine-based nuclear-tipped warheads that are capable of flying and detonating at very low altitudes. The Starfish Prime testing of six decades ago focused on HEMPs—high-altitude electromagnetic pulse detonations."

"That's all I'm familiar with," said Blair.

Cort wandered through the middle of the group. "I can tell you why the low-altitude nukes have been developed. It actually follows the lead of the Russians in a way. Moscow had successfully used cyber attacks against critical infrastructure in the past as a precursor to a ground incursion. Georgia, Estonia, and, later, Ukraine are all examples of this. By taking down the power grid and disabling communications, the smaller countries were incapable of fending off the Russian invasions."

"So we plan on invading Mexico or Canada?" asked Meredith, who'd become intrigued by the conversation. Her husband rarely *talked shop* in front of her.

Cort chuckled. "Yeah, um, not on the drawing board to my knowledge. However, the use of a targeted EMP is an ideal way to disable an enemy's electronics without causing similar harm to its neighbors. For example, we could take out the command and communications structure in Damascus, Syria, without destroying the electronics in nearby Beirut, for example."

"Exactly right, Cort. Again, it goes back to our military capabilities. The launching of a high-altitude EMP requires a rocket, with booster separation, the whole nine yards. The sub-launched low-altitude EMPs come flying out of the bottom of the ocean, race toward the detonation target at hundreds of miles an hour, and barely leave a trace at detonation."

Ryan wrote this information under the column marked *Philly*. He sighed and shook his head. He had turned to ask for people's opinions about U.S. military involvement when they were interrupted.

CHAPTER 51

Haven House
The Haven

The rest of the group had made their way into Ryan's study, leaving Charlotte Echols behind to keep an eye on Hannah, who was watching television alone in the family room. She had finished clearing the table of glassware when she heard a gentle knocking at the door. Initially, she thought about hollering for Ryan or Echo to answer it, but then she shrugged it off. At the Haven, she'd never felt safer despite what was happening around the country. Besides, the bad guys don't knock.

Charlotte opened the door and was astonished to find a shivering and bloodied Skylar standing in front of her. "My goodness, child. What has happened to you? Come in, come in."

"Okay," said Skylar sheepishly as she stepped through the massive wood doorway. "Um, I'm sorry to bother you, but is my dad here?"

"Why, of course, Skylar. He thought you'd be at home with your brother."

"Hey, Skylar!" greeted Hannah, who'd heard her new friend's voice. "Wow! Did you wrestle a bear?"

Mrs. Echols shut the door and rushed off to find Delta.

"Hey," began Skylar. "I, um, you're never gonna believe this. I saw an all-white raccoon."

"No way!" Hannah was genuinely intrigued.

"Way. It was dark and I saw it in the road. It looked like it was glowing, like a ghost."

"I wanna see it!"

"Yeah, maybe tomorrow. Um, I kinda need to talk to my dad first."

Delta rushed into the room with the rest of the group in tow. "Sky, baby girl, what happened? Where's Ethan?"

"Sorry, Daddy. That's why I'm here. Um, I fell down on the road, but I'm okay except for my hand."

Delta turned around and searched for Blair. She was already headed for the bathroom to retrieve some first aid supplies and waved to him as she left.

"Come here, honey. Sit down at the dining table and tell us what happened."

"I'll get a glass of juice, or do you want hot chocolate?" offered Charlotte.

"Hot chocolate, please."

"Baby girl, are you okay?"

"I'm fine, Daddy. Ethan never came home today. After Hannah and Miss Meredith dropped me off, I started painting and, um, the next I knew, it was dark out, and Ethan wasn't home."

Delta glanced around at the curious faces and then closed his eyes. He couldn't decide who to berate first, himself for leaving his young daughter unattended, or his son, who'd disappeared, shirking his responsibilities to watch over his sister.

"I'll call the front gate and let Alpha know what's going on," said Echo, who walked toward the fireplace to place the call.

Meredith and Hannah sat next to Skylar. Meredith fixed the child's disheveled hair while Hannah picked out a few more pebbles that remained embedded in Skylar's jeans. Blair returned with a wet cloth, some gauze, and Neosporin to clean up Skylar's wounds, which were not significant, but likely painful, nonetheless.

"Delta, wasn't your son working with Alpha this afternoon on his drone-surveillance project?" asked Ryan.

Delta rose and turned to Ryan. He rubbed his temples and then ran his hands down his face in a sign of exasperation. "Alpha touched base with me at midday and said Ethan was enthusiastically taking to the project. He didn't have a set time to finish for the day, and I just assumed he'd be back at the cabin before dark, as I instructed."

"That was two hours ago," interjected Meredith in a slightly condescending tone of voice. Delta took the hit. No matter how safe the Haven was, you should always know where your children are.

Echo returned to the group. "Alpha is notifying the security team. He's sent guys to the barn and also around the property."

"Good," said Ryan. "I have an idea. Join me in the study. Echo, call Alpha back and tell him to come to the house."

"He's already on his way," said Echo.

"Ryan, I need to go look—" started Delta before Ryan interrupted him.

"I understand, but hang on until Alpha arrives. Let's go look at the drone footage. Also, this may relate to something else that happened today."

"What?" asked Delta.

"First, let's take a look, and then we'll discuss this with Alpha."

The guys headed back into the study, where Ryan settled into his chair and powered up one of the television monitors on his wall. With a few keystrokes on the computer's keyboard, he pulled up a program that displayed the names of all six drones in the Haven's air force. In a spreadsheet fashion, the monitor displayed when the drones had last provided aerial footage to the computer's hard drive. The only active camera that sent a recorded feed during the day was H-Quad-1. The other cameras could've been active, just not recording.

While Ryan ran through the footage at four times normal speed, Alpha entered the room and addressed the group. "Okay, the last time I saw Ethan was around two thirty or a quarter to three. Thereabouts. He seemed to be doing fine, although I didn't speak with him."

"That coincides with the footage," added Ryan. "Man, he was all over the place. Really, he was flying too fast to effectively surveil anything."

"Does he have a cell phone?" asked Cort. "Let's try to call him."

"Nah," said Delta. "His battery died and I told him I'd find a charger for it. Frankly, all he wanted to do was contact his mother, who's on a cruise and would create all kinds of complications, so I put him off."

Alpha took a deep breath and exhaled. "Well, I might have screwed up that program."

"Whadya mean?" asked Delta.

"Well, the boy asked me whether you'd been looking for the charger, and I told him I didn't know anything about it. Sorry, man. If I'd known—"

"Crap," said Delta.

"Yeah, well, I showed him where they are," continued Delta and then added, "You know, his attitude changed a little bit, but I thought it was just a teenager thing. You know, moody and all."

"Here we go," interrupted Ryan. "I know this property. Dammit, Alpha. The sheriff was right."

"What? The sheriff?" asked Delta.

Ryan paused the video at the point where Ethan had made multiple passes along the perimeter fence near the farmhouse adjacent to the Haven. Then he pressed play as the H-Quad-1 suddenly changed its orientation and flew at a high rate of speed before being shut down at the barn.

Alpha gave his opinion. "He saw what he was looking for and made his move."

Ryan added, "Do you think the kid was smart enough to shut down the video feed via the controller?"

"Yeah," replied Alpha. "It's not that difficult for a tech-savvy teen. We could pull the feed from the other drones, but what I just saw is far from coincidental."

"Would you guys please tell me what you're talking about?" asked Delta.

Ryan leaned back in his chair and clasped his fingers behind his head. "Late this afternoon, just before dark, I got a call from the front gate when the Burke County sheriff paid us a visit. He actually wanted to come in and look around, but I took a hard stance with him. Turns out his hunch might have been right." Ryan looked at Alpha, who furrowed his brow and nodded.

"What did the sheriff want?"

"The old couple at the adjacent farm had their car stolen this afternoon. He wasn't accusing anyone, but it's part of his job to check with the surrounding residents to see if they'd seen anything. I think he was also curious and was using the car theft as an excuse to look around. We sent him on his way since he didn't have a warrant."

"Jesus," said Delta as he began to aimlessly walk around the room while rubbing his hands through his hair. "He stole a car. I mean, what the hell?"

Alpha's radio squawked to life and the room became silent as he spoke to Bravo. "Go ahead."

"There's nothing out of the ordinary at HB-1 other than a go-bag missing from one of the lockers. I'm checking with the team to see if anyone pulled it for some reason."

"Are all the quads there?"

"Affirmative."

Alpha signed off and returned the radio to his utility belt. "Delta, Ethan has a charger now and can be reached by phone. I suggest you try to call him."

Delta nodded and pulled his cell phone out. He called several times, but his son didn't pick up the call. He left messages each time and then added text messaging to his contact attempts.

He shrugged and then collapsed into a chair in front of Ryan's desk. "What should I do? I mean, I've gotta go find him, right?"

Cort spoke up. "Listen, I don't profess to know anything about teenage boys from a dysfunctional family. Please, I don't mean to be insulting, just truthful. But you'd never find him out there. Maybe he's heading back home. Maybe he's decided to go to Florida for the winter. All I know is this. There's a frightened little girl out there that needs your help. I have one of those and I understand them. She needs her daddy and doesn't deserve to be abandoned while you go on a wild-goose chase."

"That's pretty blunt, Cort," said Delta angrily. "He's my son."

"Yes, and from what you've relayed to us all, he's also very independent. Listen, I'm just throwing in my two cents' worth. If you wanna go after him, by all means, go. We'll take care of Skylar. But if you're gonna chase after him to Philly, where the power outage is wreaking havoc, and take that young girl with you... Well, to me, as a dad, that's the height of irresponsibility."

The men in the room allowed Cort's words to linger. It was tough talk, but perhaps it was what Delta needed to hear.

Chapter 52

Cofer Road
South Richmond, Virginia

Ethan Hightower was dejected and scared. He'd driven a little over half of his five-hundred-mile journey when the Oldsmobile he'd stolen developed a loud ticking sound under the hood. He didn't know anything about cars. The Olds was hard to drive at times because it was larger than his mom's Toyota, but he quickly got the hang of it.

It was much faster than his mom's car. When there was a clear stretch of highway, the opposite of the busy southbound lane of I-95, Ethan opened up the throttle, allowing the gas-guzzling Oldsmobile to reach ninety miles an hour. He cranked up the radio, rolled down the windows, and searched for a functioning radio station to listen to. He was having the ride of his life and he intended to enjoy every moment.

The car's motor hadn't been tested like that in two decades, and the oil gaskets were none too happy. Soon, a leak developed, and as Ethan squandered gas, the engine lost its oil.

He'd made it to South Richmond and pulled off at an exit in search of a gas station. With only a few dollars and some loose change he'd found in the glove box, he hoped to pay for some gas and steal the rest. He never got the chance.

He turned west off the interstate and drove around in search of an open gas station. He smiled as he saw the lights of the Emerald Fast Mart near Cofer Road. The Olds limped toward the station; the pinging sound of the engine had now turned into a full-blown clatter.

Just as he entered the parking lot, the motor seized and shut down. All of the lights on his dashboard lit up with various shades of red and yellow, indicating the death of the Oldsmobile. Ethan sat there in disbelief. He turned off the ignition and tried to start the motor. It wouldn't turn over, prompting him to beat the steering wheel in anger.

"Now what am I supposed to do?" he asked aloud as he studied his surroundings. There were no cars at the fuel pumps of the convenience store, but there were certainly plenty of patrons milling about the entrance. Young men carried on animated conversations amidst clouds of cigarette smoke. Brown paper bags with the necks of beer or liquor bottles were in their hands as they argued about world events or sports or the weather.

Ethan didn't know or care. He needed help, so he approached the men. Shy and unsure, Ethan finally mustered the courage to speak to the men, who'd given him the once-over but didn't acknowledge him.

"Hey, um, do you guys know anything about cars? Mine broke down and I think—"

One of the men cut him off before he could finish. "Man, we don't care nothin' 'bout you or your busted-up old car. Go ahead on and don't go bustin' in on our conversation."

The rest of the men started laughing and toasted their liquor bottles together, allowing the loud clink of glass to put an exclamation point on the man's admonition to Ethan.

Ethan—young, naïve, and idealistic—persisted. "Come on, guys. I'm from out of town. My mom is missing, and I could use a break."

One of the men grinned, his gold teeth glimmering in the fluorescent light shining from the gas station's canopy. He was the largest of the group and appeared to be the drunkest. He spun the cap onto his bottle of wine and forcefully shoved it into the chest of the first man who'd addressed Ethan. He was flexing the fingers on his right hand as he stood a little taller and approached Ethan.

"Look here, man. You don't listen too well."

The man had a swagger, a side-to-side swaying movement, as he walked toward Ethan. Ethan stepped back, but it was too late. A right fist connected with his jaw, spinning him around like a top until he landed facedown on the oil-covered pavement.

Ethan tried to raise his arm to beg the man to stop, but his plea for mercy was ignored. Egged on by his drunk friends, the heavyset man kicked his size fourteen Air Jordans repeatedly into the side of Ethan's body, knocking the wind out of the boy and likely fracturing several ribs.

Ethan couldn't breathe. He tried to crawl away, occasionally looking up for someone, anyone, to come to his aid. He was alone except for the pack of attackers, who were driven insane by the blood gushing out of Ethan's mouth.

Suddenly, the large man stopped kicking him. Instead, he grabbed Ethan by the jacket and stood him upright. He wrapped his arms under Ethan's armpits and held him tight against his chest.

The rest of the men took turns punching and kicking Ethan, battering the fifteen-year-old's body beyond recognition. When the attack was over, his shoes and jacket were taken, as were his cell phone and the few dollars from his pockets.

His body was left unconscious on the cold, dark concrete next to a dumpster in South Richmond, Virginia. Ethan Hightower's day was done.

CHAPTER 53

Front Gate
The Haven

It was dark when Hayden pulled up to the front gate of the Haven. Several guards stood at attention with their weapons slightly raised. The appearance of her truck immediately placed them on alert. To assuage their apprehension, Hayden rolled down her window and yelled to the guards, "Don't shoot. I'm Hayden Blount."

Alpha's baritone voice bellowed back to her, "Foxy! It's about time!"

"Yeah, well, traffic was bad. How're ya doin', Alpha?"

A flashlight lit up her face, and then another appeared at the passenger side of the Range Rover, drawing an angry hiss from an inhospitable Prowler.

"Just fine," he responded as he stopped just short of sticking his head in her window.

Hayden immediately cautioned him. "I wouldn't do that if I were you. Prowler didn't take too kindly to the last guy who stuck his head through a window. There are still pieces of his face inside here."

Alpha let out a hearty laugh. "Yeah, sure. From that furball."

Hayden shrugged and leaned back in her seat. "Okay, big guy. Go ahead. Give it a try. Stick your head in and try to grab me."

By this point, Prowler was in full defensive mode and was standing on the passenger seat with his back arched. Alpha wisely chose not to test Prowler's mettle.

He declined. "Nah, it's too late to wrestle cats. We haven't gotten much sleep around here."

"Have you had trouble?" she asked, looking ahead impatiently, as she was ready to find her cabin and curl up under the covers.

"No, not really. We've had a few issues, but nothing we couldn't handle. I hate to have you do this, but we've got a protocol to follow, you know. I need you to step out of the truck while we do a quick search."

"I get it," said Hayden as she noticed a guard approaching her vehicle with a German shepherd on a leash. "Who's that?"

"That's Rex, one of our bomb-sniffing dogs."

"Seriously? Bomb-sniffing."

"Not really, although maybe. He was a former law enforcement K-9. One of two trained dogs here at the Haven now. Um, you might want to keep Prowler safe."

Now it was Hayden's opportunity to burst out laughing. "From that?" she asked, pointing at the shepherd. "It's the other way around, trust me."

She motioned for Prowler to join her, and he quickly made his way across the console and crawled into her arms. As she walked past Alpha, Prowler's eyes lowered and glared at the large man.

"Jeez, he is a killer, isn't he?" asked Alpha.

"You bet he is."

Hayden waited patiently until Alpha's team gave him the thumbs-up. "Okay, Foxy, you're good to go. I'll let Ryan and Blair know you've arrived. She said you guys were on a call when something went down."

"Yeah, and somehow I stomped on my phone during the melee. Let her know I'm here and safe. I assume we still have our regular morning briefings at the barn?"

"Absolutely," replied Alpha. "Bring your weapons and ammo, and we'll get them secured for you. Plus, we've picked up some new artillery since we saw each other last. We'll get you checked out on it tomorrow sometime. Obviously, we've had to limit our range practice due to circumstances."

Hayden and Alpha bumped fists. It was a rite of passage that occurred every time she'd come to the Haven. It was the point where she transitioned from being Hayden Blount, the president's legal counsel, to Foxtrot, one of the defenders of the Haven.

She loaded Prowler back into the truck and made her way down the dark gravel roads. The tires crunched on the melted and then refrozen snow. As she passed the cabins on the main drive, she noticed lights were on inside almost all of them. Her remaining headlight reflected off the license plates from many states east of the Mississippi, from Florida to New York. She rounded a bend, and then the sight of one particular vehicle caused her to slam on the brakes, forcing Prowler to dig his claws into the leather seats to stop from tumbling onto the floorboard of the truck.

"Well, would you look at that?" she asked as she stared at the GMC Yukon with the blood-red-painted hood. "Hello, and Godspeed to you, too."

CHAPTER 54

Front Gate
The Haven

Richmond SWAT eventually showed up at the intersection near the Rankin home, and the enemy combatants who'd squared off for nearly an hour fled in all directions. Even the Guardian Angels, who ordinarily were praised by law enforcement for their nonviolent approach to neighborhood watch, decided not to stick around for the inevitable questioning by police. In anticipation of a dangerous physical confrontation with the various factions brought together to wreak havoc on Richmond, many of the members wielded weapons ranging from stun guns to pepper spray. They did not, however, break out their firearms.

After the uproar subsided, Tyler approached his vehicles, full of apprehension. He'd prepared himself for the worst case, which included his new truck being vandalized and his belongings stolen. When he arrived at the truck-trailer combination, he shook his head in disbelief. Through it all, his trucks hadn't received so much as a scratch.

The family had packed everything they thought they'd need, and Tyler expertly loaded the vehicles, maximizing every available square foot of space. Tyler and Angela focused on the basics—food, water, medical supplies, and bedding.

They also packed small appliances and things that might come in handy in the event they would be there for an extended stay. The kids brought games, Tyler loaded up tools, and Angela focused on hygiene. As a doctor, she recognized that bacteria, if left unchecked, could be just as deadly as a bullet. Once their things were loaded, the family stood in the foyer and said goodbye to their home.

It was near midnight, forty-eight hours after the attacks, when they pulled up to the front gate of the Haven. Before he addressed the guards, his mind wandered back to Richmond and those final moments in the home they loved.

"Mom, do you think we'll come back?" asked J.C.

"Of course, honey. I hope this is temporary and I hate that we even have to do it. But nothing is more important than our family."

"I know, Mom," said J.C. with a slight whine. "But all of our things are here, and Dad said the trucks are full."

Tyler placed his arm around J.C.'s shoulder and gave his son a squeeze. "Hey, no worries, buddy. We can replace things and houses. But we can't replace Rankins."

Everyone allowed the statement to soak in for a moment, and without another word, they loaded up in the truck for their new adventure.

Remarkably, unlike other travelers on that day, their trip south to Henry River Mill Village was uneventful. The oversized fuel tank gave Tyler plenty of gasoline to make the three-hundred-mile trek. Angela carefully monitored Tyler's emergency radio and the Bearcat scanner to listen to first responders being dispatched. That enabled them to avoid the bedlam that had overtaken Durham, North Carolina. Taking back roads delayed their travels by about an hour, but at least they arrived alive.

After a brief delay at the gate while the security team checked out their trucks, the Rankins pulled into their cabin located on the bank of the Henry River. All of the lights were off in the nearby cabins except for the one immediately adjacent to them.

"Look, we have a neighbor now," began Tyler, pointing to their right as they made their way along the wet gravel road. "I never thought they'd sell that cabin to anyone."

"Why's that, Dad?" asked Kaycee.

"Supposedly, it's haunted," replied Tyler. "Your mom and I thought that would be kinda cool, but it was only a one bedroom, so we took the one next door instead."

"Yeah," interjected a now wide-awake J.C., who'd slept the entire trip. "A ghost house would've been the best." J.C. turned in his seat and slid onto his knees so he could crane his neck to look at the allegedly haunted cabin.

"What do you think, Mom?" asked Kaycee.

Angela looked in her side-view mirror at the dimly lit cabin and the black conversion van with trailer parked at its side. "Yeah, Peanut, I bet it's full of spooks and boogeymen."

CHAPTER 55

Haven House
The Haven

"Just another day in paradise, right?" asked Ryan as he tried to find a place in a bed full of girls. Invariably, he was the last one to make his way to bed at night. Once Blair had her spot and the two sixty-some-pound bulldogs staked their claim on the perfect place to sleep, Ryan had to make do with what was left. It was a game of Twister that he never tired of playing.

"Ryan, I like Delta, I really do. But we don't need this kind of drama."

"I understand."

"I mean, here's the thing. I'm not a kid person, don't get me wrong. And I get that he hasn't had a lot of practice over the last couple of years. Still, shouldn't he have made an effort to make sure his two offspring were safely tucked into bed at their cabin? It's not like he lives twenty miles away, for Pete's sake."

"Honey, I can't disagree. We both suggested that he bring them to the house. Now I've got a problem. Ethan has run off, stealing a car in the process. That brings unwanted attention to the Haven from the sheriff."

Blair sat up in bed and gritted her teeth. "Not to mention that we don't know where Delta's head's at. Cort was shooting straight with him, and I appreciate it. But will Delta follow the advice or resent his bluntness? And will he ask us to babysit Skylar while he gallivants off to Philly?"

"I don't know," said a stressed Ryan.

214

Blair wasn't finished. "Plus, Ryan, what if he doesn't come back? You've heard the stories from the Cortlands and Sheltons. It's getting worse, and now it appears that some puppet master, or maybe several, is pulling the strings."

Ryan propped his head up on a pillow. "Like Leland Gaunt."

"Yes, for once you're right, Mr. Smart."

Ryan fell back on the pillows and began to laugh. The girls both stretched and groaned a little bit. It was their way of politely telling their parents it was time to go to sleep.

Ryan thought for a moment and then he said, "Sometimes, I hate it when I'm right."

Chapter 56

X-Ray's Cabin
The Haven

The only light in X-Ray's cabin came from the bluish glow of his computer monitors. He'd sat there, staring mindlessly at the screen, for the better part of an hour. As Ryan had requested, he'd been compiling information from news sources around the country and creating a daily report of conditions on the ground, together with the government's response. It was a logical task that needed to be performed, and X-ray was the right guy for the job.

He did consider himself the right guy for his side job. When he'd received instructions from his benefactors just after his arrival at the Haven, he found the request to be odd and likely harmless. He didn't know this Michael Cortland, and he didn't even bother to research the name online. He was in the process of unpacking and setting up his gear, not to mention trying to assimilate into his new community.

Now it appeared he'd been drawn into some kind of conspiracy. One that involved the chief of staff to a powerful senator. X-Ray looked through the Google images of Cort standing with his beautiful wife and daughter at various Mobile social functions. They were a loving family. *Why is he anyone's target?*

He swapped windows and studied the coverage of the downing of Delta Flight 322. The reporting focused on the death of Congressman Pratt and the impact his demise would have on impeachment proceedings against the president. There was no mention of a Michael Cortland being a survivor of the crash.

Was the information given to him by Alpha false? Was Cortland not on the plane? Or was his name scrubbed from media attention for a reason?

Besides all of that, X-Ray was genuinely bewildered as to how his handlers knew Cortland would be there in the first place.

There were more questions than answers, and X-Ray's head began to pound as he tried his best to compartmentalize what he knew. He considered leaving it be, chalking it up to much ado about nothing. Yet the coincidences were too great and the cryptic message he'd received earlier in the day was emphatic.

Tell no one. Will advise.

"When?" he shouted the question aloud, instantly covering his mouth as if he'd just yelled *Fire!* in a crowded movie theater.

X-Ray stood and wandered about his small cabin. He ran his fingers through his hair and wished he'd smuggled a bottle of gin into the Haven. A Tanqueray and tonic would hit the spot, he thought to himself as the burner phone in his pocket came to life, vibrating relentlessly.

He quickly pulled the phone out of his pocket and flipped it open. He pushed the select key to change the display to the text function. He read the message and then collapsed back into his swivel office chair.

Beware of those around you.
All is not as it might seem.
Godspeed, Patriot.
MM

"What?" he shouted again. "Beware of who? You? Jesus!"

In a rare show of anger and raw emotion, X-Ray flung the phone across the room, where it careened off a lampshade and landed safely on the leather couch in front of the fireplace, its light-blue screen continuing to illuminate despite the attempt to kill it.

THANK YOU FOR READING
DOOMSDAY: ANARCHY!

If you enjoyed it, I'd be grateful if you'd take a moment to write a short review (just a few words are needed) and post it on Amazon. Amazon uses complicated algorithms to determine what books are recommended to readers. Sales are, of course, a factor, but so are the quantities of reviews my books get. By taking a few seconds to leave a review, you help me out and also help new readers learn about my work.

And before you go …

SIGN UP for Bobby Akart's mailing list to receive special offers, bonus content, and you'll be the first to receive news about new releases in the Doomsday series. Visit: www.BobbyAkart.com

VISIT Amazon.com/BobbyAkart for more information on the Doomsday series, the Yellowstone series, the Lone Star series, the Pandemic series, the Blackout series, the Boston Brahmin series and the Prepping for Tomorrow series, totaling thirty-plus novels, including over twenty Amazon #1 Bestsellers in forty-plus fiction and nonfiction genres. Visit Bobby Akart's website for informative blog entries on preparedness, writing, and a behind-the-scenes look into his novels.

Made in the USA
Middletown, DE
26 February 2019